death by discount

death by discount

A MARA GILGANNON MYSTERY

mary vermillion

alyson books
los angeles

MANUFACTURED IN THE UNITED STATES OF AMERICA.

THIS TRADE PAPERBACK ORIGINAL IS PUBLISHED BY ALYSON PUBLICATIONS,
P.O. BOX 4371, LOS ANGELES, CALIFORNIA 90078-4371.
DISTRIBUTION IN THE UNITED KINGDOM BY TURNAROUND PUBLISHER SERVICES LTD.,
UNIT 3, OLYMPIA TRADING ESTATE, COBURG ROAD, WOOD GREEN,
LONDON N22 6TZ ENGLAND.

FIRST EDITION: OCTOBER 2004

04 05 06 07 08 **a** 10 9 8 7 6 5 4 3 2 1

ISBN 1-55583-863-4

LIBRARY OF CONGRESS CATALOGING-IN-PUBLICATION DATA

VERMILLION, MARY.

DEATH BY DISCOUNT : A MARA GILGANNON MYSTERY / MARY VERMILLION — 1ST ED.

ISBN 1-55583-863-4 (PBK.)

1. AUNTS — CRIMES AGAINST — FICTION. 2. LESBIANS — CRIMES AGAINST — FICTION.
3. DISC JOCKEYS — CRIMES AGAINST — FICTION. 4. DISCOUNT HOUSES (RETAIL
TRADE) — FICTION. 5. WOMEN DETECTIVES — IOWA — FICTION.
6. IOWA — FICTION. I. TITLE.

PS3622.E746D43 2004

813'.6 — DC22   2004048572

CREDITS

COVER ILLUSTRATION BY NICK STADLER.

COVER DESIGN BY MATT SAMS.

for B.D. Thiel,
the love of my life

one

If you speed, it's about three hours on I-80 from Iowa City to Aldoburg. I was barely doing seventy-five, but my steering wheel vibrated in protest. One set of taillights after another vanished into the darkness, leaving me alone with my thoughts and my house-mate, Vince. He'd begged me to take the passenger seat, but driving gave me a much-needed feeling of control. I hoped he could wait a while longer before bombarding me with questions.

We'd been in the middle of a huge fight when the phone rang. It was Hortie Riley, my Aunt Zee's best friend, her voice thick with tears. Zee needed me. Glad was dead. Murdered. In back of the radio station she and Zee had run since 1967. Since I'd been a little girl.

Vince tugged at the seat belt that strained against his girth. He crossed his legs tightly and clasped his hands over his top knee. "How could it be a hate crime?" he asked. "Everybody loved your aunts."

I pressed my glasses into the top of my nose and gave myself a lecture. Vince was my best friend. He had immediately

offered to come with me. He too loved Glad. "There was something written above her body." My voice caught. "They spray-
painted *dyke* on the back wall of the station." I squeezed the
steering wheel. Zee and Glad loved KGEE almost as much as
they loved each other. They'd been roommates in college and a
team ever since—in business and in life.

"What happened?" Vince whispered.

I'd asked Hortie the same thing. What I'd really meant was
How was she killed? What did they do to her?

"What was Glad doing in back of the station?" Vince asked.

"She might have been checking the rain gauge." I didn't
want to believe someone had lured her outside. Someone she
knew. "Maybe she wanted a smoke."

The smell of cigarette smoke always made me think of Glad.
When I was a kid, she read me all sorts of fairy tales—my
choice, not hers. I'd sit next to her on the sofa, and she'd offer
me books on Johnny Appleseed, Clara Barton, and Abraham
Lincoln. *Real people*, she'd urge. But I always insisted on a large
Brothers Grimm volume that belonged to my older sister. Glad
would finally give in and rest the tome on her lap. Her legs—
long as Jack's beanstalk—jutted way beyond the book. I nestled
underneath one of her arms, and the smell of cigarette smoke
whisked me away to the magical worlds of Thumbelina,
Sleeping Beauty, and Rapunzel.

Tears burned my eyes. I blinked them back and focused on
the semis streaming past on the other side of the interstate.

Once I asked Glad if I could grow my own hair as long as
Rapunzel's. She snorted the way she always did when she
thought someone was being ridiculous. I tried to imagine exactly how her snort sounded, and a tear rolled down my cheek.

"Sure you don't want me to drive?" Vince handed me a
Kleenex.

"I'm fine."

He stroked his goatee. He's seldom at a loss for words, but whenever he is, he rubs his chin. "We don't have to talk about it anymore," he said.

"There's nothing else to say. Hortie wasn't very coherent. She needed to get back to Zee." I wondered how my aunt was holding up. What would she do without Glad?

Vince gave me another Kleenex. I blew my nose and scowled at the red numbers on my car's clock. It would be 2 A.M. before we made it to Zee's. Before I could offer her any comfort.

"Remember when I first met your aunts?" Vince asked.

I nodded. We'd both been in a university production of *Romeo and Juliet*. He played Mercutio, and I was the nurse.

"Backstage after the show, Zee was so effusive," he said. "I was the best Mercutio she'd ever seen. So handsome in my costume. She couldn't believe I was just a freshman. I should have had the lead." Vince turned up the air conditioning. "But Glad just smiled at me and said, 'Not bad.'"

"That's Glad in a nutshell. She was hard to get to know."

"She loved you," Vince said.

Did she? I thought of her strawberry-blond hair glinting in the sun, her arms outstretched as she waited for me at the bottom of Redwing Park's biggest slide. There was no question Glad loved me when I was a kid, but things changed after I moved in with her and Zee my sophomore year of high school.

That year my mom discovered me kissing Susie Sorenson. Dad remained blissfully oblivious to everything except his precious patients, but Mother resolved to shape me into a happy heterosexual. Unaware of the irony, she asked a nun—her second cousin from Omaha—to talk to me about the pleasures of conjugal love. When that didn't work, she signed me up for a Mary Kay makeover and a sewing class. Finally, she

3

sent me on a date with her best friend's nephew—a gangly cross-country star from exotic Des Moines. He talked about how he wanted to be a pediatrician and responded to all my conversational gambits with an overenthusiastic "No kidding." After I politely explained that he was cute and sweet but I liked girls, he tried to unhook my bra. I packed my bags and moved across town to my aunts' faster than you could say "alternative lifestyle."

Zee was thrilled to add me to their household, but raising a teenager wasn't on Glad's top-ten list of cherished dreams. Glad seldom joined in our Trivial Pursuit or Monopoly marathons, and she never went shopping or hiking with us. When she and Zee thought I was asleep they argued about me.

"Do you know you're doing eighty-five?" Vince interrupted my thoughts.

As I eased my foot off the gas, my headlights flashed on a white semi with bold red and blue letters:

WAL-MART

WE SELL FOR LESS

ALWAYS

The discount giant wanted to open a store on the south edge of Aldoburg, and for the better part of a year, Zee and Glad had been campaigning against it. The last time Zee visited me, we combed my station's archives for anti–Wal-Mart programs even though I gently reminded her that KICI—and Iowa City—had lost their battle with the store.

I nibbled at a hangnail. "I should call Orchid," I said.

Vince gave an exaggerated shudder.

Orchid is the kind of lesbian who gives the rest of us a bad name. She hates men and feels superior to everyone who has ever slept with one. She doesn't trust women who shave their legs, and she thinks line dancing is patriarchal. She is also my boss and nemesis. I used to dream of becoming the program director at the alternative radio station where I DJ. That dream ended when guess-who got the position.

"She'll probably be delighted by my absence," I said. "Now she'll get to handle the GLBT reading series her own way." I didn't like the bitterness in my voice, but it was a relief to fall into the routine of griping about work. "She won't admit it, but she vetoed my first proposal because she doesn't want any bisexual or transgendered writers. And I know she vetoed my second one because there were too many men." I passed three cars and turned down the air conditioning. "She's trying to take the series away from me," I said. "Get this: She vetoed my most recent list—which included almost all lesbians—because she doesn't want any mystery writers. She says that mysteries valorize violence. Give me a break."

I whipped back into the right lane and sighed. My ranting hadn't taken my mind off Glad.

The Texaco off the Deep River exit was so brightly lit you could perform surgery while filling your tank. But fortuitous lighting it was, since I had to search for my backpack before finding it wedged in between Vince's two monster suitcases. The man doesn't know the meaning of traveling light. Like nature, he abhors a vacuum. He had filled the floor of my once clutter-free backseat with supersize pumps and stilettos that could have doubled as lethal weapons. They were destined to adorn the cast of *La Cage aux Folles*, a community theater production in which Vince was both the star and, as he would say, the "wardrobe consultant." What would I find the next time he borrowed my car? Falsies on the passenger seat?

As I slung my backpack over my shoulder and lifted a nozzle from the pump, Vince stretched his arms above his head and inhaled dramatically. "Ah, fresh country air. What is that fragrance? *Eau de Hog Lot?*" He always made fun of Iowa. Never mind that he chose to live here instead of his beloved Chicago.

I triggered the gas and gazed at Vince: black pleated shorts, a purple polo shirt, Birks, and a leather ankle bracelet. His dark wavy hair was pressed flat because he and the entire cast of *La Cage* had been trying on wigs to see which ones captured the "essence" of their characters.

Said wigs were piled high on our coffee table when I arrived home with my date. My first date, mind you, since Anne left me fourteen months ago, claiming that I was "emotionally unavailable." My lovely date and I had waited weeks to find a time that worked for both of us. Then finally, after struggling through awkward small talk over dinner and shoving aside my self-doubt, I promised her a romantic nightcap at my place. Instead we found a houseful of men in various states of *dishabille*. Three drag queens riffled through a mound of makeup on the dining room table. A slender man with a triangle tattoo on his shoulder wrestled with a pair of panty hose on the couch. And Vince—who had promised to be in absentia so I could have the house to myself—fluttered about in a gold evening gown two sizes too small, offering beers to his entourage. My beers. When he saw me he fussed with his white feather boa and suggested everyone head to the Alley Cat. His friends took the hint; unfortunately, so did my date. She followed a fuchsia evening gown out the door.

The scene that ensued hadn't been pretty. Then Hortie called.

Murder. How could that be?

I wrenched the nozzle out of my car and headed inside the gas station. Winding my way through a narrow aisle of cookies and crackers, I found the ladies room, which reeked of disinfectant. I followed the directions on a cardboard sign and jiggled the toilet handle after I flushed. Pink liquid soap oozed down one side of the sink. I pumped some onto my hands and stared into the mirror. I was still in date attire, but I didn't like what I saw. My black tank top accentuated my garishly red hair, anemically pale skin, and flat chest. I'd hoped to make an impression, so I'd opted for a real bra instead of a jogging one, but you couldn't tell. Flat is flat. I'd also swept my unwieldy hair back with a barrette instead of braiding it, hoping my date would find me classically Romantic or at least quasi–Pre-Raphaelite, but with my hair puffing out at the sides of my neck, I looked like a scrawny Bozo the Clown on estrogen. What had I been thinking?

I emerged from the den of disinfectant, grabbed a Coke, then headed back to the cookie aisle, where I seized a single-serve bag of Chips Ahoy! and regular size package of Double Stuf Oreos. Near the cash register I snagged some Twizzlers for good measure. As I handed the clerk my credit card, I glanced outside. Vince was washing my windshield.

Wonders never cease. Since he moved in six months ago, not a day has gone by without me asking him to pick up after himself. Let me set the record straight. I am not a neat freak. Nor am I the sort who strives for the *Better Homes and Gardens* look, but I have to draw the line when I find Vince's stack of old *TV Guides* teetering on the back of the toilet, which has its seat up yet again. I also take umbrage at the pine shavings that make their way from his guinea pigs' cage onto the floor of every room. And I loathe the Ricky Martin poster he hung next to my

Georgia O'Keeffe in the living room. Try being a thirty-five-year-old lesbian who has to explain Ricky Martin to your guests. It gets old fast.

As I passed a car and gnawed on a Twizzler, Vince punched buttons on his cell phone, seeking a hapless soul to tend his menagerie. On his third try he began cajoling. The guinea pigs were no trouble at all. Norma Desmond, his favorite cat, was a tad excitable, but all the cats got along beautifully. No, the cats never attacked the guinea pigs. Or the hamsters. Of course, all the cages and litter boxes had just been cleaned.

The hapless soul finally relented, and Vince called his assistant director at the animal shelter to explain he'd be away a few days. Vince had begun volunteering at the shelter his second year of college and had worked his way up to director. I was happy for him and jealous as hell. What would Orchid say when I called?

I polished off the Twizzlers, took a swig of Coke, and asked Vince to open the Chips Ahoy!

"Someone has a sweet tooth," he cooed.

I held out my hand for the cookies and turned on the radio. I surfed the static until a tune came in: Kenny Rogers's "The Gambler," one of Glad's favorites. I shut it off and chomped on a cookie. "Want one?"

"Better not," he said. "I've got to lose weight for the show." Vince always has a reason for losing weight—a new boyfriend or a pair of bargain jeans that are the eensiest bit too tight. He thinks his goatee and mustache slenderize his face. When he had to shave them off for *La Cage*, his offstage histrionics about his lack of cheekbones would no doubt rival his onstage performance.

Vince punched in more numbers and canceled two dates. He called one of them *schmookims*, and I started to wish he hadn't come along. I had no one to call but Orchid. Vince always had a date, and he took them out to expensive restaurants even when he still owed me for last month's bills.

"Jared didn't seem very interested in rescheduling." Vince pouted and folded his arms over his chest.

"Is he the bathroom hog?"

"Not sweet Jared," Vince said. "He's a natural beauty."

"*Someone* was in there for almost an hour. What was he doing? Cleansing his pores one by one?"

"It's not a sin to take good care of yourself."

We rode in blessed silence for a couple of minutes.

"Can I have a cookie after all?" Vince asked.

"It'll have to be an Oreo," I said. "The Chips Ahoy! are history."

He tore open the package. "You've consumed a lot of sugar," he said, "even for Mara the Metabolic Wonder." Vince made yet another call, this one to the director of *La Cage*. "Just a few days. Word of honor. I've got my script with me." He turned off his cell and stared out the window.

"Sounds like George was giving you a hard time." I often did the lights and sound for the theater, so I knew how anal-retentive George could be, and I felt touched that Vince had risked his lead role on my behalf. Then I felt guilty for being angry with him and envying his career and love life.

I passed three semis—all red, white, and blue—all belonging to Wal-Mart. "I've seen at least seven or eight of those tonight," I said.

"They're everywhere," Vince quipped.

"They *are* everywhere," I said. "They may soon be in Aldoburg."

Vince twisted an Oreo apart. "Sorry, Mar-Bar. I forgot about your aunts' campaign."

A Wal-Mart truck eased up on my right as we went down-hill. "I wonder what'll happen now." I reached for an Oreo. "Zee's up against pretty big odds. Wal-Mart opens a new mega-store every two days." I didn't add that Wal-Mart is the world's largest privately owned business, that its annual revenues exceed the gross domestic products of entire western European nations.

"I once dated someone who worked there," Vince said. "He despised that horrid blue smock, and he wasn't thrilled with his salary either."

"Glad thinks—" I corrected myself. "Glad *thought* Wal-Mart lowered wages and working conditions all over the world." I sighed and tried to stretch my left leg.

"I bet Aldoburg can stave off Wal-Mart."

I appreciated his attempt to encourage me, but only one Iowa town has ever successfully pressured Wal-Mart to with-draw. The town is much bigger than Aldoburg, and the last time I drove through it I saw a Wal-Mart entrenched on its northern edge.

I grabbed another cookie, and Vince put the package in the backseat. "You're going to be sick," he said, "and I'm going to lose my girlish figure."

We sped along in silence. I pictured Glad at her computer keyboard, pounding out ads and speeches against the "discount devil." She always attacked the keys as if she were furiously playing a Beethoven sonata. "You're going to break that thing," Zee would say. Glad would lean back in her swivel chair, arms atop her head, and grin. Zee would sigh, kiss Glad's forehead, and call her a "big lug." But that was just a game. Not a real fight like the kind they used to have about me.

"Do you think your parents will be with Zee when we get there?" Vince asked.

"Maybe."

"Didn't Hortie say?"

"Vince," I said, "no more questions for now, OK?" But I couldn't stop the questions spinning through my own mind. Who killed Glad? Would the murderer go after Zee next?

two

We entered my aunts' house without knocking. On the sofa Zee huddled under one of Hortie's long arms and clutched a crocheted pillow in her hands. Their dear friend Winker Mason sat next to them, his wooly eyebrows pinched together.

"Zee," I called softly.

She rushed to me and hugged me hard. I started crying. We broke our embrace but grasped each other's hands, needing to hang onto something. She looked vulnerable without her glasses, her brown eyes dull and rimmed with red. Her oversize T-shirt made her look shorter and heavier than usual.

Winker eased himself from the couch, and Hortie fluffed its pillows until it was her turn to hug me. "I'm ten kinds of sorry," she told me. As she wrapped her arms around me, I smelled cigarette smoke and french fries. She'd come straight from the Chat 'n' Chew—hadn't even bothered to remove her frilly apron.

Winker lumbered over and placed one of his huge hands on my shoulder. As editor of the *Aldoburg Times* he made his living with words, but he didn't have any now. He squeezed my shoulder, his eyes glistening.

Call me sexist, but I can't stand to see a man cry. "You remember my friend Vince?" I asked.

Winker nodded, and Hortie managed a smile in Vince's direction. She had a gold crown on one of her front teeth, and her short curly hair was dyed raven-black. Had been for as long as I could remember. "We should get going," she said, "and let you be alone. I'm sure you all have a lot to talk about." She and Winker headed for the door. "I'll bring by some food, but call me if you need anything else—anything at all."

"That goes for me too," Winker said.

Vince followed them. "I'll unload the car."

Zee sank back to the couch and slipped on her glasses. They were silver like the braid that fell almost to her hips. She wore gray sweat pants and a lavender T-shirt that advertised Stuff, a consignment shop that bought a lot of airtime from KGEE.

I sat next to her. There was nothing I could do that would ease her pain, so I did what came naturally. I went for the facts. "Tell me what happened. Why was Glad at the station on a Sunday night? Where was Parker?"

"Oh, Mara," Zee said, "I tried calling you earlier tonight." Her lip trembled.

I panicked. "What? What happened to Parker?"

She rested her hand on my arm. "His dad passed away yesterday afternoon."

I was speechless. Parker's father, Bill Honig, was Zee and Glad's next-door neighbor—one of the sweetest men I knew. He and his wife, Barb, had been so kind after I moved in with my aunts. They often had us over for homemade ice cream, but they never once asked me about my parents or why I wasn't living with them. Whenever I baby-sat Parker, Barb always made my favorite chocolate chip cookies, and Bill always watched until I made it safely back home.

"It was a heart attack," Zee said.

I couldn't believe it. Glad and Bill both dead.

"He was only fifty-six," she added, "but he had heart trouble."

I wanted to comfort Zee, but all I could think about was the unfairness—the unpredictability—of it all. He and Barb were both so active. When Bill wasn't working at his hardware store he was loading his truck for a hunting or fishing trip. And Barb was even more energetic. She taught aerobics at the Y, and rumor had it that her routines made women twenty years her junior whimper in pain. She was the shortstop for the coed softball team that Honig's Hardware sponsored, she played doubles with my dad in the town's tennis league, and she never missed RAGBRAI—biking across Iowa in ninety percent humidity was her idea of a dream vacation. Barb also sewed most of her own clothes and baked scrumptious cakes. When her kids were in school she was the PTA president, the leader of countless scouting troops, and the winningest Little League coach in Aldoburg history. If I aspired to motherhood, domesticity, or athleticism, I'd envy her.

Thinking about Barb and Bill was a lot easier than thinking about Glad.

"Was Barb with him?" I asked.

"She was at the store," Zee said. "Your dad had to prescribe her a sedative, but she's been resting pretty well since then."

Zee could surely use something too, but I'd have to convince her of it first.

"It's a blessing that Parker is home for the summer," she said.

I nodded. Poor Parker—not even out of college, and his father is dead.

"Glad was real torn up about Bill's death." Zee's voice

caught. "I've never seen her so upset. We didn't find out about it until late last night. Now tonight, Glad..."

I rested my hand on Zee's back. "So Glad was taking Parker's shift," I prompted.

Zee nodded, her face a mass of worry lines. "Jack couldn't work because his mother is in the hospital in Des Moines again."

Jack was the evening announcer Monday through Friday. His mother had lung cancer.

"I should have taken the shift. But I had a headache." Zee clenched her hands in her lap. "A measly little headache."

"It's not your fault."

Zee unclenched her hands.

"How did you know something was wrong?" I asked.

"Dead air." Zee practically choked on the words. "Glad was playing Garth Brooks's newest CD. The last song faded away, and then there was nothing. I knew something was wrong right away."

I took Zee's hands in mine.

"I called 911 and got in the car." She squeezed her eyes and mouth shut for a moment. Her entire body shook as she fought against her tears. "When I got to the station there was a boy who looked to be about twelve dressed in a police uniform. I didn't know him. He told me someone was dead in back of the station. It looked like murder, he said, and I wasn't allowed on the crime scene. *Crime scene.* I couldn't believe it. I thought Glad had gone outside to smoke, that she'd fainted or fallen. I never dreamed that..." She couldn't bring herself to finish the sentence.

I put my arm around her. "Then what?"

"I had to see for myself. I ignored the cop and ran to the back of the station." Zee fell silent.

I saw what I knew she was seeing—Glad's body crumpled on the ground.

"I didn't want to believe it. I was reaching down to touch Glad—to see if she was really dead—but Chuck Conover yanked my hand back."

Chuck Conover. Aldoburg chief of police. I'd gone to school with him. A thick-necked, thickheaded creep who stole my first girlfriend and told everyone I was a "lezzie" like my aunts. The perfect man to investigate a potential hate crime.

"He ordered the young cop to take me home. Said no one could do anything until the medical examiner gave the OK." She shook her head indignantly. "The examiner wasn't even there yet. He was coming from Des Moines."

"Who could have done it?" I asked.

"It must have been strangers passing through. No one who knows Glad could have killed her."

"But how would strangers know she was gay? How would they know she'd be in back of the station smoking?"

Zee frowned.

"Have you received any threatening notes or phone calls?"

"No. Not really. None that have anything to do with Glad's—"

"Someone's threatened you?" My heart started racing.

"No one's threatened anyone, Mara. Glad and I just got a few angry calls about our campaign against Wal-Mart. That's all. A few folks didn't like the noon shows we did, especially the one with a former Wal-Mart manager."

"Who complained?" I asked.

"Stuart Peterson."

"The mayor? How angry was he? What did he say?"

Zee massaged her temples. "I don't remember."

"Who else called? Did they use the word *dyke*?"

"Mara," she snapped, "Glad's death had nothing to do with any phone calls. Or with anyone in this town."

"But maybe—"

"No buts," Zee said. "You can't suspect everyone who disagrees with you of murder. Are you going to suspect Winker? He called about Wal-Mart too."

The front door banged shut. "I've got everything out of the car," Vince said.

Zee held her arms out to him. "It was so good of you to come."

After they quit hugging, we stood in silence.

"You both look exhausted," Zee said. "How about some coffee?"

"Why don't you just let me tuck you in? It's nearly 3 A.M."

"Don't be silly," she said. "I need to leave for the station at 5."

"What?" My voice shot up an octave. "You're not setting foot out there until we know what happened."

"That's what Chuck said, but you're both mistaken."

She knew I wouldn't like being linked with him, but I wasn't falling for her ploy. "He's right," I said. "It's dangerous."

Vince sat down, wisely refraining from our argument.

"The city council votes on a zoning ordinance for Wal-Mart next Monday night," Zee said. "That's a week from today. This Friday there's a public forum. Glad and I planned to barrage our listeners with anti–Wal-Mart information." She took a deep breath and kept her tears at bay. "I have to honor her memory by finishing our plans."

"Do you really think she'd want you to risk your life?"

Zee didn't respond. We both knew the answer.

"The closest Wal-Mart is eighty-five miles away," she said, "and I intend to keep it that way."

"But the station is so isolated."

"This is none of your business." Zee would sooner vote Republican than admit fear.

"I could take a shift," Vince said.

So much for wisdom. "I don't want to lose either of you." I glared at Vince. "Besides, you don't know how to run the board."

"You could teach me," he said, "or I could be your body-guard."

"Right. And you'll protect us how? With your feather boa?"

"Temper, temper," Vince said. "We could all three go and protect each other."

"Zee needs some sleep."

"I need to go to the station," Zee said. "I can't just sit here and do nothing."

Working had always been her lifeblood. It had to be. KGEE was a small operation—just Zee, Glad, Jack, Parker, and Charlene Conover, their longtime business and ad manager. When Zee wasn't DJing she was selling ads or covering some civic event. And when she wasn't doing station work she was gardening or producing various and sundry craft items for various and sundry church bazaars even though she hadn't set foot in a church since I'd been confirmed.

"I'll keep the doors locked," Zee said, "and I'll stay inside. And of course, we'll close early for the visitation and the whole day of the funeral. If you or Vince must accompany me to the station, so be it."

"Who will relieve us?" I asked. Zee usually opened KGEE Monday through Friday. Then Glad came in at 11:30, and they did a noon news show together. Glad worked until 6, and Jack took over until the station closed at 11. He and Parker also covered the weekends. "Jack and Parker are out of the picture for now," I said. "Are you going to ask Charlene to fill in?"

"Of course not. She's far too busy with the books."

I knew Zee was more concerned about her old friend's safety, but I kept my mouth shut.

"Besides," she said, "I don't need any relief."

Vince raised his eyebrows, but I wasn't surprised by my aunt's bravado. "I don't want you there when it's dark." I fought to keep my voice calm. "I'll open the station and work until 1. Then you and Vince come in and work until 7. Then we close."

"I don't like the idea of you being out there by yourself," Zee said.

"I'll keep the doors locked, and I'll stay inside." I smiled at her. "That was your plan, wasn't it?"

Zee narrowed her eyes. "What about when you're walking from your car to the station?"

"It'll be pretty dark when you open." Vince fingered his goat-ee.

They were spooking me, but I'd be damned if I let them know. "I've got Mace," I said. I wasn't sure whether this was true. Orchid had given some to every woman at the station in honor of Take Back the Night, but I wasn't a hundred percent certain mine was in my backpack. I locked eyes with Zee. "If Glad really was killed by strangers who were just passing through, then we have nothing to worry about."

Zee headed toward the kitchen again. "8 o'clock," she said. "I'll just work until 8. It's still plenty light out then." She yanked open the fridge and pulled out a box of eggs.

I almost told her not to bother, but I knew that cooking comforted her. We would all need a lot of that.

three

After persuading Zee to get some rest and Vince to stay with her, I couldn't sleep, so I left early for the station. At 4 A.M. there were no other cars on the road. I drove through town past several darkened houses and an abandoned gas station. Then for a couple miles there was nothing but corn. I rolled down my window and let the muggy breeze blow through my hair.

Aldoburg's new baseball-softball complex came up on my right, and KGEE was about a mile farther on my left. A floodlight shone on white call letters, but I could barely see the brick building behind them. I had told my aunts they needed more light.

My car rattled as I turned it off. I riffled through my backpack, looking for the Mace that Orchid had given me. Of course, it wasn't there. I closed my eyes, trying to remember where I'd seen it last. Next to my sunscreen on my dresser in Iowa City. I made a fist, with my keys jutting out between my fingers, opened my door, and scurried toward the station. Gravel crunched under my feet. A dog barked in the distance, and the wind rustled through the corn stalks. Glad's killers could have easily hidden in one of the fields that surrounded the station, waiting for her to leave the building—even daring to watch as the police arrived.

I breathed a sigh of relief as I entered the station. Its front room was Charlene's domain. She was Chuck's mother, but I didn't hold that against her. You can't help who you spawn. Her desk sported three coffee mugs. One said, "A lack of planning on your part does not constitute an emergency on my part." Her desk calendar was encircled with photos of children and grandchildren. Taped to the front of her desk were several crayon masterpieces. Most featured dinosaurs. One was devouring an unfortunate stick figure.

I forced myself to the back of the station, turning on lights as I went. A lump formed in my throat as I passed the studio. Glad had spoken her last words into that microphone. Unless she'd tried to reason with her killer. Or *killers*. Hate crimes usually involve groups of young men trying to out-macho each other. I tried to recall what else I knew about hate crimes. I didn't want to picture Glad surrounded by a band of name-calling brutes.

Crime-scene tape spanned the back door. I shouldn't have been surprised, but I was.

Next to the door hung a flashlight for checking the rain gauge at night. I flipped the light on to make sure it worked. I wouldn't cross the tape. I didn't want to ruin any chance the police had of catching Glad's killers, so I went back out the front door and walked around the building. I'd told Zee I wouldn't go outside, but I hadn't exactly promised. I hoped she was right, that strangers had done it and they were miles away. The cornstalks whispered, and dew chilled my sandaled feet. The first time I walked into a cornfield I was five or six. Rain-soaked soil tugged at my feet, and leaves scratched my skin.

Cornstalks had always seemed tiny from the backseat of my parents' car, but they loomed above me once I was in the midst of them.

I rounded the back corner of the station and found more yellow-and-black tape. Carefully stopping a couple of feet behind it, I let the beam of my flashlight fall to the ground, and I studied the tiny light that shone on one side of the back door. The light was rigged so that it always came on after dark, but its dull glow hadn't kept Glad safe. Beneath it was a lawn chair and a Folgers can, Glad's ashtray. I raised my flashlight and moved it toward the other side of the door. There it was. White spray paint on brick: DYKE. The cramped letters slanted to the right, and they were a lot smaller than I expected, more like a lesson on a chalkboard than a hateful scrawl. Such tiny letters.

I moved the beam down to the cement patio.

Nothing.

I'd expected a chalk or tape outline where Glad had lain. I'd expected blood.

I thought about Matthew Shepard. Pistol-whipped, tortured, lashed to a fence, and left to die. I hoped that Glad died right away, that she hadn't been tormented first. Still, it was strange that there was little evidence of struggle or violence.

A twig snapped. Someone was behind me.

I clutched the flashlight. If there was only one of them, I could whirl around and hit him with it. I cursed myself for forgetting the Mace, for not listening to Orchid when she urged me to take a self-defense class. I grasped the flashlight with both hands.

Another twig snapped. Whoever it was sounded huge.

"Mar-Bar, could you shine that light over here? I can't see a thing."

I shone the light right at Vince's face to get back at him for scaring me.

"Hey!" He shaded his eyes. "I come out here to check on you, and you try to Ray-Charles me?"

"You scared the crap out of me!"

"You said you'd stay inside. The gay bashers could still be around."

I flashed my light on the spray-painted letters. "I don't think they were ever here."

Mr. Coffee gasped and chugged in Zee and Glad's office. I sat at Glad's desk and picked at the crumbs of the chocolate doughnut Vince had brought me. "Chuck Conover must not know much about hate crimes," I said. "Most are committed by strangers. White males under twenty."

"Plenty of those in small-town Iowa." Vince's Hawaiian-print shirt featured hot-pink parrots. He sat at Zee's desk, peeling away the outer layer of a cinnamon roll.

"How would strangers know Glad was a lesbian?" I countered. "It's not like she and Zee did lesbian radio shows. No one in Aldoburg even uses the word *lesbian*." I nibbled my doughnut. Most Aldoburgians referred to my aunts' relationship as *different*—a catchall euphemism that conveyed a tinge of disapproval. It was *different* when Kelly Skelley got her tongue pierced. It was *different* when Parker Honig graduated high school a year early. *Different* when Hortie Riley's second oldest adopted two Korean girls.

"Maybe this hate crime is atypical," Vince offered. "Maybe it wasn't strangers."

I poured coffee into Glad's mug. There was a stain around

the rim. Steam brushed against my face. I couldn't bear to think someone who knew Glad had killed her. "Aren't most hate crimes intended to make a public statement?" I asked. "What kind of statement did these killers make? Why spray-paint the back of the building? Why not do it out front?"

"Maybe they were in a hurry. They didn't want to get caught."

"Then why spray-paint anything? Why such small letters? Why didn't they at least leave their message below the light that's back there?"

Vince had no answer.

"If they really wanted to make a statement," I said, "they could have bought themselves some time by putting on another CD. They could have trashed the station and Glad's car."

"Maybe it was their first time and they were spooked."

"Why are you insisting this is a hate crime?"

"Why are you insisting it isn't?"

I hated it when he answered my questions with questions. "Think about Matthew Shepard," I said. "He was tortured." I tried not to think about Glad's final minutes. I needed to remain logical. "There isn't even any blood in back of the station."

"Maybe the police cleaned it up."

"Then why leave the crime-scene tape?" Nothing made sense.

I gazed at Glad's desk. To the left of her computer was my senior portrait, complete with an unfashionably broad collar and a miserable attempt at feathered bangs. The photo was a disaster, but I was touched—and surprised—that she kept it on her desk. Tension had been high between Glad and me during my senior year. She was a light sleeper, so she always woke up when I came in—even if it was really late. Once I tried to make amends by weeding the garden. Turned out I couldn't tell the difference between crabgrass and Glad's treasured irises.

There was a photo of the garden on Glad's desk. She and Zee stood proudly in front of it— Zee, short with long hair, and Glad, tall with short hair. Their temperaments were opposite too. Zee was a constant whir of activity; Glad was a workhorse, both at the station and about her causes, but otherwise she loved to relax. When she and Zee gardened together, Zee attacked the weeds, her gaze fixed on the ground. Glad pulled a few, then stepped back to survey her work. She clasped her arms atop her curls. Her gray eyes traced the rows of blooms and lingered on Zee. When they finished gardening, Zee was ready to vacuum the living room or try a new casserole recipe, but Glad went for her rocker every time. She kicked off her shoes, stretched her legs straight in front of her, and folded her hands on her ample belly. "Got to rest my bones," she said. I must have taken too much of her energy. She was visibly relieved when I left for college.

"Earth to Mara. Come in, please." Vince stood next to me, playing with the collection of windup toys on the other side of Glad's computer. They were mostly animals except for Nunzilla, a square little nun who spits sparks as she marches. She was a gift from me, perfect for Glad, a recovering Catholic.

"I'll grant you this," Vince said, "it's pretty rare for lesbians to be gay bashed. Men are way more likely to be victims."

"So now you're agreeing with me?"

"I was just playing devil's advocate before."

I rubbed my eyes underneath my glasses. "Vince," I said, "you wear me out." Glad's chair squeaked as I stretched. "I've got to get on the air."

"Say no more," he said. "I'll quietly finish my cinnamon roll while looking up hate crime online."

I stood and cracked my back. "Could you please go back to Zee's and look it up? I don't want her alone."

"What about you? She's got neighbors to look after her, and you're out here by yourself. Sneaking up on you was as easy as most of the men I date."

"Nothing is that easy."

"Ouch." Vince clutched his chest.

I smiled a little and told myself I didn't mind being at the station alone.

I leaned my elbows on the counter in front of the soundboard. All the knobs had intimidated me when I started DJing, but Zee rested her hand on my shoulder and imposed order on the chaos. Most of the knobs were volume controls. Everything, she explained, had its own separate control—the mike, the carts that played ads and public service announcements, the news, the phone patch-in, and the turntables. CDs didn't exist back then, and there was nary a computer to be found.

Sometimes thirty-five seems very old.

Back in the Stone Age—when I was in high school—I had to arrive at least fifteen minutes before my shift to gather and organize the ads, PSAs, jingles, and music for my first hour. If I worked ahead I'd have a pile of tapes a couple feet high and a big stack of records. Now my stacks were replaced by two computer monitors. The one on my right contained all the station's ads. The one directly above the soundboard contained the live log, which detailed the day's programming. For most of the items on the log all I had to do was grab the mouse, point, and click. At the bottom of the log were several "hot buttons" that featured frequently played jingles: mostly station IDs and news and weather sounders. The log also contained most of the station's music, although you wouldn't know it from the walls of records that surrounded me on three sides. Those walls hadn't changed since I started working at the station, except that the pale green record covers had turned brown and crinkly along their edges.

Zee had taught me how to select a good variety of music, and she'd sat by my side during my first night on the air. Near the end of Country Countdown I accidentally started a Willie Nelson song on high speed. He sounded like a manic woman, and my eyes widened in horror. Zee chuckled. "Your first mistake. You're an official DJ." She told me to let the record finish and say it was a Crystal Gayle remake of a Willie Nelson tune. I thought we'd never get away with it, but someone requested it the next day. Whenever Zee and I wanted to make each other laugh, all we had to do was say "Crystal Gayle."

I flipped on the mike, gave the station's call numbers, and introduced the ABC news. The announcer had barely begun the top story when the blinker on the studio phone went off.

"Where's Zee?" asked a fragile voice. Most of KGEE's listeners are old. They don't like change.

"She's not feeling well." Zee didn't want me to say anything about Glad until she'd contacted her close friends. Which, I thought, consisted of the entire listening area. But I let Zee play things her way.

I put down the phone, and instantly it lit up again.

"Where's Zee?" a gruff voice asked. "What happened last night? You went off the air without a warning."

"Technical difficulties." I hung up before he could ask anything else.

As I announced the local news—weather, crop prices, Little League scores—the phone blinked madly. I clicked on a thirty-second commercial and answered the phone. It was a variation of the first two calls. By the middle of the Brownfield Agribusiness News, I'd handled nine others.

I was thinking about turning off the phone when the ceiling light wired to the front door flashed on.

Someone had entered the station.

Vince was right. I should have let him stay.

I left the studio—keys in my fist—and tiptoed toward the front.

I peeked around the corner and saw Charlene Conover rummaging through her front desk drawer. Of course. I'd locked the front door, and she'd opened it with her key. I took a deep breath that came out as a sigh.

Charlene's harried face told me she knew about Glad. Her bright red lipstick had been applied in haste, making her mouth seem puffy. As we hugged, the rhinestones on her shirt pressed into my chest and her perfume stung my eyes.

The phone rang, and she picked it up on her own desk.

I dashed back to the studio and clicked on a commercial for Stuff. I scanned the live log. Dixie Chicks next. Then a PSA.

Charlene stood in the door of the studio. Huge glasses that went out of style years ago rested far down on her nose. Her hair was pure peroxide and permed into a helmet of curls. "I can't believe it," she said. "Who would do such a thing?"

She didn't expect an answer.

"You gone out there?" She jerked her head toward the back.

I nodded. "Thanks for coming in early." Zee must have gotten her out of bed. Charlene usually didn't arrive until 9. And who could blame her if she didn't want to come in at all?

"Zee told me not to come in," she said, "but I knew the phone would be ringing off the hook, and I needed to do something besides bake a damn casserole."

I smiled in spite of myself and held up my hand. "You're lis-

tening to KGEE: country, soft rock, and golden oldies. It's 6:32
A.M. and seventy-eight degrees. How 'bout some Dixie Chicks
to get you goin'? But first this message." I started the public
service announcement.

Glad's voice. Low and resonant—perfect for radio—yet gentle like a slow-flowing stream. But not so gentle in this
announcement.

Some people say Wal-Mart will bring jobs to Aldoburg.
Not true. For every two jobs that Wal-Mart creates, it destroys
three. And most Wal-Mart jobs are part-time with no benefits.

Slow, mournful music swelled behind Glad's voice.

Some people say Wal-Mart will bring money to Aldoburg.
Not true. Wal-Mart sends all its money to banks in
Bentonville, Arkansas—Walton family headquarters.
Some people say Wal-Mart will bring better shopping to
Aldoburg. More consumer choices.
Not true. Wal-Mart will destroy our downtown. Then it will
pack up and leave us high and dry with no place to shop.
Urge your council members to vote no on the new zoning ordi-
nance. Stop Wal-Mart. Save Aldoburg.

I didn't trust myself to give the time and station ID, so I
clicked on the Dixie Chicks.

Charlene sighed. "Sad, isn't it—hearing her voice like that."

The ceiling light flashed again.

"Didn't you lock the door behind you?"

"Of course I did." Charlene's anger faded into fear.

Neither of us budged.

The studio door opened, and in tromped Chuck Conover.

At the sight of her son, Charlene relaxed, but I tensed up, frozen.

Chuck was trailed by an ash-blond woman who looked considerably better in her cop uniform than he did. His face was red. "What the hell are you doing?" he sputtered.

"Playing the Dixie Chicks." I told myself to chill. Chuck's uniform was at least a size too small, and his chin was more than double. It's such a pleasure when people you don't like age badly.

The woman was in her late twenties, hair swept up in a bun. She had a good inch on Chuck. Great muscle definition in her forearms too.

Chuck turned to his mother. "What are you doing here?"

"I work here," she said.

Score one for Charlene.

"Not after a murder, you don't. I told Zee to keep everyone away."

I held up my hand so I could open the mike.

"Pipe down, Chuck," Charlene said.

His lips tightened into a thin line. His eyes were metallic blue, and his hair, Aryan blond. Seeing him made me feel sixteen again: a scrawny redhead who felt desperately out of place in Aldoburg. He'd made everything worse by asking Susie Sorenson—she of my first passionate kiss—to the homecoming dance. Then he started taking her to the movies every weekend, and somewhere along the way he outed me to the entire school. Since this was long before the era of lesbian chic, I ate many a solitary cafeteria lunch.

As I announced the next song, Chuck folded his arms over his chest. "It isn't safe here."

The jerk had a point. I'd been scared out of my wits three times, and it wasn't even 7 A.M. "How did you get in?" I asked.

"Your aunt gave me a key. My men and I have an investigation to conduct."

Blondie flinched. Perhaps she didn't consider herself one of his "men."

"Investigate," I said. "Don't let me stop you."

The Dixie Chicks crooned and strummed. I wasn't caving, and Chuck was losing face.

"Keep the door locked," he said, "and stay away from the crime scene."

"Mara wasn't born yesterday," Charlene said.

Chuck glared at me. "Sorry about Glad."

"Thanks." I tried not to sound angry. After all, he was in charge of finding Glad's killers. "I haven't touched the scene, but I do have some questions about it."

"I'll mind the board for a while," Charlene offered.

Chuck scowled at his mom and made a show of checking his watch.

"We can talk in the office," I said.

Blondie followed us. Her silence was beginning to bug me. I whirled around and extended my hand. "I'm Mara Gilgannon. My aunt owns this station."

Her grasp was firm. "Neale Warner." Her voice was lower than I'd expected. A good radio voice.

Chuck jumped in. "This is her first job out of the academy."

No wonder she was so quiet. "Coffee?" I asked.

"Never say no to coffee," Chuck said. At least we had that in common.

He hiked up his pants and sat. Neale crossed her willowy legs at the ankle. Her posture was military-straight.

"I'd like to hear your version of what happened to Glad." I handed him and Neale steaming Styrofoam cups.

"Somebody cracked her skull," Chuck said.

Neale raised her eyebrows.

Chuck certainly wasn't worried about sparing my feelings. "Were there other bruises?" I asked.

"None that I saw, but we'll have more information after the autopsy." He sipped his coffee.

"When will that be?"

"Shouldn't be long. Cause of death looked pretty obvious."

"Did you already clean up back there?" I asked.

Neale studied me. I'd never seen such green eyes.

"We didn't touch a thing except her body." Chuck took another sip. "That's protocol."

"There wasn't any blood on the patio?"

"Nope." He shifted his back against the chair, obviously tired of my questions.

"What makes you think Glad's murder was a hate crime?" I asked.

He looked at me as if I were a moron. "You saw what they wrote."

"Yes," I said, willing myself to be tactful, "but my understanding of hate crime is that it's very violent."

"There's an exception to every rule." Red splotches appeared on his neck and worked their way toward his buzz cut.

Neale blew on her coffee.

"Do you have any suspects?" I asked.

"We just started."

"What have you found so far?"

"We'll have to wait a couple days for fingerprints. A bigwig from Des Moines came and took photos, but he said there didn't appear to be any impressions in the grass. Killers must have stayed on the cement."

I thought about the tiny patio and sidewalk in back of the station. The killers—if indeed there was more than one—had carefully avoided the grass. It was hard to imagine someone in a homophobic frenzy being so meticulous. And restricting themselves to a miniscule message on the back of a building. "So," I said, "you're assuming my aunt's death is an atypical hate crime?"

"I don't assume anything," he said.

Neale caught my eye over her coffee.

"Officer Warner," Chuck said, "I'd like to speak to Mara alone."

A flicker of irritation and she was gone.

He held his coffee in his lap, staring at it.

"I know there's no love lost between us." He suddenly met my eyes.

What could I say?

"But I'm going to do the best I can to catch the thugs that killed Glad." He paused.

Was I supposed to voice appreciation?

"If my men and I didn't have to worry about you and Zee being out here we could give more time to the investigation."

"No need to worry about us," I told him. "We'll keep the doors locked, and we'll stay out of your way."

"You couldn't close for just a week?"

"Why a week? Are you going to catch the killers by then?" I couldn't resist taunting him.

The red patch on his neck crept back toward his ears and face. "It would be easier if you cooperated."

"If I did things your way, you mean."

He set his coffee on Zee's desk, probably biting his tongue. "You can't feel good about Zee working out here after what happened."

"The campaign against Wal-Mart meant so much to Glad," I said, "that Zee is determined to finish it."

33

When I mentioned Wal-Mart, his jaw tightened. "If you're not going to close, then I need a favor."

I couldn't believe it. Chuck Conover asking me for a favor.

"I don't feel good about my mom being out here," he said. "If you could get her to take a vacation, I'd owe you one."

I completely understood his feelings, but empathy had never been so disconcerting. "Zee or I could try talking to her, but I doubt it'll do any good. Maybe one of your men could stand guard—"

"This isn't Iowa City," he said. "I don't have the manpower for that."

I warmed up my coffee. "Maybe we could swap favors. I try to convince her to work at home if you consider the possibility that my aunt's death wasn't a hate crime."

"I don't need you to tell me how to do my job," he growled.

I bit my own tongue and headed for the door.

He blocked the exit. "I could order the station closed, you know."

"Then why haven't you?" I snapped. We were so close I could smell his aftershave. I resisted the urge to step back as he glowered at me.

"You should watch your back," he said. "There's somebody out there that doesn't like your type."

Charlene was playing a Pizza Hut ad when we went back into the studio. She smiled and ushered me to the swivel chair in front of the soundboard. I grabbed a pen and tried to keep my hands from shaking. I was angry that I had let Chuck rattle me.

"Where's Officer Warner?" he barked.

"Out back," she said.

Chuck marched out of the studio. He probably didn't want anyone at the crime scene without him.

"That girl has the patience of a saint," Charlene muttered.

As she headed back to her desk, I examined the live log. I could have sworn there had been anti–Wal-Mart announcements every half hour. I scrolled down the schedule but found only two until Zee's shift started. Then, sure enough, there was one every half hour. While I was fighting with her son, Charlene had changed my part of the schedule.

four

Marshmallow brownies, strawberry pie, angel food cake. Zee's kitchen counter looked like an all-you-can-eat dessert buffet. Hortie had brought some Champion Chippers, the supersize chocolate chip cookies she serves at the Chat 'n' Chew. I opened the fridge. It was jammed with Tupperware containers and plates covered with Saran Wrap or tin foil. Zee's friends must have whipped out their cookbooks as soon as they heard about Glad's death. I moved a plate of deviled eggs and grabbed a Coke. Then I grabbed one of Hortie's cookies and headed for the living room.

Sinking into the sofa, I reviewed my morning at the station. Chuck had refused to consider Glad's death as anything other than a hate crime, and he seemed uncomfortable when I mentioned Wal-Mart. His mother removed several anti–Wal-Mart spots from the live log. I wanted to ask Zee why Charlene would do that, but I didn't want to upset her again.

I popped open the Coke and took a long swallow. The cold carbonation soothed my throat, but my stomach growled. I bit into a cookie that was bigger than my head. Hortie had perfected supersize long before it was even a flicker in the McDonald's corporate imagination. I licked some chocolate off my thumb and glanced around the living room. Lace curtains hung in both windows—Zee's taste all the way. Across the street a lanky teenager lazily shot hoops. The sun shone on the love seat under the front window. It was covered with an afghan Zee had crocheted. Crocheting is what she does for fun when it's too cold to garden and when she's not pursuing the latest in the world of arts and crafts. Back in the seventies she made more macramé than she knew what to do with. Tucked away in the recesses of my bedroom closet is a macramé belt and owl, along with several other of Zee's creations—Christmas reindeer made out of pinecones and pipe cleaners, endless jars of potpourri, ceramic cats, and countless cross-stitch renditions of Norman Rockwell paintings.

But no such kitsch appeared in the living room. Above the fireplace hung an oak-framed mirror. On the mantle was a vase of slightly wilted pink roses and my sixth grade class picture. I nibbled on my cookie and walked over to it. There I was— immortalized with braces and a too-curly perm. Little Orphan Annie meets the orthodontist. I looked beyond the photo into the mirror. I'd lost the braces, but it was a good thing I worked in a field where appearance doesn't matter. The neck of my faded T-shirt was stretched out and wrinkled. My hair hung in a thick braid, and my tortoiseshell glasses rested midway down my freckled nose. Funny, I was a combo of Zee and Glad. I was short and nearsighted like Zee—with her penchant for braids— and I had Glad's coloring even though I wasn't related to her. Not by blood, as my mother puts it.

The phone rang. I raced to the kitchen and snatched it up, my heart thumping.

"Mar-Bar?" A country song twanged in the background.

"Vince," I said, "what's wrong? Is Zee OK?"

"Everything's fine. She just wanted me to check in on you."

I took a deep breath and sat on a stool next to the desserts. The country song segued into a jingle. "How's she doing?"

"She says she doesn't need a baby-sitter and that I should go home and support you, but don't worry, my fair Mar-Bar—I'll not be swayed from my mission."

"Is she really OK?"

"Yes," Vince said. "She's fine. Just like you."

His sarcasm wasn't lost on me, but I let it pass.

"So," he said, "how'd things go with Orchid?"

I should have called her hours ago. She'd have a tough time finding a replacement for me on such short notice, and she might actually have to work my shift herself. Passive-aggressive? You bet.

"Want me to call her?" Vince asked.

I said no, which was a lie, and then we hung up.

Outside, a finch pecked at the bird feeder Glad had hung so she could bird-watch when she did the dishes. The dish drainer was filled with plates she'd probably washed. She was almost always on cleanup detail. When I first moved in, I offered to dry the dishes, wanting Glad to see how helpful I could be. She declined my offer. "That's what a dish drainer's for," she'd said. What she meant was that there was nothing I could possibly do to earn my keep, to make up for being a thorn in her side.

Maybe another Coke was in order. And perhaps some peach cobbler.

I studied the desserts again and picked at the burnt edges of an apple pie crust. Maybe I should go outside, take a walk, clear my head. Then I'd call Orchid. No, I'd call her, get it over with, and reward myself afterward.

I punched in her office number, wondering what she'd do about the reading series while I was gone. Would she replace all the mystery writers with authors she deemed more socially responsible? After five rings, her voice mail picked up. Ah, the joys of modern technology.

I stepped outside and plopped myself down on the front step. The sun had disappeared under a cloud, but the humidity more than made up for its absence. Weeds peeked through the cracks of Zee's driveway, crisscrossing the cement like a giant green spiderweb. A boy whizzed down the sidewalk on a scooter, his golden hair sticking out of his baseball cap. A block behind him an equally blond girl wobbled on a bike that still had training wheels—neither of which quite reached the ground. Her tiny legs worked madly to keep up with the boy. "Wait for me!" she squealed.

I could relate. My mind was churning fast but getting me nowhere. Glad was dead—murdered—and I had stupidly agreed to help Zee remain in harm's way. She wouldn't be safe at the station until the killer was caught. Maybe she'd never be safe since Chuck refused to look at all the facts.

A neighbor's phone rang faintly, but someone picked it up mid ring. The last time I spoke to Glad had been on the phone. I grunted a greeting and asked for Zee. I didn't even ask Glad how she was doing. Of course, she didn't ask me either.

The sky rumbled and grew grayer. A few houses down a mother yelled for her kids to get home this minute if they knew what was good for them. Unless I wanted to get stuck in a downpour, a walk was out of the question. I headed to the driveway and began yanking weeds. A losing battle, Zee called it.

I straightened my back and scanned the neighborhood again. The Honigs had obviously been doing battle with their shrubs. What had once been a meticulously trimmed hedge now looked like a pruning session gone bad. The part of the "hedge" farthest from me reached its prickly branches over most of the sidewalk, but the part closest to me had been chopped down to gnarled stumps. Since it wasn't yet raining, I strolled over to investigate.

I'm not the type of lesbian who worships power tools, but if I were, I would have been drooling over the impressive saw that lay on the ground, flanked by a shovel and a couple of clippers. The tools were shaded by the uncut part of the hedge. It was brown underneath. Only the newest growth was green. Around two of the stumps was a huge hole and a complicated network of roots. The largest roots looked like rats' tails except that they were a dull orange and wider than my arm. Extracting them would be grueling given the high humidity. I'd been outside only a few minutes, and I was already sweating under my bra and around my hairline. I felt a raindrop on my shoulder and then another on my head. Several more pelted me, covering my glasses and transforming Cedar Street into a blur. I turned to run for Zee's when I remembered the saw and other tools. They'd be ruined if it kept raining. Of course, Barb could always get new ones. After all, she owned a hardware store. It rained harder, and my T-shirt clung to my skin. I was rationalizing. The truth was I didn't want to see Barb; I didn't want to talk about her dead husband. I had enough grief of my own.

Barb answered the door in a bright blue terry cloth bathrobe. It looked worse for the wear, and so did she. Her dark hair hung limply to her shoulders; her eyes were red, and her complexion paler than usual. She'd lost some weight, so her front teeth—which had always been too big for her delicate features—seemed even larger.

"Sorry to bother you." I nodded toward the saw I was clasping to my chest. "I was afraid this would get ruined in the rain."

Her brow furrowed, and the TV droned.

"It was out by your hedge." The rain kept pounding, making my braid heavy on my back. "If you open your garage door, I'll slip it in there for you."

Barb flashed a smile of recognition, whether for me or the saw I wasn't sure. "Aren't you sweet?" She opened her screen door wider. "Get in here," she said, "before you get any wetter."

I shook my head. "You've got more tools out there." Before she could protest I set the saw on a huge mat in the entryway and sprinted to the hedge.

When I returned I placed the dripping tools next to the saw and noticed a pair of men's work boots, probably Bill's. The air conditioning raised goose bumps on my arms, and I floundered for an excuse to leave. "Sure you don't want me to put your tools in the garage?"

She smiled faintly. "It's such a mess the car won't even fit in there. Bill had been meaning to clean it." Her smile faded.

Behind her the TV flickered on a coffee table laden with desserts. I spied Hortie's cookies and several other familiar delectables. Clearly the church ladies had made double batches.

Barb followed my gaze. "We just keep getting more food. Thank God Parker is here, or it'd all go to waste."

"I'm sorry about Bill," I said.

Barb's face tightened. She and Bill had celebrated their thirtieth wedding anniversary a few years back. I couldn't begin to fathom her grief.

"I'm sorry for your loss too," she said. "Murder. That must be so hard." She idly tapped her front teeth with her fingers. "My Mama always said the good Lord doesn't send us any more than we can handle."

I wondered if that platitude brought her any comfort. It only served to piss me off.

The TV blared the praises of Swiffer Wet, and Barb adjusted the tie on her robe. "I sure admire you and Zee, keeping the station open so you can fight against Wal-Mart. Glad would be proud. Bill too."

"Thanks," I said, surprised at the knot in my throat. Barb was the first person I'd heard praise Zee's decision. "Your store must mean even more to you—" I hesitated, "now that Bill is gone."

"Oh, Mara," she said, "you don't know the half of it."

An infomercial urged us to buy a contraption that made perfect pancakes every time—even heart-shaped ones. "What will they think of next?" Barb mused.

From the back Barb could have passed for a teenager. Teaching aerobics kept her slender; Miss Clairol or some such stuff kept her hair dark, and her jaunty shoulder-length cut kept her from looking like the grandmother she was. But grief had made her face look far older than its fifty-some years, and the contrast between her face and the rest of her unnerved me. "I should let you get back to your show."

Barb dismissed my comment with a wave of her hand. "Want a cookie?"

I clasped my stomach, thinking about all the sweets I'd just eaten.

"Oh," she said, "you've probably got plenty of your own."

We both stared at her coffee table.

"How about some ice tea? You must be thirsty from all that running."

"I don't want to get your furniture wet."

"Don't worry," Barb said. "I'll grab you a towel and a lawn chair from the garage."

Ice cubes clinked in the kitchen as I toweled myself off on the mat and scanned the living room. The olive couch was faded and threadbare, and the shag carpeting had seen better days. There were photos everywhere: on the end table next to the couch, on top of the TV, around the oversize wooden fork and spoon that adorned the paneling. The bookshelf was filled with photos instead of books. On the top shelf were high school portraits of Parker and his older sister, Frannie. They both had their mother's coloring—dark hair, porcelain skin, blue eyes—but Frannie had inherited their father's meaty build. She was just a couple years younger than me, but we'd never been close because she'd been a jock and I was a card-carrying nerd. Parker was thin like his mother but far more serious, barely smiling in his black sweater. Most of the other photos featured Frannie's children in various regalia: party hats, dance costumes, First Communion veils, scout uniforms, soccer gear. The only thing missing was the obligatory bathtub shot.

"Adorable, aren't they?" Barb said. "Parker took most of them. He's turned out to be quite a photographer." She handed me a green-and-white lawn chair.

I unfolded it and took the ice tea she offered me. Now I was stuck. I cast about for something to say as Barb sank into her sofa. "Looks like you've got quite a project going out front," I said.

"Bill started that for me a couple weeks ago. I want to put some flowers in."

"That'll look nice." I gulped my tea. The sooner I finished it, the sooner I could leave.

"Those bushes just got out of control."

"They can do that," I said, as if I were an expert on lawn upkeep. I took another gulp. "Does Parker take lots of pictures?"

Barb grinned. "He takes great ones of people. This past spring break he was in the Yucatan tutoring grade school children. You should see the pictures he took of them. So beautiful. I'm going to mat and frame most of them."

"That'll be nice," I murmured. "I'm sure it'll mean a lot to Parker."

Barb crossed her legs. "Does Chuck know anything about Glad's death?"

Her abrupt subject change startled me. "He thinks it's a hate crime," I told her. I hoped she wouldn't ask any more questions. "The murderer spray-painted the word *dyke* on the back of the station." I swallowed hard.

"How awful." Barb's hand went to her mouth and she began absently tapping her teeth again. "You know," she said, "This past spring a couple of high school kids beat up a boy they thought was homosexual. Timothy O'Rourke. He wasn't permanently hurt, thank God, just bruised up real bad." She sprang up, tightened her robe, and scooped up our empty glasses. "Timothy isn't really homosexual. I'm on the Altar and Rosary Hospitality Committee with his mother, and she says the girls are always fawning over him. Calling every night."

"Who beat him up?" I prodded.

Barb's eyes met mine. "Stu Peterson and Collin Conover."

"Stu Two?" I asked. "The mayor's son?"

"Yes, and Chuck's boy."

So Chuck Conover had raised a gay basher. That didn't surprise me. What did surprise me was Chuck's pigheaded refusal to consider Glad's murder as anything other than a hate crime. Why was he purposefully pursuing an angle that would cast suspicion on his own son?

five

When I returned to Zee's house, my clothes were still wet and my muscles were in knots, so I got in the shower. As the water pounded against my back, I resolved to take a nap until Zee and Vince got back from the station. I tried not to worry about them or think about everything that had happened since Glad was murdered.

God. It hadn't even been twenty-four hours.

Just as I stepped out of the shower, the doorbell rang— probably somebody with a casserole or dessert. I'd had enough sweets and condolences for one day, but I rushed to towel myself off.

The bell rang again.

I wrapped a towel around my hair, fumbled for my glasses, and grabbed the robe on the bathroom door. It was Vince's—red silk with embroidered gold dragons. The sleeves drooped below my fingertips. I was drowning in silk. I thrashed around in the robe, pushing up the sleeves and hiking up the bottom. As I foundered down the stairs, the visitor started pounding on the door.

I opened it mid-knock and found myself facing the willowy blond cop from the station. Maybe she and Chuck had caught Glad's murderer!

She gave me the once-over. "I've caught you at a bad time."

I felt no need to deny the obvious. "Do you have news about my aunt's death?"

"May I come in for a moment?" Her tone was subdued.

They hadn't caught anybody.

"I have a lead," she said.

I stepped aside, and she glided across the living room, her ballerina grace at odds with her uniform. She sat on the sofa amid crocheted pillows and fanned herself with her slender fingers.

She had lovely hands. I could see them rippling up and down a keyboard or—

"It's close to a hundred degrees out there," she said, "even after the rain."

I tried to think of something clever to say.

"Could I trouble you for a glass of water?"

"Water?" I said. "Sure." I wondered if Vince's robe made me look extra scrawny. "We've also got ice tea and pretty much any kind of dessert you can think of, Officer—" Damn. I couldn't remember her name.

She smiled and tucked a wisp of hair behind her ear. "I'd love some ice tea, and please call me Neale."

Carrying two beverages while doing battle with a huge robe is no easy task. When I handed Neale her tea I spilled a bit on a dragon that danced across my knee.

"Oh, I hope that doesn't stain." She grabbed a napkin and patted my lower thigh.

Her touch sent a wave of warmth through me. My face was no doubt turning redder than the stupid robe. "I'll get another napkin." I rushed back to the kitchen and started stacking sugar cookies onto a plate. I dropped one of them on the floor and accidentally stepped on it. I needed to focus. Make some small talk and find out about the lead. Gather more clues.

I reentered the living room and sat in the chair across from Neale. "Did you know Glad?" I wrestled with the sash of Vince's robe.

"I've only been here a week," she said.

"Where were you before?" Question and answer. Not so hard after all.

"Chicago."

Same as Vince. I bet she shared his snobby attitude toward all things Iowan. "What brought you here?"

"Long story," she said. "You must want to hear about the lead." She leaned forward, excited. "I called around to see if there were any other recent incidents of homophobic graffiti." She smiled, smug about her prowess as a detective. "The high school guidance counselor grudgingly admitted that a couple of jocks beat up another student and called him a faggot."

"This past spring?" I asked.

Neale's smile vanished. "Yes."

"My aunt's next-door neighbor just told me about it."

I'd cut short her moment of glory, but she didn't stay flustered for long. "OK, let's compare notes."

I sipped my tea. "Does Chuck know you're here?"

"My shift ended a few hours ago."

I took that as a no.

"I just questioned Timothy O'Rourke," she said, "but he was very tight-lipped."

"He didn't say anything?"

Neale set her glass on a crocheted daisy coaster. "Just that he's not gay and it wasn't that big of a deal. He said Collin and Stuart were just messing around."

"Did he seem scared?"

"Hard to tell," Neale said. "Do you know him?"

I shook my head.

"I thought people in small towns knew each other."

Truth be told, most Aldoburgians did know me by sight, and vice versa even though I was no longer a citizen per se. Visitors to Aldoburg almost always earned a blurb in the paper. Sometimes an ambitious reporter would even detail the events I attended with my aunts.

"What about the perpetrators?" Neale said. "Do you know them?"

"I've gone to some of their games with my aunts."

She forced a smile, no doubt wondering what kind of loser wasted time at high school sporting events. She'd soon realize they topped Aldoburg's entertainment calendar. "Stu Two is a local hero," I said. "Star quarterback and pitcher. Rumor has it several colleges are looking at him."

Neale folded her hands in her lap and waited for me to say more.

"You know Collin is Chuck's son, right?"

"Of course."

"News travels like wildfire in Aldoburg," I said. "You won't be able to keep your off-hours sleuthing a secret."

"I can look out for myself." Her voice was confident, but her green eyes darted away from mine, and she fussed with a piece of hair that had escaped from her cap.

"If Chuck finds out what you're up to—"

"Don't you want to catch your aunt's murderer?"

"There won't be any murderers caught if Chuck has to waste his time hiring a new cop," I said, "or if he decides to spend his time teaching you a lesson." I thought about how easily he'd lost his temper with me at the station. "He doesn't like to be second-guessed."

"If he catches me," she said, "I'll apologize profusely and say you put me up to it." She smiled wickedly.

My stomach fluttered. I stared at the ice cubes in my glass.

She moved to the edge of the couch. "Will you help me?"

"Why are you taking all these risks?" I asked.

She smoothed out a wrinkle in her pants. "I'd like to be a homicide detective some day."

So Miss Chicago wanted to use Glad's death as a way out of Aldoburg. What was she doing here anyway? Couldn't she get a job anywhere else? "I don't understand why Chuck is working the hate-crime angle," I said. "Why would he risk involving his own son in the investigation?"

Neale shrugged. "Maybe he never considered the risk."

Did she assume all small-town cops were idiots? "Chuck is not an intellectual giant," I said, "but he's not stupid."

"Maybe he's trying to protect someone."

"Who could he possibly want to protect more than his own son?"

That stymied her. "Look," she said. "I know you don't think your aunt's murder was a hate crime, but right now it's the only lead we have."

I couldn't argue with that.

She finished her tea. "I'd like to question Chuck's son and the other boy who beat up O'Rourke, but Collin would surely tell his father." She gazed at me expectantly.

"So you were hoping I'd do it?" Wow. This chick had a lot of nerve, wanting me to do her dirty work. Then again, I'd been hoping for more clues.

"The boys might be more likely to talk to someone who grew up here," she said.

"Do you really think it was a hate crime?"

"I think we should cover all our bases."

Our bases. Call me vindictive, but I liked the idea of going behind Chuck's back with one of his "men." Even if she was a ruthless careerist.

Since it was too wet to practice outside, the entire baseball team was lifting weights in the loft above the high school gym. The machines clanked and squeaked, and the boys grunted and groaned as if they were in the throes of ecstasy, each trying to lift more than the others. One guy with bangs down to his nose loaded too much weight on the bench press and let it fall. The crash garnered far more attention than I did. A few guys glanced my way, but nobody missed a rep. Perhaps the Aldoburg grapevine didn't include high school boys.

Stu Two strained at the leg press. He was the pride and joy of his glad-handing father, the mayor, who happened to be Chuck's best friend. Like his father, Stu Two had a wrestler's body and topsoil-colored hair. Sweat beaded on his square, lightly freckled face.

I ambled over to him. "Hey," I said, "mind if I work in?"

Stu Two got up and grunted my name. He wasn't wearing a shirt, and the machine where he'd been sitting was coated with sweat. When I sat down, it dampened the back of my T-shirt. One word: *eew.*

"What weight you want?" He yanked out the pin.

"How about 125?" A girl ought to be able to lift her own weight with her legs. I grimaced and pushed. Nothing. "Maybe a little lighter," I said.

He smirked and put the pin at seventy.

As I worked my legs, Stu Two stretched his quads.

"So how's Tim O'Rourke?" I asked.

Stu Two stopped stretching and scowled. "How would I know?"

"I heard you and Collin Conover beat him up," I said mid-rep.

"He's a faggot." Stu blew a bubble. "I don't like faggots." He glared at me. "Or dykes."

I winced. I've never loved the word *dyke,* but now it made me think of the letters above Glad's body. "Where were you last night around 10?"

His eyes darted to the bench press. "What do you care?" he snapped.

"Do my questions upset you?" I lowered the weight and stood.

"Why should they?" He put his hands on his hips.

"So where were you last night?"

Again, he looked away. "Jogging with Collin."

"Out by the radio station?" I asked.

He shrugged.

"Have you heard Glad was murdered there last night?"

He stopped chomping his gum. "Miss McAuley is dead?"

"Somebody spray-painted *dyke* on the back of the station," I said.

He finally put two and two together. "We had nothing to do with that." He swallowed hard.

"Where were you jogging?"

"All over." He began chewing again. "We usually run at least five miles."

"Did you see anybody?"

He moved the weight pin. "I got more sets to do."

When I walked away, he was sitting at the leg press, staring into space.

Collin paused mid-crunch when I greeted him, but he continued huffing and puffing through an interminable set of sit-ups on an incline bench. Just watching him made my stomach hurt. He didn't seem to have much in common with his father except for the blond buzz cut. His eyes were brown, and he was tall and thin, all arms and legs, the starting center on the basketball team. The numbers on his mesh tank top were cracked and faded.

When he quit torturing his abs he eased himself off the bench and smiled at me. "You want to use this?"

"Sure," I said. "You can never do too many sit-ups."

Collin towered over me, unimpressed. "Want me to wipe it off?"

"Nah, that's OK." I needed to work quickly before Stu Two snapped out of his reverie and interrupted our conversation. Besides, I was already drenched in one young man's sweat.

This time I'd thought of a more graceful way to begin. "You think the road out past the station is a good place to jog?"

His Adam's apple jerked up and down, and his face reddened like his father's. "There's some traffic," he said, "but it's real flat."

"Stu Two said you guys were jogging there last night."

"I wasn't paying much attention," he said, "just following Stu."

I wondered if that was often the case. "Were you just following Stu when you beat up Tim O'Rourke?"

Collin's Adam's apple went berserk, and he hitched up his shorts.

"That was an accident," Collin said. "Things got out of hand."

Sweat trickled down my back. "Did things get out of hand last night?"

Collin's eyes danced around the room until they found Stu. "What are you talking about? We were just running."

"Out by the station?"

He frowned.

"Glad was killed there last night."

Collin gulped and plopped back down on the bench. The color drained from his face. "Somebody murdered her?" he asked.

"And spray-painted *dyke* on the back of the station," I said.

He met my eyes. "And you think me and Stu did it because of O'Rourke."

I remained silent.

"Why would we hurt Miss McAuley?" His voice cracked. "She covered all our games and always cheered us on."

He had a point. Yet neither boy would say where he'd been last night.

six

I'm a living example of Murphy's Law. Just when I thought things couldn't get worse, they did. Right after I fell asleep on the couch, Vince and Zee returned from the station. Then my mom showed up with a ham loaf and a cherry pie. I have nothing against the edibles, mind you.

Vince took the food to the kitchen as Mom distributed quick A-frame hugs and guided Zee into the living room. "I came over as soon as I knew you were off the air," she said. "I was so sorry when I heard about Glad. It's just awful."

Mom perched herself on the edge of Glad's chair, and Zee eased into her own. The two sisters don't have much in common except that both were born and bred in Aldoburg, and both were named after flowers. Zee's full name is Daisy Violet. My mother is Ivy Rose, but she goes by Rose, in keeping with the pastels she always wears. Tonight it was a pale yellow jumpsuit and a mauve scarf that Vince was probably coveting. My mom is five years older than Zee, but she looks younger thanks to peroxide and Slim-Fast.

For Zee's sake I hoped my mother would have the good grace to keep her martyr act in check, that for once she would- n't urge me to stay with her and Dad. I hadn't stayed overnight there since I'd moved in with Zee and Glad, but every time I visited, Mom tried to persuade me to come "home." It's not that she really wanted me to feel welcome there—she'd never invit- ed Anne or any of my other girlfriends. Her invitations were all about making herself look good. She's Aldoburg's alpha church lady—no easy task when your sister and daughter are both les- bians and lapsed Catholics, and when your own daughter refus- es to sleep under your roof.

"They have a suspect in custody," my mother proclaimed. "Alex Riley."

"Riley," I said. "Is he related to Hortie?"

"Her grandson." Zee wrinkled her brow. "He's been living with her for the past few months."

"Rumor has it he's been bad-mouthing you and Glad all over town," my mother said.

Vince banged a few dishes in the kitchen.

"We barely know him," Zee said. "He applied for a job, but we couldn't hire him—not even as a favor for Hortie. His voice was too high for radio."

"He's trouble," my mother said. "Shoplifting and vandalism." Her eyelids fluttered. She insists on wearing contact lenses even though they make her blink funny. "Chuck has already arrested him once for drugs."

Chuck didn't need to worry about his son being considered a suspect with Alex around.

"Poor Hortie," Zee mumbled.

My mom continued, oblivious to Zee's distress. "Someone saw him riding his motorcycle toward the station a little before 10."

"It's a main road out of town," I said.

"He was carrying a can of white spray paint."

"There are plenty of things you can do with a can of paint," Zee sputtered. She refused to believe her dear friend's grandson had murdered Glad.

"It's a pretty big coincidence," my mother insisted.

"It's just a rumor," I said.

"Not in Chuck's eyes," she went on. "He's convinced the case against Alex is open and shut."

Zee's knuckles were white on the arms of her chair. Her sorrow was slowly boiling into anger.

"Let's try some of that cherry pie," I said quickly.

"None for me." Mother patted her stomach. "Besides, I've got another casserole to deliver to Barb. I just wanted to see how you two were holding up."

"We're fine," Zee said absently.

"Don't you think you should close the station for a spell?" Mother said. "It's not safe out there."

"If the murderer is already in custody," Zee snapped, "there's nothing to worry about."

Mother adjusted her scarf. "Your campaign against Wal-Mart is making things extra hard on Jonathon." Her eyes batted wildly. "You might be more considerate of the fact that he's a council member. If he votes against the store, people will think it's because you're my sister and that he cares more about his family than the good of the town."

Bottom line: My mother was afraid she'd lose some of her precious status if my dad weren't reelected to the city council.

"This Wal-Mart controversy is tearing Jon apart," she said. "It's tearing our town apart."

My mother was fond of hyperbole, but she made me wonder about Wal-Mart as a motive for murder. Maybe one of the store's proponents had killed Glad and made it look like a hate crime.

It had been more than forty hours since I'd last slept, but I always need to read before I can fall asleep. I riffled through my suitcase, searching for Ellen Hart's newest Jane Lawless mystery. Plenty of underwear and tank tops, but nary a paperback. Fortunately there were plenty of books in my old room. And plenty of memories. Zee had urged me to redecorate it shortly after it became clear that my parents and I would be happier if we didn't live together. She helped me weave a rug for the hardwood floor, and we painted the walls lavender. Two of the walls sported old posters: *Star Wars*, a herd of wild horses, and Farrah Fawcett in that unforgettable red swimsuit. The other two walls were covered with bookshelves. A thin layer of dust coated the shelf next to the bed. On the bottom shelf was my Nancy Drew collection. As a child I loved her adventures so much I'd devour two in a day. I imagined myself as carefree and efficient as the titian-haired detective—complete with a cute and helpful girlfriend named George.

I moved my eyes to the next shelf. In front of my Kurt Vonnegut collection was a photo Glad had taken of Zee and me at the State Fair a few summers ago. We both wore our hair in long braids—mine red, hers silver. Zee hugged a monstrous green teddy bear I'd miraculously won for her in the ring-toss. She laughed at my unwieldy puff of cotton candy. Glad was always behind the camera. Never in front of it. Was that her choice, or had she resented it?

I pushed this question away and continued searching for a book. I wasn't in the mood for anything violent, so that let out Stephen King. Science fiction didn't sound good either. I scanned the top shelf. *Pride and Prejudice*. Just what the doctor ordered. Elizabeth Bennet's biggest worries were her family's *faux pas*.

I put on a fresh tank top, slid under the covers, and opened the book: *It is a truth universally acknowledged that a single man in possession of good fortune must be in want of a wife.*

Money was a big motivator. Bigger than hate?

I let the novel rest in my lap. If Glad's death was truly a hate crime, Stu Two and Collin were prime suspects. They seemed to be lying about their whereabouts at the time of her death, and Collin knew the radio station well because his grandma worked there. Yet his words echoed in my head: *Why would we hurt Miss McAuley? She covered all our games and always cheered us on.*

Why? That question was harder to answer with Alex. Jobs were hard to come by, but murder? Still, he'd bad-mouthed Zee and Glad, and he'd been heading toward the station shortly before the murder. He had a can of spray paint and a history of vandalism. Circumstantial evidence, but evidence all the same.

My legs felt too warm underneath the sheets. I kicked them off and walked to the window. I'd always loved my view from the second story. The breeze ruffled the leaves on the huge oak next to the Honigs' house, and the moon shone on the chopped-up hedge that lined their sidewalk.

Next to the hedge something moved.

A dog?

I squinted: It was a person crawling on their hands and knees.

I was about to call 911 when the figure stood and wiped her brow. Through the moonlight I recognized a ponytail. It was Barb—in her own yard, spade in hand—digging out her shrubs. She lowered herself to the ground again and attacked the earth with her spade. Occasionally she stopped and tugged at the roots.

The air conditioner kicked on.

Barb had to be sweating herself silly out there trying to work her grief away.

I considered taking her a glass of ice water and urging her to bed, but then I recalled my attempts to keep Zee away from the station, and for once I opted to leave well enough alone.

But I couldn't go back to bed, so I pulled on some shorts and tiptoed down the hall to Glad's office. The door creaked as I opened it. The ceiling light seemed too bright, so I switched on a couple of lamps instead. Glad's room, like mine, had two walls of bookshelves: gardening books, travel guides, Russian novels. On the shelf tops were philodendrons, their vines draped over the highest row of books. Next to the window was a Northern pine about my height. There was a speck of tinsel on its lowest branch. Glad must have missed it when she removed her Christmas decorations.

My head throbbed as I resisted the urge to cry. I sat in Glad's easy chair, its leather cool on my legs. On the floor next to it was her most recent reading: a seed catalog, a Joan Hess, and an anti–Wal-Mart book. It was a red, white, and blue paperback called *How Wal-Mart Is Destroying America*. I turned to one of the pages Glad had marked:

ONE STATE'S DEATH TOLL
A 1995 survey in Iowa shows what Wal-Mart has done to the state since arriving in 1983:
  50% of clothing stores have closed
  30% of hardware stores have closed
  25% of building materials stores have closed
  42% of variety stores have closed
  29% of shoe stores have closed
  17% of jewelry stores have closed
  26% of department stores have closed

I shut the book. Some of those closings were undoubtedly caused by the farm crisis, but it was no wonder Glad wanted to fight Wal-Mart. I felt guilty for the occasional shopping I did at Iowa City's Wal-Mart. But when you can barely pay your rent and electric bill, you can't always spend more on underwear and toothpaste to support local businesses. Can you?

"Mar-Bar?" Vince was wearing emerald silk pajamas. At least he didn't shop at Wal-Mart.

"Vince," I said, "do you think that politically correct spending is a luxury or an obligation?"

He sat at Glad's desk, a beautiful oak piece that matched the floor. "Girlfriend, you think too much."

I flipped through the Wal-Mart book, found the page I'd been looking at, and handed the book to him. "It was by Glad's reading chair," I said.

Vince skimmed the numbers.

"It's why she was fighting."

"You're torturing yourself." He stood up. "You need some sleep. Come on, let me tuck you in."

I shooed him away from Glad's desk and gazed at the sea of paper on its surface. "I won't disturb things," I said. "I'll just look at the top layer."

Vince sighed as he settled into Glad's easy chair. "I'll keep you company, but when the clock strikes midnight I'm dragging your skinny ass to bed." He started flipping through the Wal-Mart book, and I studied Glad's desk.

There was an empty pencil holder half hidden by her computer. Next to it was a tiny photo, the only photo on the desk. I must have been about four. The wind had whipped one of my pigtails into my face, and I was grinning wildly because of the piggyback ride Glad was giving me. Had the photo always been on Glad's desk, even when I was living with her, pulling up her irises and keeping her awake nights?

I picked up a pile of papers. "Vince," I said, "here's some stuff about Wal-Mart that Glad must have printed off the Internet." There was a site called Sprawl-Busters, and another that celebrated Gig Harbor, Washington's successful fight to keep out the "multinational monster."

I handed them to Vince, and he squinted, too vain to wear his glasses—even on his way to bed.

I glanced back at her desk. A pale green Post-it note stuck to the front page of the *Aldoburg Times* caught my eye. On it was written:

WM

SP

CC

I peeled it off the paper, my heart pounding, and held it out to Vince. "WM," I whispered, "Wal-Mart. What if Glad was killed because of Wal-Mart?"

"You're delirious. No one gets killed because of a discount store."

"But her death doesn't seem like a hate crime. There has to be some other motive."

"And that's why you're snooping through her office?" Vince said. "I thought this was part of your grief process."

Vince could have easily been a lesbian given his penchant for processing other people's issues—especially mine.

"I just want to find out who killed her," I said. "I don't trust Chuck Connover. According to my mother, he's so sure of his arrest that he won't even consider other suspects."

Vince leaned back in his chair. "I don't blame you for not trusting small-town police—"

"I don't mistrust them because they're from a small town. I mistrust them because Chuck's son may be involved." I told Vince about Collin and Stu Two's gay bashing.

"What delightful young men," Vince said. "If you think they did it, why are you obsessing over Wal-Mart?"

I told him everything Zee and Mom had told me about the Wal-Mart controversy. I also told him about Charlene and the deleted ads.

Vince rubbed his goatee, deep in thought. "If that Post-it is a clue," he said, "WM could be someone's initials."

I didn't want to say what I was thinking. "Winker Mason. You met him last night—the editor of our paper. But he couldn't have done it. He's a dear friend of Zee and Glad's. He taught me to make paper airplanes when I was a kid."

"You're too sentimental to be a good detective," Vince said.

I took that as a challenge. I opened drawers until I found a notebook and pen. At the top of the page I wrote "Wal-Mart" and "Winker Mason." Maybe Vince was right. Perhaps I was too sentimental. I sure didn't like writing Winker's name on a list of suspects. The last time I was in town, he'd taken my aunts and me to Mitzi's. We sat in the back booth, drinking and laughing about a Pork Queen contest. KGEE and the *Times* often covered the same events, so Winker had a friendly rivalry with Zee and Glad.

But with Winker in favor of Wal-Mart—what if the rivalry wasn't so friendly?

"Anybody else with those initials?" Vince asked.

I grabbed the phone book from the shelf above Glad's desk and skimmed through the M's. "Nope," I said. "One bonus of a small town is fewer suspects." Next I wrote "SP." Then I turned to the P's in the phone book. "No SP's except Mayor Peterson and his son Stu Two. Zee said the mayor is pro–Wal-Mart."

"And, of course, his son is a raging homophobe," Vince said.

I added the mayor and his son to my list and wrote "CC." Then I smiled. "What do you know? Collin Conover and his dad, Chuck Conover." I nibbled my pen. "I was thinking that Chuck arrested Alex Riley in order to protect his son, but maybe he's hiding his own crime. He seemed very uncomfortable when I mentioned Wal-Mart."

Vince stroked his goatee again. "Isn't Chuck Conover the guy who stole your first girlfriend?"

"So?"

"It's not very sporting to suspect someone of murder just because you don't like them."

"He got really huffy when he thought I was challenging his investigative skills."

"So his manhood is easily threatened," Vince said. "That doesn't make him a killer."

I wrote Chuck's name on my notepad and glared at Vince.

"His son has the same initials and an actual motive." Vince said. "And he fits the profile of a typical gay basher."

I wrote "Collin Conover." Then my throat tightened.

Charlene.

"His mother has the same initials too," I whispered.

"The woman who deleted the anti–Wal-Mart ads today?"

I nodded.

"Maybe Chuck and his mother are partners in crime."

"Charlene would never kill someone. She might have deleted the ads by accident."

"Then why didn't she tell you?"

I couldn't bear the thought of my aunts' longtime friend and employee turning on them. She was their first and only business manager. I called her Aunt Char when I was little, and she still sent me birthday and Christmas presents.

I turned to the C's in the phone book. No other CC's. I rubbed my eyes and stared at the list.

Wal-Mart
Winker Mason
Stuart Peterson
Stu Two
Collin Conover
Chuck Conover
Charlene Conover

I tried to imagine Chuck raising a jagged rock over his head, bringing it down on Glad's skull. "I can't see any of these people killing Glad," I said. "Not even Chuck." I was beginning to understand Zee's need to believe that strangers had done it.

seven

As I slid into my car the next morning, something crinkled under my butt. A sheet of paper. I tilted my hips up and pulled it out.

GO HOME
DYKE BITCH
OR ZEE IS NEXT

I yanked the door shut and locked myself in. My hands shook, and my heart raced. I stared at the note, stunned.

What was I thinking? I needed to check on Zee. Pronto.

I opened the window and poked my head out. The street was deserted, but there were lots of hedges and bushes that someone could hide behind. The sky was turning a dull pink, and the birds were already twittering away. Just another regular morning for them.

I took a deep breath. Whoever left the note wouldn't still be around. That's what I told myself as I ran for the house.

Once inside, I locked the door and shivered as the air conditioning washed over me. I dashed up the stairs to Zee's bedroom and cracked open the door. She was snoring, and she was safe. For now.

I needed to make sure she stayed that way, so I headed down the hallway to the guest room, intent on rousting Vince. I poked his shoulder.

No response.

I needed to wake him without disturbing Zee, so I called his name in my loudest stage whisper. Then I shook him.

He mumbled and pulled the sheet around his shoulders.

I glanced at the bedside table. Next to a jar of night cream and the remains of a generous slice of pie was an alarm clock. I set it so the alarm would go off immediately and stuck it next to Vince's ear. When it beeped, Vince stirred and pushed it away.

I shoved it back. "Vince." I shook him again. "Wake up, damn it."

He grunted and rubbed his eyes. "Mar-Bar?"

The alarm kept beeping. I grabbed his closest hand and tugged on it, hoping I could get him upright.

Finally, he opened his eyes.

I tossed the note at him.

He rolled himself onto one arm and squinted at the message, pulling it closer to his face. Soon his eyes were wide.

"It was in my car," I said. "Promise me you won't let Zee out of your sight. And don't tell her about the note. It'll only frighten her. I've got to go. I'm already late."

"Whoa, Mara." Vince swung his legs to the floor. "You can't be serious. We've got to take this to the police."

"Chuck would use it as an excuse to shut down the station."

"And well he should." Vince patted the bed, but I refused to sit.

"Don't you see? Chuck might have written it. Or his son. We can't take this to the police."

Vince tugged at his pajama bottoms. "You could show it to another cop."

I thought about Neale, but I couldn't trust her to keep Chuck in the dark about the note. She wanted her promotion too badly.

Vince moved the note back up to his face.

"They used such ordinary paper and type," I said. "And I'm sure they were savvy enough to avoid fingerprints." I sighed and sat next to Vince. Outside, the birds sounded a cacophony.

"Noisy little buggers, aren't they?" he said.

I bit my lip to keep it from trembling.

Vince set the note on his pillow. "Hey," he said, "every cloud has a silver lining."

"Clichés do not become you." My lip kept trembling.

Vince put his arm around me. "Think, Mar-Bar. Doesn't this get that kid in jail off the hook?"

For a moment I felt better, resting my head on Vince's shoulder, imagining Hortie's delight when Alex was cleared. But then I thought about Chuck's determination to keep him behind bars. "Not with Chuck in the picture," I said. "I can see him arguing that someone sent the note in order to help Alex. He might even accuse me of manufacturing it."

"Come on," Vince said.

I pulled away. "If he takes it seriously, he'll use it to close the station." I stood. "I just know he will. And that would break Zee's heart."

"Won't she also be a tad upset if her best friend's grandson is convicted of murder?"

"That won't happen."

Vince crossed his legs and rubbed his goatee. "Aren't you impeding an investigation if you don't come forward with the note?"

I folded my arms over my chest. "You've picked an incon-
venient time to develop scruples."

"I'm worried about you," he said. "You'd look perfectly
hideous in that prison-orange."

"Nobody else needs to know about the note," I said.

Vince picked it up and studied it again. "Don't you think Zee
has a right to know she's been threatened?"

He was right. Of course she did. "What if she insists we go
back to Iowa City?" I asked.

Vince raised his eyebrows. "Before the funeral?"

"What about after? Who's going to watch over her then?
Practically all her close friends are murder suspects."

Vince frowned and scratched his head. Finally, I'd argued
him into silence. "Just promise me you'll watch her."

"I'm going to have to leave after the funeral," he said.

My throat tightened, and I blinked back tears. "I'll just have
to find the killer before then."

"Mar-Bar, this is no time for egomania."

"Give me the note."

Vince moved it away from me. "You're going to have to take
it to the police sometime."

"Not today," I said. "As long as you can watch Zee, there's no
need to tell a soul."

"What about you?"

"I'll be careful."

Vince sighed and tucked the note under his mattress.

Out of sight, but not out of mind.

During "The Worry Bird" the DJ puts callers on the air to
discuss their "worries." As if I didn't have enough of my own.

I couldn't bear the thought of people calling in and asking about Glad, so I replaced "The Bird" with half an hour of Glad's favorite music. Such a tribute was more fitting than morbid questions about her death. I clicked on Patsy Cline's "Crazy" and started reading through a stack of *Aldoburg Times* I'd salvaged from the recycling bin. A front page featured a huge photo of two kids running through a sprinkler. Aldoburg is not a fount of hard news. I skimmed the headlines: DROUGHT WORRIES FARMERS, ZION LUTHERAN CALLS NEW MINISTER, COUNCIL CONSIDERS ZONING. Wal-Mart wanted to build south of town, but the land was zoned residential, so they couldn't build unless the city council voted to change the zoning. Council members included Mayor Stuart Peterson, Winker Mason, Hortie Riley, LaVonne Mumford, and Dr. Jonathon Gilgannon—my dad.

I already knew Winker and Stuart favored the store. LaVonne and Hortie were surely against it. Both owned downtown businesses—LaVonne's pharmacy had been her grandfather's. Dad was undecided. I wondered how the rest of Aldoburg felt, so I turned to the opinion page. Surprisingly, there were no letters to the editor, but Winker's column extolled the virtues of Wal-Mart. Low prices, more jobs, more choices for consumers. The opposite of everything on Glad's PSA.

As I refolded the paper, a photo on the back page caught my attention. My dad and Barb in their tennis gear, holding aloft a trophy. Next to them was a much younger duo with a much smaller trophy. Dad and Barb were grinning. Little did they know that in a few days Dad's sister-in-law and Barb's husband would be gone. I allowed myself to brood until Patsy finished. Then I announced Elvis's "Love Me Tender" and turned to the opinion page of the next paper. Again, Winker's column celebrated Wal-Mart. He waxed eloquent on the pride of buying

American. Rather ironic since so many of Wal-Mart's products are made overseas.

I tried the next paper. The superstore had made the top of the front page. In the middle of the article was a sentence that took my breath away: *Wal-Mart plans to build south of town on land currently owned by Ronald and Charlene Conover.*

Color me stupid. While I was busy making a list of murder suspects, I hadn't even thought about who owned the land Wal-Mart wanted. Charlene must have tampered with the live log because she wanted to sell her farm. But it had been in her family for generations. And surely she hadn't put that horrible note in my car.

I segued from Elvis to the Beatles when Chuck barreled through the studio door. "I just got an earful from the mayor. What were you doing harassing our sons—implying they committed murder?" Veins bulged in his temple and neck.

I summoned my strongest radio voice. "They beat up another student and called him a faggot. And they have no alibi."

He leaned over the counter on my right, his face inches from mine.

I was trapped.

"They were at my mother's, helping her move stuff out of her basement." Chuck moved back. "Not that it's any of your business."

"That's not what they told me."

Chuck's brow creased—but only for a moment. "I've already got a suspect in custody. Alex Riley was seen heading toward the station at the right time, and I found a can of white spray paint in his saddlebag."

"Who saw him?"

"Doesn't matter. He was carrying spray paint."

"It matters to me," I said. "Who was it?"

Chuck stared at the floor.

"Look." I struggled to keep my voice calm. "My aunt was murdered. I have a right to know about the witness."

Chuck tried to look me in the eye. "We got an anonymous note."

"What did it look like?" Maybe it was from the same person who'd visited my car.

"Just a note. Regular typeface."

The Beatles faded out. I started Bette Midler's "The Rose" and gazed at Chuck during the opening chords.

He folded his arms over his chest and worked his jaw.

"What if the murderer sent it?" I asked. "Or someone with a grudge against Alex?"

"Riley has a motive." Chuck spoke to me as if I were at the bottom of the class at Moron U. "He's been trashing Glad and Zee all over town because they wouldn't give him a job."

"Lots of people have been trashing my aunts because of their stance against Wal-Mart."

Chuck's jaw worked harder. "I bet none of them have a history of vandalism. Last year I caught Alex spray-painting Bible verses all over the bandstand at the park. He's probably one of those right-wingers that hates gays."

That was rich, given that his own son is a gay basher—and a chip off the old block. "What were the verses?"

Chuck shrugged.

"Any word on Glad's autopsy?" I kept my voice even.

He dropped his hands to his sides. "Preliminary results are just like I thought. Death caused by a single blow to the back of the head." He met my eyes. "She lost consciousness right away. She didn't suffer."

His momentary kindness flustered me. I was relieved Glad hadn't suffered, but that made the homophobic graffiti all the more puzzling. How could there be a hate crime with no suffering? There were so many things I wanted to ask Chuck: How did he feel about the potential sale of his family's farm? Where was he when Glad was murdered? But I'd cover old ground first, and for good measure I'd begin with some ass-kissing. "My aunt and I really appreciate all the time and energy you've spent investigating Glad's murder, but I still don't think it was vicious enough to be a hate crime."

"I know how to do my job, Mara." He headed to the studio door.

"Does Alex Riley have a history of violence like your son?" I can only do tactful for so long.

Chuck whirled around. "You stay away from my son and his friends or you and your aunt will both be sorry."

As he stormed out, I turned to the live log and clicked on "The 59th Street Bridge Song." At least Simon and Garfunkel were feelin' groovy.

eight

My first stop after work was the jail. It was in the back of the
county courthouse, a pale brick building across from the town
square. The baby cop seemingly in charge was working a crossword puzzle. I cleared my throat, and he dropped his pencil.

"Ma'am?" he said, his eyes wide. He had huge freckles and
huge ears.

"I'm here to visit Alex Riley."

"You a relative?" He swelled with self-importance.

"I'm his aunt." Sometimes the ends do justify the means.

I was ready to launch into a shameless tale of family dys-
function when he grinned, revealing a space between his two
front teeth. His shoes creaked as he led me down a hallway that
hadn't seen a coat of wax in years.

Alex stared at me, expressionless, through the bars of his
cell. His black Marilyn Manson T-shirt matched the circles
under his bloodshot eyes. He was pale, with a spattering of
acne on his chin and greasy dark hair that hung to his scrawny
shoulders.

Neither of us spoke until the baby cop left.

"You're not my aunt," he said in a squeaky voice that confirmed why my aunts hadn't wanted to hire him at the station.

"Mara Gilgannon," I said. "I'm a friend of your grandmother."

He slouched over a metal table that looked like a miniature version of Zee's kitchen counter. Someone—probably Hortie—had brought him several platters of cookies.

"I'm also Zee Richter's niece," I said.

He crammed his hands into the pockets of his jeans. "I didn't do nothing to Glad."

"Zee believes you." No need to state that Zee believed everyone in Aldoburg was innocent. "I'd like to get your side of the story," I said. "Maybe you can help me find out who really killed Glad."

The air conditioning droned ineffectually, and Alex grabbed the bottom of his T-shirt and mopped his brow with it.

"Someone saw you heading toward the station the night she was killed," I said.

"They're lying."

The anonymous note did seem suspicious. "Where were you?"

"Grandma's."

"Was she there?"

"I was by myself—just like I told the cops."

"When was the last time you saw Glad?"

He shoved his hands back into his pockets. I hoped I wasn't firing my questions too quickly.

"She was at the diner talking to Grandma about Wal-Mart. All Grandma talks about is how it'll hurt her precious restaurant."

"What do you think?"

"I don't give a flying fuck about anything in this town." He jutted out his chin and scowled.

He probably felt like no one in Aldoburg—except maybe Hortie—gave a fuck about him. Proverbial Midwestern friendliness doesn't extend to Goth kids. "Looks like someone brought you cookies," I said.

He shrugged. "Some guy whose dad died. He said people brought them way too much food."

Barb must have asked Parker to bring the sweets. In the midst of her grief, she'd been thinking of others, and all I'd been thinking about was my questions. I hadn't even brought Alex a damn Coke. In fact, I was concealing a note that could help him. "Did you know Glad very well?" I asked.

He shrugged again.

"How do you feel about gay people?"

"What's it matter if you think I'm innocent?"

"Just covering all the bases."

He looked me up and down. "I don't get queers," he admitted, "but I had nothing against Glad."

His statement seemed too tactless to be a lie, but I persisted. "You weren't angry that she and Zee didn't hire you?"

He smirked. "I didn't want that job. No offense, but I can't stand their music. I applied just so Grandma would quit nagging me."

"I heard that you were badmouthing my aunts all over town."

"Just their music. Ain't no law against that."

"Chuck Conover seems pretty convinced that you disliked Glad."

"He's an asshole."

I was warming up to Alex Riley—attitude and all. "I don't like Chuck either," I said, "but he told me you spray-painted Bible verses on the bandstand."

"Doesn't mean I painted anything on the radio station."

"Chuck doesn't see it that way."

Alex picked at a fingernail. The air conditioner grew louder in the silence. "This girl I was seeing was really into apocalyptic bullshit. I spray painted some stuff from Revelation to impress her." He smiled wryly. "Didn't work."

I felt pretty sure he hadn't killed Glad, but I had one last question. "Why did you have spray paint in your saddlebag?"

"Grandma wanted me to paint some chairs she got at a farm auction." He shook his head and sighed. "The one time I do something right, I get nailed for it."

I left the courthouse and strolled through the town square toward downtown Aldoburg. It consists of four blocks that dead-end at an abandoned train depot. Once a major stop for the Rock Island Rail, it's now all cobwebs and rotting wood because the town doesn't have the bucks to restore it. A few years ago the rest of the downtown got a face-lift, courtesy of the Coca-Cola bottling plant, Aldoburg's biggest employer. Traffic lights were painted black to match the newly added Victorian-style street lamps. Old-fashioned Coca-Cola ads adorn the sides of three brick buildings, and potted impatiens line each block. Their slightly wilted blooms were the only sign of life on the sweltering sidewalks except for yours truly and a window shopper two blocks down. When I was a kid, my mother cruised up and down Main Street, growing more and more indignant that there wasn't a space for our station wagon. Now the library was the only building that had more than one car parked in front of it.

I walked past a computer store and nearly collided with Charlene. She was carrying a plastic bag filled with computer paper. I told myself that people used such paper for all sorts of things besides threatening notes, but I couldn't help staring. The sun glinted off the rhinestones that dotted the collar of her denim blouse.

"Mara, you should be resting." She fanned herself with her free hand. "It's too hot to be running around. I'd be inside myself if Zee hadn't sent me to get this paper."

"She's not at the station by herself, is she?"

"Of course not. That friend of yours follows her everywhere. Drives her crazy." Charlene set her package on the sidewalk and lit a menthol. "Why aren't you home taking it easy?"

Good question. Between her smoke and the steam rising from the sidewalk, I was feeling faint. Maybe I just needed to eat. "I was on my way to the Chat 'n' Chew."

"Poor Hortie." Charlene flicked her ashes. "Her grandson has brought her nothing but grief."

"It doesn't seem like he has much of a motive," I ventured.

"Chuck says I'm not supposed to talk about Glad's death." She rolled her eyes.

"Can you think of anybody who might have a stronger motive?" I asked. The wind whipped a stray piece of hair into my face, but Charlene's hair didn't budge.

She flicked some more ashes onto the sidewalk. "I can't figure why anybody would ever want to kill somebody else."

I hoped that was true, that she hadn't done it herself. Of course, I didn't believe for a minute she had, but still, I appreciated the car that crept past. "I'm trying to find out where everybody was the night Glad died. Maybe somebody saw something unusual."

Charlene tensed. She brought her cigarette to her lips but didn't take a puff. "I didn't see anything except Collin and Stu Two carting stuff out of my basement. Chuck was there too."

Chuck hadn't told me he was with his son that night. Was

Charlene trying to give him and her grandson alibis? I weighed my next words carefully. "When I first talked to Stu Two and Collin about Glad's death, they said they were jogging."

Charlene exhaled a cloud of smoke. "Kids," she said. "They never keep track of anything."

A lot of people were confused about their whereabouts the night Glad died. Charlene's alibi depended on her grandson, and vice versa. Not exactly airtight. "I read in the paper that Wal-Mart wants to buy your farm."

She studied our shadows on the sidewalk. A woman with a cane hobbled by. I waited until she was out of hearing range. "So do you and Ron want to sell?"

Charlene frowned at the mention of her husband's name, and her wrinkles deepened. "Ron's not doing too good." She sucked on her cigarette. "He needs a drier climate for his asthma. A place like Arizona."

I felt sorry for her but not sorry enough to stop my questions. "So you'd like to move?"

"We got to," she said, "but we can't afford it unless we sell the farm. Wal-Mart's offering a decent price."

Talk about motive. Charlene deleted those anti–Wal-Mart ads on purpose, and now I knew why. I also knew why Zee insisted strangers had killed Glad. If they hadn't, then Charlene was an obvious suspect.

Or maybe Chuck had committed the murder to give his parents a better chance at selling their farm.

"Would you be for Wal-Mart if you didn't need to sell?" I asked.

"Moot point." She exhaled more smoke. "I will tell you this—Zee is shooting herself in the foot with her anti–Wal-Mart programming."

I flinched. Given Glad's murder, Charlene might have used a less violent figure of speech.

Her eyes met mine. "Sorry." She cleared her throat "But Wal-Mart offered to buy several promos for the new store. And the station could use the money."

"Is it in trouble?"

"It will be if Zee doesn't pay any mind to her listeners," Charlene said. "I'm not the only one who wants Wal-Mart. There's everybody that got laid off from IBP." Charlene coughed, and I wondered how many people had lost their jobs at the beef-processing plant.

"Folks are tired of driving an hour one way to work," she said. "And everybody wants a decent place to shop. The only people against Wal-Mart are your aunts and people who own businesses downtown. Some of them have been calling me— begging me not to sell to Wal-Mart, telling me it will destroy Aldoburg—but I gotta think of my family first. You'd do the same thing if Zee was sick and you needed money."

She was right. I would. But I wouldn't kill an old friend. Had she?

nine

At the Chat 'n' Chew, a couple of retired farmers sipped coffee in a window booth, and Hortie's granddaughter Talia smiled at me from the counter. Her ponytail swung back and forth as she brought me a glass of ice water and a menu. Talia is Korean. She and her older sister were adopted by Hortie's second-oldest son when Talia was a baby. I wondered if it bothered her, growing up in such a white town. She'd been popular in high school, a cheerleader and the homecoming queen. Still, I knew it was hard being different.

"How'd your first year of college treat you?" I asked.

"Fine."

The curt response wasn't like her. "Is your grandma in the kitchen?" I asked gently.

"She's not feeling good." Talia gazed at the counter and bit her lip. Her lipstick—a frosty pink—matched her fingernail polish.

"Look," I said, "Zee and I certainly don't think Alex killed Glad. Will you tell Hortie that for me?"

Talia gave me a tiny smile. "I'm so worried about him," she said. "He was having such a hard time even before all this. He's a really good artist, but his dad doesn't care. Uncle Frank is always pushing him to get better grades. He wants Alex to become a dentist like him." She made a face.

I promised myself I'd drop some sketching materials by the jail.

"Last year," Talia continued, "the cops caught Alex with some pot, not enough to sell, just to smoke. A month later he got a DUI. That was it for Uncle Frank. He and Alex had a huge fight, and Uncle Frank gave him an ultimatum—a treatment center or Grandma's."

Hortie had run a restaurant and raised eight kids on her own after her husband died, and now she was helping her wayward grandchildren. She had her work cut out for her with Alex.

"I'm sorry," Talia said. "What can I get you?"

I ordered a Coke and some onion rings. Not much had changed at the Chat 'n' Chew except the prices. In some of the booths, the olive vinyl upholstery had cracked, and the cloth flowers next to the condiment trays had frayed. The walls were more crowded with photos of boys and girls posing next to champion livestock. One photo featured an ostrich.

Talia set my Coke on the counter. I decided to make the most of her chattiness. "When was the last time you saw Glad?" I asked.

"She was in here with Winker. They kind of looked like they were fighting."

I thought about Winker's pro–Wal-Mart editorials. "Did you hear what they were saying?"

Talia twisted her ponytail, probably wondering whether she should admit to eavesdropping. "Waitresses must accidentally overhear lots of things," I said.

She let go of her hair. "When I brought them their food they were just talking about shopping."

"Wal-Mart?"

Talia shrugged.

"Did you see anyone else arguing with Glad?"

"No, not really."

"But something else?" I prompted.

Talia fingered her ponytail again. "She had a Coke with Stu Two and Collin one afternoon. They all looked real serious, and I heard Stu say, 'I'm afraid of what my dad will do.'"

There are two short blocks between the Chat 'n' Chew and the *Times* office. I studied the stores on my side of the street. The first block had a jewelry store, a bakery, and two vacant shops—all sporting anti–Wal-Mart posters. The bakery's display also featured a wedding cake and a sign that read BETTY'S BAKERY: HOME OF THE WORLD'S LARGEST BUTTER COOKIE.

The next block featured a so-called dime store. In my lifetime the only things that have cost less than a dime were bubble gum and—for a fleeting moment—postage stamps. Next to the "dime store" was a more accurately named consignment shop called Stuff. In its window was a display of retro clothing. A headless mannequin was dressed in a bright green tube top with denim bell-bottoms. Her feet were adorned with red sandals that Vince would die for. Their heels were at least five inches high and nearly as big around. I swung my backpack from my shoulder and felt around for my wallet. Only two dollars and some change. Vince's treat would have to wait.

After Stuff was a defunct hardware store, a law office, a plus-size clothing store, a beauty shop called the Kutting Crew, a sewing store called So 'n' So, and a Dollar Daze. If misspelled store names guaranteed success, downtown Aldoburg had nothing to fear from Wal-Mart.

On the next block I passed Mitzi's Bar, a tanning salon, one more abandoned store, and Honig's Hardware. I wanted to stop and ask if anyone besides Alex had recently bought white spray paint, but the store was closed because of Bill's death.

The *Times* office was right across the street. A bell announced my entrance, but the secretary's desk was empty. At the foot of her desk was a mass of ivy that needed to be repotted. Despite the air conditioning, a miniature fan whirred on her front desk, so I closed my eyes and leaned my face next to it.

"Mara!"

Winker's bellow made me jump. When I was a kid I was scared of his booming laugh and his bulk—his broad shoulders and his hands that were the biggest I'd ever seen. Sweat glistened on his bald head. His shirt was unbuttoned at the collar, revealing a tuft of gray hair. "You holding up OK?" he asked. "What about Zee? She need anything?"

Winker had always been kind to my aunts and me. When I got my learner's permit and couldn't master their stick shift, he let me practice on his automatic. When Glad had her hysterectomy, he sat with Zee and Hortie in the waiting room. He couldn't have killed Glad. Zee would be furious if she knew I even considered him a suspect. "Zee's fine," I said, "doing as well as can be expected."

"Wish she'd take better care of herself," he said gruffly. "It's crazy, you two keeping the station open."

Was he concerned about our well-being, or did he have another reason for wanting the station closed? Fond memories be damned. I needed information. "I've been reading some back issues of the paper," I said. "Seems like you're a real Wal-Mart fan."

"I'm no fool. Wal-Mart will buy weekly advertising inserts from me, and the *Times* needs the money."

"Aren't you afraid it'll drive your other advertisers out of business?"

"You must not have looked at the paper too closely," Winker said. "Only a handful of businesses can afford ads."

What a vicious cycle. You can't afford advertising because you don't have enough customers; without advertising, you have even fewer.

Winker followed my train of thought. "There's nothing to do about it. Zee thinks she can save downtown, but she's dreaming. It's already dying without Wal-Mart."

"There are a lot of empty stores," I admitted.

"We're lucky Wal-Mart wants to come here." He folded his arms across his massive chest.

"I suppose you and Glad had lots of discussions about it?"

"We were always fighting. Glad was stubborn as they come." His voice filled with admiration.

"What were you doing the night she died?"

He narrowed his storm-gray eyes. "For Zee's sake," he said, "I'll pretend you didn't ask that."

I met his gaze. I wouldn't turn away or blink until he answered me.

"I was watching CNN," he said.

I didn't have to ask if he was alone. His wife had died of cancer when I lived with Zee and Glad.

"Didn't know I'd need an alibi." He turned his back on me.

I was halfway to my car when I decided to go back and apologize. Through the glass doors of the *Times* office, I saw Winker on the phone, his back to me, his voice booming. "I'm telling you," he said, "she could really mess things up for us."

He slammed down the receiver, and I hightailed it up the street—no longer in the mood to apologize.

ten

Simmons Funeral Home is a study in tackiness: dull gold carpeting, chairs of fake dark wood with olive cushions, wallpaper with shiny gold stripes. Worst of all are the knickknacks designed to make the place look homey, to help you forget the casket in the next room.

Tonight William Honig was in the casket. Tomorrow night it would be Glad.

As I scanned the crowd, looking for the Post-it-note suspects, Vince signed the guest book with a flourish. I dashed over and all but ripped the pen out of his hand. "You're supposed to be with Zee."

"I know," he said. "I stayed as long as I could, but she insisted I leave. She said you needed my moral support."

I scowled.

"She said she'd be fine at the station with Charlene."

"You left her alone with a murder suspect?" I could barely keep my voice down.

"I couldn't help it." Vince fussed with his bow tie. "You didn't want me to tell her about the note, did you?"

"Couldn't you think of some other excuse?"

"Like what?" He cocked his head to one side and assumed an ultraserious voice. "Zee, Mara and I think your dear friend may be a murderer."

"You couldn't lie?" I said.

"They're coming here right after they close."

I glanced at my watch. 7:55. Even if Vince and I zipped to the station, we might still miss them. And I didn't suspect Charlene, not really.

"You might as well make yourself useful," I said. "See if you can eavesdrop on some of the Post-it-note suspects."

Vince bowed. "I'll make myself utterly inconspicuous."

In the midst of muted Sunday suits, Vince—with his pink dress shirt and black bow tie—stuck out like a sore thumb. But who was I to criticize? My formal repertoire consisted solely of the allegedly wrinkle-proof black dress I was wearing. "I'm going to find Barb," I said. "There's Winker in the far corner. Why don't you hover nearby and listen in on his conversations."

Vince started to step away, but it was too late. LaVonne Mumford bounded toward us. A navy polyester dress accentuated her pear-shaped body, and clusters of pearls at her ears made her round face look even rounder. "You poor dear," she gushed. "I'm so sorry, honey."

Damn. I knew this would happen. People would feel obligated to offer their condolences tonight, and they would feel equally obligated to come to Glad's visitation tomorrow and offer them again.

"Glad was a gem—a real gem. You tell Zee that if she needs anything from the pharmacy, just give me a call and I'll bring it by. Day or night."

LaVonne ran the downtown pharmacy, and word had it she'd begun throwing frequent Tupperware parties—which probably meant her store was hurting.

"This must be so hard for you," LaVonne said.

"You too." My throat tightened. "Glad considered you one of her best friends." I groped for a graceful way to move on. "I still haven't seen Barb," I said.

"She's in there." LaVonne nodded toward the casket room and smiled at Vince. "Who might you be?" From her tone of voice, I could tell she was picturing me in a wedding dress marching down the aisle of St. Patrick's on my father's arm. She must have forgotten about the whole lesbian thing.

"This is Vince," I said, "my housemate." I emphasized the last part and stepped on Vince's foot, signaling him to keep quiet.

It didn't work.

"I'm gay," Vince said. He loved to shock people, and the poor dear didn't get much of a chance in Iowa City.

LaVonne stammered, but she never lost her smile. "Oh, I see," she said. "Like on *Will & Grace*."

I grabbed Vince by the elbow and steered him toward the casket. We made our way past two elderly women who were discussing their late husbands' strokes. And there was Bill. His dark hair was combed more neatly than it had ever been when he was alive, and he was dressed in a black suit. I'd never seen him in one before, not even at church. His personality was evident only in the fabric of his tie, which was sprinkled with tiny black saws, hammers, and screwdrivers.

"Bill loved to fix things," I said.

Vince put his arm around my shoulder. "Is Glad going to be in a casket like this?"

"It'll be closed," I said. "She never liked people staring at her." A wave of guilt washed over me. I hadn't been helping Zee with the arrangements. Instead I'd been alienating and annoying her friends with my questions.

I pushed aside my guilt and once again sent Vince to spy on Winker. Then I walked past several flower arrangements and waited a few steps away from the group that encircled Barb and her family. In the midst of this group were my parents. I had to admit, they made a handsome couple. They're about the same height, and both are tan and trim from hours on the golf course. My father has magnificent thick white hair and black-framed glasses, which he got last year. He's a quiet, patient soul—hen-pecked, some would say. He was hurt and bewildered when I moved out, but over the years we've sort of patched things up. He even started asking about Anne a few months before she left me. Since then I've evaded his questions. As Vince would say, I haven't been in the "right space" to tell him about Anne's departure. In other words, I'm too damned embarrassed.

As Dad waited to offer Barb his sympathy, he picked up her youngest grandchild, rocking the toddler and stroking her curly brown hair. I waited for him to chuck her under the chin and ask, "How's my best girl?" He said that to every little girl he'd ever treated for so much as a stuffy nose. It burned me up inside when I was a child. But tonight Dad barely smiled at the toddler. Bill's death must have hit him hard. Dad had gone hunting and fishing with Bill, and he'd delivered all of Bill's children and grandchildren. According to Zee, Dad had also treated Bill's heart trouble.

The toddler started fussing, so Dad cooed at her. The toddler's mother, Frannie, was busy wiping her son's nose and hoisting her purse strap back onto her shoulder. Her oldest daughter clung to the vinyl handbag as if it were a life preserver. Dad shifted Frannie's toddler onto his left hip and shook

Parker's hand. Dad never tired of telling the story of how Parker got his name. When he was born, Bill and Barb were afraid that eleven-year-old Frannie would have a hard time adjusting to a new baby brother, so they let her name him. She had a big crush on Parker Stevenson of *Hardy Boys* fame. The rest is history. "Can you imagine that?" Dad said. "Naming your only son after a bad actor?"

Parker had grown up to be a good foot taller than Frannie and his mother. His hair was short and dark in back, long and bleached in front, hiding his face as he stared at the carpet. When my dad clasped Barb's shoulder, Parker glanced up and brushed his hair out of his face. My mother offered him a Kleenex while Dad squeezed Barb's hand and deposited the toddler on the floor. Then he and Mom drifted away.

The toddler hugged Frannie's knee as Barb endured several more condolences. Then it was my turn.

First, Frannie. She acknowledged my words with a nod and put an arm around her boy, whose nose continued running. Then Barb herself. The bruise-blue of her eye shadow matched the swollen circles beneath her eyes. When I hugged her I could feel her ribs.

As I shook Parker's hand, he studied his feet. "I'm really sorry," I said. "Your dad was a great guy."

Parker looked up and nodded. When I baby-sat him, his favorite activity was playing store. He'd wear one of his dad's caps and offer up his toys to me one after another. "You buy this? You buy this?" He never wanted me to sell him anything. He always wanted to be like his dad.

I touched him on the arm. "I'll be in town a few days if you want to talk."

He nodded again, and Barb clasped the hands of an older woman behind me. "I've got Parker and Frannie and the little ones with me right now," Barb said. "That makes it easier."

I checked my watch. Where was Zee?

Winker was talking with Chuck and Mayor Peterson. The mayor had thinning hair, broad shoulders, and a penchant for reminding people that he was the state middleweight champion in 1968.

Vince stood nearby, pretending to study a glass cabinet filled with miniature ceramic shoes—white old-fashioned lace-ups, dotted with brightly colored flowers. My three suspects were oblivious to the shoes. Winker looked worried, and he spoke rapidly. The mayor's bushy mustache twitched as he listened. Chuck's suit strained at the seams, and his shirt cut into his neck. Boy, what *Queer Eye for the Straight Guy* could do for him.

I didn't want to get caught staring, so I headed toward a photo display of Bill's life, where I tried to gather my thoughts about the threesome. It just didn't make sense. The mayor and Chuck were good friends, but I'd never known Winker to socialize with either of them. In fact, it was no secret that Winker and the mayor disliked each other. Winker had come out of the womb a Catholic Democrat, and Stuart was a WASP Republican. As far as I knew, they didn't have anything in common except a fondness for Wal-Mart.

I turned my attention to the photos of Bill. There was a picture of him when he was about Parker's age, shelving cans of paint at the hardware store. Next to him was a beaming man who must have been his father. In another photo Bill held a two-ish Parker on his lap, rapt with whatever the boy was babbling. Bill had never been much of a talker, but he was a joyful listener, sprinkling his part of a conversation with phrases like "Ain't that the truth?" and "How about that?" In a more recent photo Bill was selling beer and brats with my dad and Winker at a Knights of Columbus booth—probably during Aldoburg Fest. The men were laughing, and Bill held a brat aloft on a fork. Lots of photos featured Bill eating or cooking. In one of them he was grinning and turning an ice cream maker, his eyes shaded by a Pioneer Seed cap. At the edge of the photo was a slender arm. My arm. With a jolt I realized Glad had taken the picture.

I bit my lip and looked away. An ash-blond stood next to a cluster of tall fake plants, her back to me. She was talking to Lester Simms, the funeral director. Her curls streamed past her shoulders, and a teal suit revealed gentle curves. I refuse to wear panty hose, but I like it when other women do. This woman had the best-looking legs I'd ever seen—long, slender, and sinewy.

Vince caught my eye and winked.

The funeral director wandered off, and the woman turned. It was Neale.

We smiled at each other. I wanted to tell her what I'd learned, and I wanted to pour out my heart about the horrible note I'd received, but she darted her eyes toward Chuck and walked away. She didn't want him to see us talking, I thought.

The crowd showed no signs of thinning. The smell of cologne, hairspray, and funeral flowers made me long for the great outdoors—even with ninety-nine percent humidity—but I needed to keep tabs on the Post-it-note suspects. The mayor had cornered my dad, who was politely smiling and nodding. Dad liked almost everybody, but not Stuart Peterson.

The room hushed as Zee entered with Charlene. Thank God. As my aunt signed the guest book, Charlene rested her hand on Zee's shoulder, her bright pink fingernails clashing with Zee's red dress. The group of well-wishers that surrounded the Honigs swarmed toward Zee. LaVonne gave her a crushing hug, and several spindly old ladies tottered toward her. Abandoning my father, the mayor sped toward the crowd.

I rushed to him and held out my hand. "I hope there aren't any hard feelings about the questions I asked your son."

He took my hand and forced a smile. "Stu realizes what he did was wrong, and now it's in the past."

He emphasized the word *past*, warning me to leave his son alone. I wondered if he condoned his son's homophobia, and I forced a smile of my own. "Sure," I said. "Young people can get carried away sometimes."

"Exactly," he said. "Stu's under a lot of pressure. Several schools are already looking at him. I know how stressful that can be. After I won the state middleweight championship in 1968, plenty of them were after me."

I tried to look attentive, but I couldn't help thinking about Stu Two's words: *I'm afraid of what my dad will do.*

"It may sound good to have so many schools wanting you," the mayor continued, "but those decisions are tough. Very tough."

Charlene sat on a couch next to Chuck, who handed her a Dixie cup. Vince stood nearby, pretending to admire a fake fern.

"I'm very sorry about your loss," Stuart said. Politicians—even small-time ones—never forget their manners for long.

"It was quite a shock," I said. "One day she was gardening and battling Wal-Mart, and the next day she was gone."

"Glad was a wise woman and a savvy consumer," Stuart said, "Zee will be getting a tidy sum because of the life insurance I advised Glad to purchase."

"I'm sure that will be a comfort." I fought to keep the disgust out of my voice. "She's been very preoccupied with funeral arrangements and the Wal-Mart thing."

He nodded several times as I spoke. His active listening was too active for me.

"You must be pretty busy with the Wal-Mart thing yourself," I said, "preparing for the public forum that's coming up."

"Not really. There are two opposing teams, and I'm just the referee."

"You must have some personal opinion about it."

He pressed his lips together, and they disappeared under his bulky mustache. "I just try to stay objective."

"Zee said you called to complain about an interview she and Glad did with a former Wal-Mart manager."

"It was very one-sided."

"Were you worried it made Wal-Mart look bad?"

Stuart held his arm in front of him and checked his watch.

"I guess Alex Riley has been arrested." I blurted the obvious in an attempt to keep Stuart from bolting. "Somebody sent Chuck an anonymous note, saying they saw Alex out by the station." I kept my tone light. "Did you see anything unusual that night?"

"Of course not," he said. "Now if you'll excuse me, I need to find my wife."

"Were you with her that night?"

He ignored my question and headed straight for Chuck. Uh-oh. It wouldn't be long before I got another visit from my favorite law enforcement official. Or maybe another threatening note.

I checked the room for Zee. She was behind me, still mobbed, my parents and Winker at her side. Vince stood near the exit, frantically motioning me toward him. So much for subtlety.

He pulled the door open, and the humidity assaulted us.

"So," I said, "what was Winker discussing with Chuck and the mayor?"

"I couldn't really hear," Vince said. "They were whispering, and I was afraid they'd notice if I stood too close."

"Then why the histrionics?"

Vince beamed. "I heard your dear friend Chuck say to his mother, 'If she finds out what we were doing the night Glad died, there'll be hell to pay.'"

eleven

At KGEE the next morning, I listened to Céline Dion and tried to sort through a morass of details about my suspects. I needed to find out what Chuck and Charlene had been doing the night Glad was killed. Obviously, they hadn't really been watching Stu Two and Collin remove junk from Charlene's basement. They wouldn't worry about anyone discovering that. And who was the mysterious "she" they were worried about? Zee? Or yours truly?

The end of the theme song from *Titanic* interrupted my questions. I announced the time and played an ad for Dollar Daze. I really needed a sounding board, but Vince was with Zee at Bill's funeral. Not that I was complaining. I just prayed that he stayed with her this time.

The ad ended, and I started Neil Diamond's "Coming to America."

Stu Two and Collin never claimed to be at Charlene's house the night Glad died, yet they couldn't give me a straight answer about where they had been.

And Chuck. He insisted Alex was the murderer even

though the evidence was circumstantial and his motive was flimsy. Maybe Chuck didn't want anyone to consider Wal-Mart as a motive. He'd been whispering with Winker and Stuart at Bill's visitation. And those two were sure behaving strangely. Winker made that mysterious phone call after I visited him. The mayor was evasive about his stance on Wal-Mart, and his son was afraid of him.

Any of these charming folks could have killed Glad and left that nasty note in my car.

Neil Diamond faded. As I started Cher's most recent hit, my mind flitted from suspect to suspect and I felt trapped, penned in by the long counters on each side of my chair. On the counter to my left, tape equipment towered over me. On the counter to my right were two seldom-used turntables. Beyond it was a chair with an orange vinyl seat, and beyond that was a door surrounded by shelves of forty-fives. These records lined all but the back wall. Many of them had already been recorded and stored in the computers, and the rest probably crackled and hissed if you tried to play them, but there they were, a testament to days gone by.

When Cher finished, I played a Chat 'n' Chew ad and thought about Hortie and Alex. If someone didn't find the killer soon, Alex would go to trial. And then maybe to prison.

I began a Jim Croce tune and swiveled in my chair. The window on the back wall hadn't been washed in ages, and there was a slight rip in its screen. Next to the window was a bulletin board. I stood and headed toward it, hoping it contained some information about Glad or Wal-Mart.

There were high school baseball and softball schedules, a calendar from a seed corn company, a list of employee birthdays, and a *Far Side* cartoon. The cartoon featured a pudgy man in hell facing the devil and two doors. One said, "Damned If

You Do"; the other said "Damned If You Don't." Underneath it, Glad had written "A typical day in radio."

I wondered if my aunts were having a hard time keeping their station afloat. After all, Winker was struggling to find ads for his paper. I sat back down and scrolled through the computer that contained the station's ads and PSAs. There were four anti–Wal-Mart spots. A third of the ads were from businesses that wouldn't be impacted by Wal-Mart: manufacturers of feed processing systems and other farm implements, heating and air conditioning companies, car dealerships, financial services, law offices, and beauty shops. About another fourth of the ads promoted products that Wal-Mart sold: videos, soft drinks, contact lenses, deodorants. Three hundred twenty-six cuts in all.

I had no idea whether that was enough to keep KGEE in business. Back in Iowa City, I had nothing to do with advertising. I was simply the midday announcer Monday through Friday. I had no extra duties except for the reading series. But my aunts were the original multitaskers. In addition to their on-air shifts, they had a hand in all the financial stuff. Glad covered most of the county's sporting events, and Zee handled all the other live coverage. How could she possibly find someone to replace Glad?

Of course, Glad could never be replaced.

But Zee would need to find someone willing to work twelve-hour days, and that someone would need to be independently wealthy or totally in love with radio because I doubted Zee would be able to pay much more than minimum wage. And who would fill in when I had to leave?

I told myself that Zee was a resourceful woman. Jobs were scarce in Aldoburg, and someone would jump at the chance to work at the station. Alas, guilt never does defer to logic—at least for those of us raised Catholic.

I clicked on an ad for Farm Bureau Insurance.

Insurance. What had Stuart said? Something about Zee getting a tidy sum from some life insurance he'd sold Glad. I'd dismissed his comment as mere self-promotion, but maybe the "tidy sum" would enable Zee and the station to weather hard times. I wondered how much coverage Glad had been able to afford.

The insurance ad ended, so I started a Coke commercial.

The clock said 10:11. My morning was creeping along. I had places to go, people to interrogate. I needed to talk with Charlene, but she wouldn't be in until after Bill's funeral and the luncheon that followed. I was alone at the station.

Then it registered. I was free to snoop.

I checked the mailboxes first. Zee and Glad had nothing but bills and junk mail. Charlene's was empty, Parker's held Peace Corps information, and Jack's contained a computer catalog and several advertisements from record companies.

I announced Lee Ann Womack and headed for Charlene's desk. Under a tiny potted cactus was a stack of folders. Much to my dismay, none of them were marked "Wal-Mart" or "Secret Activities." In the center of her desk were some bills and an adding machine, which I moved aside so I could look at her desk calendar.

I sank into her chair.

On the day of Glad's murder, Charlene had written "9:30." A mere half-hour before Glad had been attacked. Charlene had carefully noted the location and purpose of all her other meetings, but not this one. Her puzzling notation had to be connected to her son's comment at the funeral parlor. What had they been doing the night Glad died?

After my shift I went to the Chat 'n' Chew, where I found Hortie slumped over the counter, idly picking at a tuna melt. I could hear the clanking of dishes in the kitchen. In the booth behind me, a toddler whined for ice cream. He and his mom were the only customers besides me.

Hortie followed my eyes. "We're extra slow today. Most folks went to Bill's funeral. Church was packed."

"How'd Zee hold up?" I asked.

"Like a trooper."

"She seemed shaky when she arrived at the station. I tried to convince her to let me work her shift, but—"

"I know, I know. She wouldn't hear of it." Hortie stood and took my order. As she headed to the kitchen, I wondered how Barb and Parker were doing after the funeral. Part of me wished I'd been there—Bill was such a sweet guy, and I wanted to be there for his family and Zee. But part of me was relieved to have been at the station. Glad's visitation was tonight, and her funeral tomorrow. Two funerals in two days was too much for me. I hoped Zee would make it through.

Hortie slid a Coke and an egg salad sandwich in front of me and gazed at the remains of her own sandwich. She hadn't eaten much.

"How are you doing?" I asked.

She tugged at the waitress cap that perched on top of her hair. "It's mighty hard to keep going with Bill and Glad dead and Alex in jail."

"Zee and I don't think Alex did it."

"The police do." She pushed her sandwich away. "That boy's no angel, but he's no killer either. His parents are beside themselves. I was supposed to straighten him out, and look what happened." Her lip trembled.

I wanted to give her some hope for Alex. "I don't think Glad's death was a hate crime," I said. "I think it had something to do with Wal-Mart."

Hortie pulled her cigarettes out of her apron pocket and chain-smoked while I told her about Glad's Post-it note and everything else I'd discovered.

"I don't like thinking that somebody I know killed Glad," she said.

The mother and her whiny boy made their way to the door. Hortie merely nodded at them. I'd never seen her so lethargic.

When they were gone, she sighed. "Maybe I should close for a few days. Just until Alex is cleared."

For as long as I could remember, Hortie had closed the Chat 'n' Chew only on Christmas Eve and Christmas. "But where will I eat my lunch?" I tried to rally her.

She flicked her cigarette in the ashtray. "If Wal-Mart comes, you can eat it in their snack shop. They always have a snack shop. Next thing you know there'll be a McDonald's."

Golden arches clearly spelled doom for Hortie. I tried to think of something comforting to say.

"Everything is going down." She shook her head sadly. "Bill had lunch in here a few days before he died. Said things just weren't moving in his store. And I know LaVonne don't sell much in her pharmacy besides prescriptions. Hard to make a living on that."

So LaVonne did need to sell Tupperware. It made me sad to think of her peddling the latest line of brightly colored bowls to friends whose cupboards already overflowed with freezer-proof containers they'd bought at her last party. "What about Winker?" I asked. "How badly does he need Wal-Mart's ad inserts?"

"Winker's oldest lost his job when IBP shut down last March. Been out of work since, and the poor thing has three kids and a mortgage." She frowned. "Rumor has it Winker cosigned it."

I swirled my straw around in my Coke. "Do you suppose Winker thinks his son will get a good job with Wal-Mart?"

"He's a fool if he does. Wal-Mart don't put anybody full-time." She lit another cigarette. "That way they don't have to pay benefits."

"What about the mayor?" I asked.

"His oldest was also at IBP, but I can't imagine Stuart cosigning a mortgage."

"What about his insurance business?"

Hortie rolled her eyes. "He's always pestering folks to buy insurance. He'd insure my daily special if I let him."

"You think he's struggling?"

Hortie shrugged. "Like the rest of us."

"Why do you think Stuart favors Wal-Mart?"

"When he got elected he promised to attract more business to Aldoburg, but he ain't done it yet." Hortie took a long drag and exhaled. "Next year's election year, so he needs to do something fast. The fool thinks Wal-Mart is his ticket to a political dynasty."

Hortie's information made me want to question the mayor again. His insurance office was sandwiched between the bank and Zion Lutheran Church, right across the street from the Chat 'n' Chew. Spoiled by the smoke-free restaurants in Iowa City, I took a deep breath of fresh air and jaywalked.

No one was waiting in Stuart's waiting room unless you count the secretary waiting to go home. The twenty-something woman looked up from filing her nails. She seemed to have a fondness for lip gloss. "Can I help you?" Her tone implied no great eagerness.

"I'd like to talk with Stuart."

She said something polite that nevertheless implied *I have no idea when he'll be back. Get away from my desk and leave me alone.*

I didn't budge. "How's business been?"

She put down her nail file. "Pretty slow."

I could tell by the thick stack of beauty magazines on her desk that she was telling the truth.

"People don't realize how important insurance is," she said.

I had no desire to hear her canned speech on the virtues of insurance, so I followed her advice and took a seat. Hanging next to her desk was a framed poster that said *Farm Bureau Insurance: Because You Have a Lot to Lose.* I scanned the darkly paneled walls. Waiting rooms never have clocks. "What time is it?" I asked.

Nail File checked her wrist. "3:25."

I longed for a nap, but I needed to narrow my list of suspects—and fast. Orchid awaited me in Iowa City. I glanced at Nail File's desk. Under the beauty magazines was a desk calendar that I wanted to see. "Miss," I said, "maybe you could help me. I need some information about long-term care insurance."

Nail File flashed me a smile, reached into her desk drawer, and pulled out a brochure.

Damn. I needed her away from the desk. "I also need some information about insuring pets," I said. "Exotic pets. I've got a depressed Komodo dragon and a python with a lot of unidentified health problems."

Her smile faded. "I don't think we insure such dangerous animals."

"I ran into Stuart last night," I said, "and he assured me it would be no problem. In fact, he promised to get some quotes ready for me. Maybe they're on his desk?"

Eager to be free of me, she all but sprinted to Stuart's office.

I was at her desk in a flash. Stuart's appointments were all written in fat curly script—undoubtedly Nail File's penmanship. There was nothing on the day of Glad's death. Not surprising since it was a Sunday.

I dashed back to Stuart's office.

Nail File was staring blankly at his desk.

"Let me help." I slid a few pages aside so I could see Stuart's desk calendar. On the day Glad died, it said, "9:30 P.M."

Fate. Providence. Destiny. Whatever name you give it, I don't believe in coincidence. Stuart and Charlene had planned to meet the night Glad died. As I strolled down the street, I wondered if Chuck had also been in on the plan, and I thought about what he'd said to his mother at the funeral parlor: *If she finds out what we were doing the night Glad died, there'll be hell to pay.* Of course, Chuck might not have been referring to his mother. Maybe he'd been with someone else, and Charlene had been with Stuart. But when I asked Stuart for an alibi, why hadn't he told me he was with Charlene? It was hard to imagine anyone lusting after Stuart or Charlene, but there's no accounting for the foibles of the human heart.

I passed a florist, the JCPenney catalog merchant, and Fisher Photo. On one of its windows was a sign painted in neon colors:

CONGRATULATIONS, SENIORS!

WIN A NEW FORD MUSTANG

DETAILS INSIDE

I studied the senior portraits on display: a lanky blond girl posing with an Irish setter, a freckled guy leaning against a tree, a girl with her face surrounded by pom-poms, and Parker in a black sweater. He'd graduated three years ago, the valedictorian of his class. Perhaps the photographer was trying to imply that successful kids had their pictures taken at his studio. Parker had been the first Aldoburgian to graduate a year early, and he'd won a free ride to Drake University.

On the next block, I passed Olsen's shoes, a tanning salon and beauty shop, a men's clothing store, NAPA Auto Parts, and an empty space that once housed Joann's Book World. I used to save my allowance so I could buy books from Joann's. Then I'd go next door to Mumford's Pharmacy and read while slurping a root beer float from their soda fountain.

I entered the pharmacy on a nostalgic quest for root beer. Neale and my dad were talking in the oral-hygiene and eye-care aisle. She was wearing khaki shorts and a clingy black tank top. Her hair was swept off her neck with a single tortoiseshell barrette. Her neck, like her legs, was long and lovely. I was in the throes of what Vince calls the Wordsworth Effect. Your soul leaps up, dances with the daffodils, that kind of thing.

I forced my eyes toward my dad. He wore his usual brightly colored tie, designed to please his younger patients. This one featured the Road Runner and Wile E. Coyote.

I slipped into the next aisle, where I squatted next to a shelf of tampons and shamelessly eavesdropped.

"So how are you going to vote on the Wal-Mart issue?" Neale asked.

I hadn't told Neale about the Post-it note. Maybe she had her own reasons for suspecting Glad's death was related to Wal-Mart.

"I'm not going to make up my mind until after the forum."

My poor dad, the swing vote. Stuart and Winker in favor. Hortie and LaVonne against.

"I bet lots of people are curious about your vote. Has anybody been pestering you about it?"

Neale was definitely pursuing the Wal-Mart angle. *Fine minds think alike.* I took a lot of joy in that thought—way more than was merited by the hope of a fresh clue or a confirmation of my sleuthing skills.

"Everybody asks about Wal-Mart." Dad sounded tired.

"Has anyone seemed especially concerned?" Neale asked.

"Can't say that they have."

"What about Glad McAuley? Did she ever talk to you about it?"

"Sure did. Told me that if I voted for Wal-Mart, I could kiss downtown goodbye. I'd like to vote against it for her sake, but I have to go with the majority. I'm a representative. I can't decide things for myself."

"Seems like you're the only council member who feels that way."

Neale's lead-in worked like a charm. "It's easy to keep an open mind," Dad said, "when you don't have a personal stake. I'm thinking about moving soon. I've got a daughter and grandkids down in Florida. The fact is, I would have retired and moved a few years back, but this town really needs me."

I didn't know that. Why hadn't he told me?

"There are only three doctors in town," my dad said, "and one of them is older than I am. The other is a nice young man, but he's from Pakistan, and I'm sorry to say that a lot of folks don't feel comfortable with him. I can't imagine he's very happy here. When he leaves, we'll really be up a creek. It's getting harder and harder to convince new doctors to practice in small towns."

"You must really love this place," Neale said.

"The point is, Wal-Mart isn't going to impact my livelihood." Dad said. "People are going to keep getting sick and having babies with or without a huge discount store."

My right leg was starting to tingle. I hadn't squatted for such an extended period of time since an unfortunate attempt to play catcher the summer after fourth grade.

"What do *you* think about Wal-Mart?" Dad asked.

Silence. Neale must have been surprised by his turnabout. "I just moved here a little over a week ago," she said, "from Chicago."

"You must have some opinion."

More silence. "To be honest," she said, "I don't quite get the controversy. One store isn't going to save or destroy a town."

My dad chuckled. "You'll want to keep that thought to yourself. It won't win you any friends."

Neale backpedaled. "I suppose lots of people are afraid Wal-Mart will change the town's culture."

"Such as it is," my dad laughed. "I bet you miss the big city."

My other leg began to tingle, so I slipped away and resumed my root beer quest.

LaVonne was near the back of her store explaining a medication to an elderly couple. "Take it on a full stomach," she said loudly. The couple must have been hard of hearing.

When they left, she glanced at me and lowered her voice. "You're not sick, are you, honey? Stress can take its toll." The pencil behind her ear stuck out of her chestnut hair at a rakish angle.

"I'm fine." I said. "I just had a craving for one of your root beer floats."

LaVonne beamed. "Coming right up."

As I followed her to the fountain I glanced behind me. No one was nearby, so I figured I might as well ask her a few questions.

"Do you think it's possible Stuart and Charlene are having an affair?" I asked.

LaVonne laughed so hard she snorted. "Oh, honey, who told you that crazy tale?"

So much for my powers of deduction. I decided to completely change the subject. "Do you know if Glad had any enemies?"

"*Enemies* is a strong word, honey." LaVonne scooped vanilla ice cream into a tall glass. "Do you know what Glad was up to before she died, besides the Wal-Mart thing?"

"That was it. Leastways, that's all she talked about."

"When did you see her last?"

"Let's see..." She fell silent as she filled my glass with root beer. "Last time I saw Glad, she was in here getting some vitamins." LaVonne stuck a spoon and straw in the fizz and handed the glass across the counter to me. "I was the only one minding the store, except for Lucy at the fountain, and wouldn't you know it, we had a rush. Maybe five or six people in line. The first needed some kind of skin cream I'd never heard of. Then Bill Honig—God bless his soul— slowed things down because he needed some sleeping pills and there weren't any on the shelf; I had to go in the back to find some. Glad was next, but I was in a hurry and I didn't say two words to her."

I broke in on LaVonne's guilt before it could mushroom. "How did she seem?"

"Same old Glad. Looked like she was stewing on something, though. Probably Wal-Mart."

"You and Glad were on the same side of that issue," I prompted.

"You'd better believe it," LaVonne said. "Wal-Mart would destroy my Lucy's dreams. She's got one year of pharmacy school left. Then I'm going to make her my partner, just like Dad did for me."

I wondered if Lucy really shared her mother's dream.

"The pharmacy is doing OK now," LaVonne said, "but Wal-Mart would price us out of business." Her face flushed. "And I sure wouldn't want to work for them. Pharmacists in Texas and Colorado are suing Wal-Mart for overtime pay. That store treats its employees lousy."

"Who's its strongest advocate?" I interrupted LaVonne's tirade.

"Officer Warner just asked me the same thing."

Once again I felt a thrill of excitement that Neale and I were on the same trail. "What did you tell her?"

"I said that a lot of fools think Wal-Mart can perform miracles, but the mayor is the biggest fool of them all. He thinks that it'll help him get reelected, but you mark my words—when folks see their downtown die, they're not going to feel too friendly at the voting booth."

She waved away the five I tried to hand her. I set it on the counter. No way was I going to accept a freebie from a woman who had to sell Tupperware to make ends meet.

"Come to think of it," LaVonne said, "I saw Stuart talking with Glad a few days before she died. Right in front of his office. They both looked upset."

twelve

"Don't Komodo dragons eat small children?" Vince scruti-
nized a yellow Jell-O salad while I regaled him with tales of my
sleuthing. We sat at Zee's kitchen table, which was covered
with desserts and casseroles Vince had taken out of the fridge.

"I had to say something." I bit into a raisin-oatmeal bar.

"And you just happened to be thinking about Komodo dragons?" Vince lifted the lid on a casserole dish. "Mar-Bar, you
worry me." He peeked under another lid. "Four green-bean
casseroles with fake onions on top." He grimaced. "You people
put cream of mushroom soup in everything."

"Vince," I said, "I need you to focus."

He sat up straight and folded his hands in front of him on
the table. "I'm all ears. Ready to play Watson to your Sherlock."
My Watson happened to be wearing a bright red tank top that
showed an alarming amount of chest hair, but you take what
you can get.

"First, let's review motives," I said. "Charlene has the
strongest one. She wants to sell her farm to Wal-Mart and move

her ailing husband to Arizona. Winker and Stuart also have monetary motives. Winker wants Wal-Mart's weekly ad inserts, and he probably thinks his unemployed son will get a good job with the store. Stuart thinks Wal-Mart will help him get reelected as mayor, and he too has an unemployed son."

"You think one of them killed Glad in order to end your aunts' Wal-Mart campaign?" Vince asked.

I sighed. "I can't imagine Charlene or Winker killing Glad. They're her old friends."

Vince walked to the fridge and grabbed a gallon of milk. "Stuart is too obvious. It's never the most unlikable character that turns out to be the murderer." He plucked two glasses out of the dish drainer and returned to the food. "What about the youngsters?" He poured our milk, and I reached for a cupcake.

"Are you still thinking Glad's death was a hate crime?"

"What if the little Neanderthals killed Glad in order to help their families?"

I couldn't tell whether he was joking. "You mean, maybe Stu Two realized his dad needed Wal-Mart to get reelected or that his big brother needed a job?"

"Voilà," Vince said. "Two motives for murder. People have killed for less."

I chuckled, feeling punchy. "Maybe the boys worked together to help both their families."

Vince reached for a macaroon. "Gotta love those family values."

"Seriously, though," I asked, "if the boys did it, why would they make it look like a hate crime? Why cast suspicion on themselves?"

Vince nibbled his cookie, deep in thought.

"And what about the adults?" I continued. "None of them would want to cast suspicion on the two boys."

"Winker isn't related to either one, is he?"

"He and Charlene are old friends," I said. "He wouldn't do anything to hurt her grandson. He knows it would tear her apart. You should see how upset Hortie is about Alex."

"Maybe whoever killed Glad wanted to frame Alex so that they could upset Hortie. Maybe that was part of the plan."

I thought about Hortie's despondency, her desire to close the Chat 'n' Chew. Who would want to make her feel so defeated? "Wal-Mart proponents." I answered my own unspoken question. "They wanted to take the fight out of Hortie. They wanted her to resign her seat on the city council."

"Whoa," Vince said. "She hasn't resigned yet. And why didn't the murderer just kill Hortie?"

"That would be too obvious."

Vince sighed dramatically.

"You're the one who started with the whole Hortie thing," I said.

"I was trying to get you to think outside the box. I hate to say this, Mar-Bar, but there's always the possibility that Wal-Mart and the Post-it note have nothing to do with Glad's death."

My gut told me he was wrong, but what if he wasn't? Then what would I do? I inched Saran Wrap off some cinnamon rolls.

"What are you trying to do?" Vince said. "Become the next Miss Diabetes?"

I pushed the rolls away. "It helps me think."

"I thought *I* did that." Vince faked a pout. "Alas," he said, "you turn to the Pillsbury Doughboy while your own sweet, dependable Watson pines away, abandoned, his razor-sharp intellect unappreciated."

I smiled in spite of myself. "What about eavesdropping tonight at the visitation?"

"Spies 'R' Us." Vince said. "You should also enlist the aid of that cute cop you were eyeballing last night." He licked his lips.

"Vince," I said, "my aunt just died."

"Exactly," Vince said, "you need to take your mind off your grief."

I took a sip of milk. "She's probably not interested."

Vince shook his finger at me. "Nothing ventured, nothing gained."

"I don't have the time or the energy for anything but finding Glad's killer."

"So you *do* like her. Come on, fess up." He was all smiles and singsong.

"What does it matter?" I said. "I'll have to leave in a few days."

Vince's smile faded, and he started lifting casserole lids again.

"What?" I asked. "What's wrong?"

He peered at a mysterious noodle dish. "I forgot to tell you. Orchid called when you were out. She needs you back at the station right after the funeral."

"But that's tomorrow," I wailed. "There's no way I can leave tomorrow."

Vince stood. "Don't shoot the messenger."

"I've hardly spent any time with Zee."

"Mar-Bar," he said. "Don't beat yourself up. Aren't you trying to find the killer so Zee will be safe?"

"*Trying* is the key word," I said. "How did Orchid sound?"

"Hard to say."

"Pissed?" I asked.

Vince smiled weakly.

I asked him to warm up something for supper, and I trudged up the stairs to Glad's office.

✧ ✧ ✧

It was on the same side of the house as my room. Neither got much afternoon sun thanks to the Honigs' big oak. I sank into Glad's chair. She used to sit in it doing nothing—or so it seemed to me in my younger days. But now I knew she must have been daydreaming, working through problems, or praying. My aunts and I weren't churchgoers. I wondered what Glad's idea of heaven had been. Probably lots of steak, flowers, and books—and Zee, of course. But Zee was here, and Glad was there. Wherever *there* was.

I stood up. That train of thought wasn't doing anybody any good. I opened Glad's closet. The floor was covered with old issues of *The New Yorker* and the *Aldoburg Times*. The bottom shelf was a catchall: boxes of stationery, playing cards, coupons, a rock I painted during my one and only year as a Brownie. There were three boxes on the middle shelf. The first one I opened housed all the extension cords you could ever need. The second contained Glad's postcard collection. My parents had sent her several from Florida and at least one from each of their other travels: Ireland, London, Turkey, and Egypt. Winker had sent one from Scotland, and I'd sent one from every vacation and road trip I'd ever taken with my ex—New York; Chicago; San Francisco; West Bend, Iowa's own Grotto of the Redemption; Willa Cather's birthplace. All signed *Much love, Mara and Anne.*

I pushed them aside and found several cards I'd sent from Japan the summer after my sophomore year of college. Back then, Iowa City had seemed like a monstrous metropolis, and if it hadn't been for Zee and Glad's prodding, I'd never have studied in Tokyo, never seen the giant Buddha shrouded in the mists of Kyoto. I flipped over the card that bore his image and read a message from my younger self:

Hi, Zee and Glad!
So many beautiful and ancient things here. This is my favorite—
it reminds me of you somehow.
Much love, Mara
P.S. I've been studying haiku. Here's one by Basho.

How admirable!
To see lightning and not think
Life is fleeting.

I remembered why that looming, lovely statue of Buddha reminded me of my aunts. They'd been a calm, rock-solid presence for me—even Glad with her grumbling about my late hours and her habitual retreats to her office. I assumed my aunts would always be there for me. I didn't know the meaning of the word *fleeting*. But maybe nobody ever does until someone they love dies.

I sat on the floor and began placing the cards around me. Some were from people I'd never heard of, and some were blank on back. Maybe friends had bought them for her, or she'd bought them herself. Exotic flowers, African textiles, spectacular sunsets. Glad also seemed drawn to humorous cards from small Midwestern towns like Aldoburg. Most featured gigantic ears of corn.

I've never collected anything except books, but I admired Glad's cards. They revealed her connections with family and friends, her taste and perseverance. She must have been collecting postcards for more than half her life.

I went to the window. A young boy zoomed down the sidewalk on a Big Wheel. From the kitchen came the smell of chicken baking. I wouldn't have much time for the third box before dinner.

When I opened it I found more postcards: mostly sepia-tone shots of Aldoburg and the Lincoln Highway that Glad must have found in antique shops. Yet there was also a bright new photo of the Sculpture Garden in Minneapolis. I picked it up and turned it over. A child's signature—spidery purple crayon, undecipherable—dwarfed the words penned below it:

> *Dear Bill,*
> *The kids just loved this place,*
> *but they miss their grandpa.*
> *Wish you were here.*
> *Love,*
> *Barb*

Her careful handwriting leaned sharply toward the address side of the card, which bore several scribbles courtesy of the crayon-wielding grandchild. Nearly obscured by a bright waxy yellow, the postmark was just a couple months old. I wondered if Bill had missed his last chance to see his grandkids.

If I'd known the postcards would make me so melancholy, I wouldn't have looked at them. But since I'd opened Pandora's box, so to speak, I examined some more. The top few were addressed to Bill Honig. I checked farther down in the box. They too were addressed to Bill.

A knock on the door startled me.

Zee smiled at the pattern I'd made on the floor with Glad's cards. "I see you found Glad's collection. She'd like that."

Would she? Why hadn't she ever shown it to me herself?

Zee put her hand on my shoulder and squatted next to me. "Mara," she said. "You know Glad loved you."

I forced myself to nod.

"She just didn't always know how to show it. She kept a lot of things to herself. Sort of like you."

Glad hadn't kept anything to herself when she and Zee were arguing about me, but there was no need to bring up ancient history. Zee had enough on her mind already. "It looks like Bill gave Glad tons of cards," I said.

Zee drew her brows together and looked through the third box. "That's Bill's collection," she said. "He and Glad were going to create a display at the Chat 'n' Chew." Her voice quavered, and she pulled her silver braid forward so that it hung down one side of her chest. She studied the end of it in an attempt to gain control.

"Maybe we could still do a display," I said gently. "I could take Bill's cards back to Barb and see what she thinks."

Zee looked up, still frowning.

"If you think it's a good idea," I added.

"It's lovely." She leaned on my shoulder and hefted herself to her feet. "I'm just worried about Alex. Chuck came to the station today and asked me all sorts of questions about him. Can you believe it?"

I was thankful Vince had been there.

"He actually thinks that poor boy did it. I was so rattled I couldn't find any of the anti–Wal-Mart spots. It was the funniest thing. I checked both computers in the studio and the one in the production room. Glad's spots weren't to be found. I made new ones, but they weren't as good as hers." She bit her lip. "I hope we don't have a virus."

I had scrolled past the lost spots that morning. Then Charlene had returned from Bill's funeral and insisted on speaking with me in the studio. One thing was for sure: We didn't have a virus—unless its name was Charlene.

thirteen

You need great social skills to be a funeral director. You have to be friendly but not cheerful, sympathetic but not intrusive. Lester Simmons, of Simmons Funeral Home, was all this plus a firm handshake and slicked-back hair.

We arrived fifteen minutes early as instructed, and he offered us little gold angel pins, which we declined. Next, he gave us each a remembrance card. On the front was a pastel mountain scene. Inside it read:

Gladys Eileen "Glad" McAuley was born on April 15, 1944, on a farm near Red Oak, Iowa. Her parents were Mary Katherine (Dougherty) and Patrick McAuley. Growing up, she was active in the Catholic Youth Organization, and she played saxophone in the Red Oak High School marching band.

Glad attended the University of Iowa, where she studied journalism and met her lifetime companion, Zee Richter. In 1967 they started KGEE, Aldoburg's first and only radio station. Glad's coverage of high school sports and other local events meant a lot to her. She was the announcer for all the home basketball games.

She also enjoyed reading, gardening, and collecting postcards.

Glad was preceded in death by her parents, and she is survived by her partner, Zee Richter.

A whole life in four paragraphs.

Vince stuck his card in his suit pocket and offered to take mine.

"Don't worry about bending them," Lester said. "I'll laminate one for each of you."

I shoved my card into the pocket of my linen jacket next to a pack of Kleenex.

"You might want to have some time in the next room before everyone arrives." Funeral directors are also adept with euphemisms. He wanted to know if we wanted to see the casket.

It was adorned with a huge spray of orange and purple flowers. Glad would have loved them. I closed my eyes. I refused to think of her in that box. Instead I saw her refinishing a dresser with Zee, sipping a beer while grilling shish kebab, flying a kite with me on my twelfth birthday.

Vince put his arm around me. We left the room so Zee could have some time alone.

Once I start crying it's hard for me to stop. So I kept myself busy responding to condolences, making sure Zee was holding up, and watching for clues. The first visitor, LaVonne, must have come straight from the pharmacy. A pencil was still tucked behind her ear. "Glad's death is a huge loss to the whole town," she said. "We'll all miss her."

I wondered if Glad was missing Aldoburg. Or Zee. Or me.

"She loved you to pieces, honey," LaVonne said. "She was so proud of you. When you got your job at that radio station in Iowa City, she talked about it for months."

A lump formed in my throat. "Really?"

"I couldn't get a word in edgewise." LaVonne squeezed my arm. "Don't you worry about Zee. We'll all look after her."

Barb and Parker were next in line. Zee and Barb clasped each other's hands. Parker put his arm around his mother and brushed his hair out of his eyes. He mumbled a sorry and gave me a long, sad look.

"Glad was a great friend and neighbor," Barb said. "A good mentor to Parker."

Zee's lip trembled, and Barb drew her into an embrace.

"She and Bill were the best," Zee managed.

Both women were crying. I joined Parker in staring at the floor.

After he guided his mother away, Zee and I readied ourselves for the next round of condolences.

Winker threw his huge arms around Zee, but he shook my hand coldly. Zee frowned at his frosty manner. I hoped she would forget it by the end of the evening.

After Winker was a group of women in flowery dresses who all seemed to be in their seventies. They said that they listened to Glad on the radio every day, and they were all crying and hugging me. One of them left snot in my hair.

I was discreetly attending to my hair with a Kleenex when the mayor approached. I wasn't sure which was worse: his cologne or his platitudes (*It must have been Glad's time; God works in mysterious ways*). As I shook his hand, I hoped his secretary hadn't mentioned my visit to his office.

Stu Two stood behind his father. He had spiked his hair and donned a black tie, but his eyes were listless and his handshake limp. He seemed nothing like the swaggering boy I'd talked to in the weight room.

Chuck wasn't far behind the mayor. The polyester sleeves of his suit coat rode up on his arms as he shook Zee's hand. "At least you can take some comfort in knowing that me and my men have apprehended Glad's killer."

Zee squared her shoulders. "I appreciate your efforts," she said, "but I certainly don't think that Alex killed Glad."

Chuck reddened. He opened his mouth, then closed it, wisely deciding that it would be poor manners to argue with the bereaved.

There was no use in prolonging an awkward social situation—even at Chuck's expense—so I held out my hand and thanked him for coming. I was rewarded with a cold smile. Given all the chilliness coming my way, I should have worn a sweater.

Collin slouched behind his dad, wearing a dark green tie that was far too short for his lanky frame. His eyes were puffy, and his nose was red. Had he been crying about Glad? As I pondered his tears, I shook several more hands.

Before I knew it, there was Neale in a formfitting skirt and jacket.

I fussed with my hair. I had removed all the snot, hadn't I?

"I'm so sorry about your loss. Your aunt sounds like someone I would have liked." She leaned forward and whispered in my ear, "I have something important to tell you when you get a chance." She touched my arm lightly and moved on.

My curiosity—and whatever else I might have been feeling—disappeared when I heard my mother ostentatiously telling Zee how sorry she was. Dad stood quietly to the side in a navy pinstripe suit. When he saw my mother was going to be a while, he walked over to me and gave me a hug. "I'm so sorry," he said softly. "This must be terrible for you."

I nodded.

"I bet you're a big comfort to Zee."

Dad and I didn't talk often, but he always knew what to say. Much to my chagrin I felt a twinge of my childhood self, the little girl who always wished Daddy had more time for her.

I was trying to return to adulthood when my mother hugged me and brushed my hair away from my face. "You're exhausting yourself, Mara—working so hard at the station—you should try to get some rest." She always gave advice that was easier said than done.

"Maybe you and Zee could come over for dinner before you leave town," Dad said. He hugged me again, and they strolled away.

Lester Simms got a chair for Zee, and she sank into it, clutching a wad of Kleenex. She crossed her ankles in front of her and smoothed out her burgundy dress. I checked my watch. An hour and a half of visitation to go. Lester offered me a chair, but I waved it away.

I put my hand on Zee's shoulder. "You need a break?"

"Lots of Glad's friends are still waiting to see us."

At the head of the line, in an eggplant polyester pantsuit, was Charlene. She took both of Zee's hands in hers, and the two old friends gazed at each other. No words needed. I told myself that Charlene would never do anything to hurt Zee and Glad, that I was making too much out of the anti–Wal-Mart spots she'd deleted.

Lester's air conditioning was losing the battle with the crowded room. Before accepting more sympathy I needed some alone time, so I squeezed Zee's shoulder and headed to the restroom.

The ladies' room lounge featured mirrors with fake gold frames and faded olive carpeting. A woman was changing her baby's diaper on the couch. I made a mental note never to sit there and went into the restroom.

I splashed cold water on my face and peered into the mirror. Freckles. I'd forgotten sunscreen as of late. My beige jacket gave me a washed-out look, but it was baggy enough to allow me to do a few stretches. I reached my hands above my head and bent to touch my toes. I slipped off my Birks and felt the cool linoleum on my feet.

The door creaked as Neale entered. She bent to check the stalls and make sure they were empty, her skirt tugging slightly against her hips. "I followed a hunch and went to the baseball complex today," she said. "I found something: a bat with a faint blood stain on it—like someone had tried to wash the blood away."

It took a while for the news to sink in. I tried to absorb it without picturing the bat.

She brushed away a wisp of hair. "The team shares bats, but even so, Stu Two and Collin are looking better as suspects."

"How did Chuck react?"

"He doesn't know yet."

"He'll insist that anyone could have used it," I said. "And unless Alex Riley's prints are on it, he's going to be very angry."

She leaned against the bathroom counter, keeping her back perfectly straight. "I contacted the lab in Des Moines, and they sent someone for the bat. We should know something soon."

I studied her ash-blond curls, her slender fingers and ankles. "Why are you risking your job over this?"

"I'm *doing* my job." She edged away from the counter.

"You know what I mean."

"What did Stu Two and Collin say when you talked to them?"

I stepped toward the door. "I've gathered lots of information," I said, "but I need to get back to Zee right now."

"Of course." The energy went out of her voice, but she touched my arm and smiled.

Underneath her navy jacket was a silky blouse, its top two buttons undone.

"See you later," she said.

I couldn't take my eyes off those buttons.

"Mara?"

I forced myself to meet her eyes. "We'll talk soon," I managed.

As she left, I reached for the faucet and splashed more cold water on my face.

Zee was talking with LaVonne again, so I surveyed the crowd. Vince was next to the clump of tall plants, attempting to chat with Stu Two and Collin. Even from a distance they both looked grief-stricken. I still didn't believe they were guilty, despite the bat that Neale had unearthed. I wanted to ask them about their conversation with Glad at the Chat 'n' Chew, but I couldn't do it with the mayor and Chuck around. I could, however, talk to Chuck. The crowded room would be a nice, safe place to ask him about his alibi.

He was holding up the wall in the far corner. He'd loosened his tie and jacket, and he scowled when he saw me approaching.

"Your son seems very upset," I said.

Chuck squinted in his son's direction and shook his head. He was obviously baffled by Collin's grief.

"I couldn't help hearing Zee tell you she doesn't think Alex is guilty," I said.

"Your influence, no doubt." He shook his head again, this time in disgust.

I chose my next words carefully. "The night Glad died, did you see something odd that made you think Alex did it? Something besides the spray paint and the anonymous note?"

He folded his arms over his chest. "Isn't that enough?"

I wracked my brain, trying to think of another subtle way to ask him about his whereabouts the night of Glad's murder. "Zee said you arrived at the station shortly after she did."

"I was on the other side of town, trying to catch speeders."

Another lie? "Your mother said you were at her place with Stu Two and Collin."

His lips pressed into a fine line. "I dropped by," he said, "but I didn't stay for long."

"Charlene made it sound like you were there for the evening."

"You must have misunderstood her." He forced his taut lips into a smile.

Why on earth didn't Chuck want me to think he'd spent the evening at his mother's?

Visitation was almost over when Hortie entered. She'd exchanged her waitress uniform for a denim skirt and red-checkered blouse. There was a slight indentation in her raven hair where her waitress cap had been perched. Despite the hush that fell over the room, she strode forth in her no-nonsense waitress shoes. She loved Glad, and she had nothing to be ashamed of. Her grandson was innocent.

I should have known she'd recover her old spunk.

Lester dashed toward Zee, ready to avert any unpleasantness. Everyone else watched to see how Zee and I would react.

Hortie ignored the stares.

I pumped her hand. "We're so happy you're here," I said loudly.

Zee hugged her. "Glad loved you very much," she said.

Hortie pulled a Kleenex out of her skirt pocket and blew her nose. "They don't make them any finer than you two," she said. "I feel so much better knowing Mara is trying to find the killer."

Zee raised her eyebrows.

Uh-oh. I should have told Hortie to keep our talk mum.

"Don't you worry," she said. "Everyone at the Chat 'n' Chew will have their eyes and ears open for more clues."

Zee glared at me.

I fled to the bathroom again, filled a Dixie cup with water, and gulped it down. Zee was going to have some choice words for me. I was supposed to be comforting her, but instead I'd pissed her off. And for all my trouble, I had nothing but wild suspicions and theories. I threw the cup away and wondered what Glad would think of my sleuthing. It would probably merit one of her derisive snorts. That was what I usually got from her. But she had told LaVonne that she was proud of me.

I started crying, and I didn't stop until a woman and her toddler interrupted me.

"Mommy, what's wrong with that lady?"

The mother flashed me an apologetic smile. "Shush. Don't stare. She's very, very sad. That's all."

Mother and child slipped into a stall, and I gazed into the mirror. My face was flushed—almost as red as my hair—my eyes were swollen, and my nose was so stopped up that I had to breathe through my mouth. I also had to go face Zee's wrath. And Chuck's. And Stuart's. That's all.

When I finally forced myself back into the fray, the crowd had dwindled. LaVonne smiled at something Vince said, and the seventy-something contingent of women gossiped frenetically. At the far side of the room Stuart, Chuck, Charlene, and Winker huddled in a circle. Chuck's entire neck was an angry red, and he scowled at his mother. I imagined him moments earlier, criticizing her attempt to give him an alibi.

Vince and I followed Zee across the nearly empty parking lot. As soon as we reached the car, she let me have it. "What are you thinking," she asked, "accusing my friends of murder?" She flipped on her lights and jerked her car into reverse. "Aldoburg is my home."

I fought to keep my voice calm. "You said yourself you don't think Alex is guilty."

"I don't think anyone in this town is guilty, and you know it." She pulled onto the street.

"What if you're wrong?" I said. "You could be in danger."

"Then you're in danger too, asking all these questions."

We drove through downtown. There were four or five cars parked in front of Mitzi's Bar. I longed to imbibe one of the beverages advertised by its neon lights. "I'm just trying to help."

"I don't need that kind of help." She hit a bump, and her engine rattled. "If you're going to keep asking my friends insulting questions, you can leave with Vince after the funeral tomorrow."

We rode in silence the rest of the way home.

fourteen

The morning sun illuminated the stained glass windows of Saint Patrick's Catholic Church. In between the windows were statues of the disciples, each holding an object that signified the way in which he was martyred. Most held swords, but then there was good old Peter with his upside-down cross. As a child I whiled away many a Sunday morning enraptured with Peter's insistence on an unusual death. But I was tired of thinking about murder, and I sure didn't want to ponder it during Glad's funeral. It was time to celebrate her life, to say good-bye.

The organ brayed in a decidedly minor key, dueling with the whir of ceiling fans. Zee sat at my right in a slate-blue dress. Her eyes were closed, and her lips trembled slightly. To her right were my mom and dad, both staring straight ahead. I prayed Zee wouldn't tell them about my detective work. Then I felt a flood of guilt. How dare I worry about myself when Zee was in so much pain?

I glanced around the church, trying to spot Vince. It was nearly full, and people were still filing in.

The murderer had stolen Glad from all of us, stolen parts of our futures Glad would never share. She wouldn't receive a postcard from my mom and dad when they traveled to Italy in the Fall. She wouldn't see Vince star in *La Cage aux Folles*. She wouldn't celebrate her anniversary with Zee this November. And never again would she trade her mushrooms for my pepperoni when Zee ordered a combo pizza.

I refused to start crying before the funeral began, so I returned my attention to Zee. She clutched a handkerchief so tightly that her knuckles were white. She wore an opal ring that Glad had given her nearly forty years ago—longer than I'd been alive.

Father Kelly stepped to the podium and asked us all to pray. His deep voice didn't fit with his scrawny physique, and his wire-rimmed glasses were far too big for his wrinkled face. They kept slipping down his nose until he gave them a final nudge and announced a hymn, "I'll Fly Away." Before the end of the first verse, Zee began crying, and I soon followed suit.

Father Kelly was a member of Zee and Glad's gardening club, and he used plant metaphors in his eulogy. The thought of Glad alive and tending other living things made me cry harder. Near the end of Mass, we recited the Twenty-third Psalm: *The Lord is my shepherd; I shall not want.* Not true. I wanted plenty of things. I wanted Glad back. But since I couldn't have that, I'd settle for finding her murderer.

For the burial we gathered in the shade of a sprawling sycamore. I pulled Zee close even though I was sweating. My parents stood on her other side. Next to them Parker gazed toward the highway and brushed a lock out of his face. Barb wiped tears away with a handkerchief. She knew all too well what Zee was going through. On my other side stood Vince. Next to him were LaVonne and Hortie, their arms around each other.

Zee's eyes were fixed on the casket, but I couldn't watch Glad's body being lowered into the ground. I took a deep breath and scanned the crowd. There, on the edge, all alone, stood Neale. Somewhere within me, something flared—lust or joy— but only for a slender moment. Then I was simply staring across the cemetery, angry at myself for being so easily distracted. Neale was watching the crowd for suspicious behavior, and I needed to do the same.

It was a huge crowd. Glad had so many friends—a county's worth—but no relatives to mourn her passing. She'd often joked about how she belonged in *Ripley's Believe It or Not!*—an only child in a Catholic family. But I wondered if she'd been lonely—especially after her parents died.

I eyed my own parents. Mother was holding Zee's hand and blinking back tears. Dad had his arm around Mom, but he was studying Barb, his brow deeply furrowed. I should spend more time with him—and I would—as soon as Glad's killer was behind bars.

Zee moved from my side, tossed a handful of soil into the grave, and returned to my arms. I held her tightly and clenched my jaw. I felt like sobbing, but I willed myself to stay strong and shifted my eyes to the edge of the crowd again. Neale had been joined by Chuck, who gazed at Hortie, his face blank.

I turned my attention to the other Post-it-note suspects. The mayor had his hands folded in front of him, his eyes on his son and Collin. Both young men seemed mesmerized by the grave. Winker kept squeezing a handkerchief that he'd wadded in his fist. Next to him Charlene sniffled and blew her nose loudly. I hoped all the sorrow was genuine.

✧ ✧ ✧

The funeral luncheon was in the basement of St. Pat's. As president of the Altar and Rosary Society, Mother had rallied the church ladies on Glad's behalf. Never mind that Glad was a lapsed Catholic and a lesbian to boot—her family and friends still deserved roast beef, mashed potatoes, green bean casserole, and various salads that featured Miracle Whip or cherry Jell-O.

LaVonne was talking with Vince under a basketball hoop— the basement doubled as a gymnasium—when Zee and I entered. Winker and my parents swept Zee toward the buffet, but I made a beeline toward Vince and threw my arms around him. "I'm so glad you're here," I whispered.

"It was a beautiful service, honey," LaVonne said, "just beautiful."

I nodded, and LaVonne patted my arm. I wanted to speak with Vince alone, but LaVonne guided us to the end of the buffet line—right behind Charlene and the mayor. They halted their conversation when they saw me.

The line inched along. Talia and her sister were examining the pie table with Hortie.

Vince followed my gaze and watched the two young Korean women. "The gathering at the dessert table is more diverse than your entire town."

I don't consider Aldoburg "my" town, but Vince was right. The predominantly Irish-Catholic town's idea of celebrating diversity was letting Protestants on the school board.

Vince scooped a mound of potatoes onto his plate. "At least this place makes me feel young," he said.

I knew what he meant. Since Iowa City is a university town, most of its population is under twenty-five. In small-town Iowa, most folks are over fifty. "Instant Oil of Olay," I said. It felt good to joke.

"Be sure you try some of my green bean casserole," LaVonne said.

Vince and I spooned some onto our plates, carefully avoiding eye contact. I grabbed a dinner roll, and we made our way to a corner table. Vince and LaVonne ate in silence as my Jell-O melted into my mashed potatoes. In front of me, a few tables away, Stu Two and Collin picked at their food. I wondered if guilt or grief kept them from devouring their lunch in the usual vulturish way of teenage boys. At the table next to theirs, Neale nodded politely as the funeral director held forth. She was wearing another silky blouse. This one had pearl-shaped buttons running down the center.

"Eat, honey," LaVonne said. "You need your strength."

I forced myself to take a bite of green beans. "Your casserole is really good." I took another peek at Neale. Her hair was in some sort of complicated knot, and her earrings matched the buttons on her blouse. She looked away from Lester, and for a moment her eyes met mine. I poked at a slice of roast beef and glanced to the right. Parker was pouring coffee for his mother and a very agitated Hortie. I heard the words *Alex* and *jail*. Barb—her own eyes red, her brow creased—offered Hortie a Kleenex and asked if Chuck had found any new evidence.

LaVonne cleared her throat. "Glad was pleased as punch that you were helping her and Zee with their Wal-Mart research. She said your station in Iowa City produced lots of features against urban sprawl when Wal-Mart first considered coming there."

I had no idea Glad talked so much about me.

LaVonne sighed and ripped open a package of Sweet'N Low. "But don't you have two Wal-Marts now?"

"One of them is a Supercenter," Vince said.

LaVonne stirred her coffee furiously. "How many pharmacies do you have left?"

"Are you a pharmacist?" Vince asked.

I was in no mood for LaVonne's lament about "her Lucy's" slim chances of taking over the family pharmacy, so I asked a question of my own. "What would happen if one of your council members were unable to vote on the Wal-Mart zoning issue?"

Vince shook his head. Whether he was disgusted by my question or his array of casseroles, I couldn't tell.

LaVonne poured some cream in her coffee. "The alternate would fill in. Lester Simms."

"So," I said, "let's say Hortie is so worried about Alex being in jail she can't come to the meeting and vote."

"Oh, honey, Hortie wouldn't miss that for the world."

"But say she did. Then Lester would have her vote?"

LaVonne nodded, stirring her coffee again.

"How does Lester feel about Wal-Mart?"

"He thinks it's the wave of the future," she said. "Tidal wave, more like."

"You'd be the only vote against Wal-Mart," I said. "Lester, Stuart, and Winker are all for it. My dad's vote wouldn't matter anymore."

Vince loaded his fork with some pasta salad. "Mara thinks someone framed Alex so Hortie would temporarily abandon her council seat."

"Goodness, honey, that's quite a theory."

I took another bite of green beans and discreetly nudged a huge portion of them under my scalloped potatoes.

"Right now," she said, "your dad is the swing vote."

I braced myself.

"You're a persuasive young lady. You could get him to vote against Wal-Mart."

I hated asking either of my parents for anything. Mother inevitably returned to the past—reprising her role as rejected parent. Dad, in contrast, always focused on the future—ever hopeful that he and I would develop a closer bond—never mind the fact that he had no time to bond with anyone except his patients and golf buddies. "Maybe I'll talk to him later," I mumbled. Or maybe I'd just forget about lunch and have a piece of pie.

"It might be best to do it before the public forum tomorrow night," LaVonne said.

I excused myself and headed to the pie table with Vince on my heels.

"Are you really going to talk to your dad about Wal-Mart?" he asked.

"I suppose." I stared glumly at an assortment of meringues.

"I wish I could stay."

I wished so too. Without Vince, Zee would be in more danger. I couldn't watch her all the time if I wanted to find the killer.

"I still think you should take that note to the police," Vince whispered.

"Your ride will be here soon," I said.

"I'd stay if I could."

"I know."

He wrapped his arms around me, and I rested my head on his shoulder. When he pulled away, I forced myself to smile. "Break a leg."

"And you," he said. "Be careful. Get that lovely cop to help you."

Most of the evergreen bushes outside the church were dried brown. Weeds sprung out of cracks in the sidewalk.

"Is it a relief to have the funeral over?" Dad asked.

I nodded, and realized it was.

"Your friend couldn't come?" he said. "I was hoping to meet her."

It was the first time he'd expressed such an interest. Too bad Anne had dumped me. "She's swamped at work," I said.

He pulled off his jacket and loosened his tie. "You and Zee need anything?"

"No thanks, we're OK." I knew he didn't have the time to baby-sit Zee at the station, and he certainly wouldn't want my mother out there. "We're keeping pretty busy with the Wal-Mart thing," I said.

We walked a block in silence, my dad frowning. A car eased around a teenage girl skateboarding down the street.

"Every night I get seven or eight calls about Wal-Mart," Dad said. "I tell them I'm going to vote according to what the majority wants, and then they try to persuade me their view is the majority view." He rolled up his sleeves. "Makes me sorry I ever even heard of council—let alone ran for it. My nerves are so on edge that I snapped at a patient the other day. I've got to focus on my practice. It comes first, you know."

I knew all too well. His priorities had always been work first, everything else second—including me. While I hated being second, I admired his devotion to his patients. And to his principles. I was proud he would vote whichever way most of the town wanted—not simply to please himself, my mother, my aunts, or me. But I was also hurt he would choose his allegiance to an abstract majority over the people he loved most. Over me. With Dad, duty won over love every time.

We strolled past a yard cluttered with lawn ornaments: fake deer and squirrels, spinning flowers, a politically incorrect black boy holding a lantern, a statue of Mary, a miniature windmill, and the brightly painted rear-ends of a man and woman bending over their garden.

"Who's been bugging you to vote for Wal-Mart?" If I couldn't influence my dad's vote, at least I could pump him for information.

"I'm sure Zee has told you who Wal-Mart's big fans are."

A stereo pulsed as a car crept by.

"What really makes me mad," he said, "is when other council members call me. They should be trying to figure out what the town wants, but Stuart says folks here don't always know what's best for themselves."

"Maybe he's right," I told him. "Look who they elected mayor."

My dad chuckled, but as we rounded the corner, his face turned grim. Parker and Barb emerged from the basement of St. Pat's. "I told her to stay home today—take it easy—try not to upset herself."

It was a good thing he didn't know about Barb's attempts to comfort Hortie or to decimate her hedge by the light of the silvery moon. "Maybe she needed to say good-bye to Glad," I said.

Dad watched Parker help Barb into their car, still frowning.

"Have any council members besides Stuart called about Wal-Mart?" I asked.

"They've *all* called." My dad quickened his pace. "And more than once."

"What'd they say?"

"Oh, Mara, I don't remember. Just what you'd expect, I guess."

We stepped off the sidewalk to make way for a woman with a double stroller.

"What about Chuck and Charlene? Have they called?"

Dad paused. "Chuck about broke my heart—all worried about his father's asthma—but I had to be honest with him. I told him I was reserving judgment on Wal-Mart until after the forum. Then he started complaining that KGEE's coverage of the issue was biased. He asked me to speak to Zee and Glad about it."

My dad shook his head at the thought of telling my aunts how to run their station, but my mind had room only for Chuck. What would he be willing to do—what had he done—to help his parents make it to Arizona?

fifteen

Zee hadn't invited anyone to her home after the funeral. She went straight to her room to lie down, and I counted myself lucky that she hadn't asked me to leave. Eventually we would have to discuss my sleuthing, but it was a conversation I was happy to postpone. First I'd get some fresh air, then I'd finish looking through Glad's postcards. I eased myself onto Zee's front step, squinting into the afternoon sun. As I wiggled my toes on the burning pavement, a sprinkler hissed a couple yards down. Barb worked on her hedge, and at the end of the block a retired couple pulled weeds in their already perfect lawn. If I had an ounce of prudence in my body, I would have left with Vince. There was no way I could protect Zee 24–7 and even less of a chance that I could bring Glad's murderer to justice. Orchid would use my extended absence as an excuse to take the reading series from me for good. She might even fire me. Then after being unemployed for months and months I'd have to eke out my bread and butter bathing dogs at the shelter. Vince would be my boss, and I'd never have another date because I'd smell like a wet dog.

Before I could borrow any more trouble, a girl biked by, cell phone glued to her ear, and I thought about Chuck's call to my dad. Was Chuck simply looking out for his parents' interests, or did he have some motives of his own? Maybe Neale would know. On TV, cops always watch each other's back, but Neale didn't seem to care much for Chuck. I could drop by her house—just for a couple minutes—but first I'd need to make sure Zee was safe.

I strolled over to Barb's hedge. She was on all fours, tugging at a root that was at least a couple feet below the surface. I cleared my throat, not wanting to startle her. She let go of the root and turned.

"You going to be out here a while?" I asked.

Barb nodded, her face flushed and glistening with sweat.

"Would you mind making sure nobody knocks on Zee's door or rings her bell? She's sleeping." I didn't think the murderer would show up at Zee's house, but you never know.

"Shouldn't you be sleeping yourself?" Barb asked.

She was right, of course. But I really needed to see Neale. I wanted to ask if the crime lab was done fingerprinting the bat, and she wanted to hear what I'd learned. In the midst of sharing my discoveries, I'd subtly ask about Chuck. Strictly a business call.

Neale's front porch was filled with empty boxes. There were also a bunch of plants and a pair of Rollerblades. I wiped the sweat off my forehead and pressed the doorbell.

I listened for movement but heard only the sound of distant music. I was about to ring again when Neale opened the door in a red jogging bra and black running shorts. There was a bead of sweat working its way down her chest.

I tried to focus on the dust cloth in her hand and attempted to speak. "Sorry-to-interrupt-you-I-just-happened-to-drop-by-to-ask-about-the-bat."

"I haven't heard from the lab," Neale said, "but I'd love to hear what you've learned." She smiled. "Why don't you come in and cool off."

We wove our way through stacks of boxes in her living room. I could hear the riff of a jazz saxophone from upstairs.

"Looks like you're still moving in." Nothing like stating the obvious when you can't think of anything else to say.

"Clear yourself a place to sit," she said, "and I'll get us something to drink."

I pushed some books to one side of the couch and sank into its plush, cream-colored cushions. Among the books was the same anti–Wal-Mart paperback I'd found in Glad's office. I flipped through its pages, but Neale hadn't marked anything in her copy. Underneath the Wal-Mart book was a Patricia Cornwell novel and a hardcover autobiography of Cynthia Cooper, former superstar of the WNBA. Near my feet was a tower of boxes. I scanned their labels: *guest room closet—top shelf, bedroom—middle drawer, keepsakes/high school.* They were typed. Of course, a wannabe homicide detective would need to be thorough. Attention to detail—it could be a good thing.

Neale returned, setting a glass of orange juice on the box next to me. She gulped half her own glass before placing the books on the floor and sitting on the other end of the sofa. Always that ballerina grace.

I took a sip of juice. It was fresh-squeezed.

"How are you doing?" she asked.

I shrugged. "It's been an emotional day."

The sun gleamed on her blond ponytail.

"This is great juice," I said.

Neale flexed her biceps playfully. "Squeezed it myself."

God, she was beautiful.

"We should hear from the lab tomorrow," she said. "I'll call you and your aunt as soon as I know anything."

I gazed at the pulp spinning lazily in my glass and tried to get back to business. "Interested in Wal-Mart?" I nodded my head toward her book.

Neale smiled. "Just keeping up on local issues."

"Yesterday at the pharmacy I overheard you talking about it with my dad."

Neale scrunched her brow and crossed her legs.

"I just happened to be in the next aisle," I said.

"Your father's a sweet guy."

"Your questions made me wonder if you think Glad's death is related to Wal-Mart."

"Why?" she asked. "Do you?" She moved to the edge of the sofa, eager to listen.

I didn't mention the note in my car, but I told her everything else I knew and suspected. She grabbed a pad of paper and started scribbling notes. When I finished, she shook her head. "You know so much more than I do."

Her tone was hard to read. "I have the insider's advantage," I said. "Small-town Iowans are friendly, but they don't trust strangers."

"But I don't have anything for you."

"What about Chuck?" I said. "You must know something about him that I don't."

Neale studied her notes.

Surely she wasn't hesitating? Given all I'd told her—and given our wee bit of flirting—I'd expected her to toss aside the cop honor code and spill the beans on her boss. "He insists on seeing Glad's death as a hate crime," I said. "He made a quick arrest based on shaky evidence. He's called my dad about Wal-Mart. And he's very worried someone will discover his whereabouts the night Glad died."

Neale drained the last of her orange juice. Outside, a car whizzed past. "I'll ask around," she said. "You'll tell me if you learn anything new?"

Neale's air conditioning kicked on, nearly drowning out the piano solo that flowed from the upstairs stereo. She adjusted her ponytail, stretching her arms over her head.

My irritation faded. I wanted to make some small talk, get to know her better, but I was tongue-tied. Me, a girl who talks for a living. I stalled by drinking my orange juice.

Neale broke the silence. "Would you like to stay for dinner? I got some fresh peppers at the farmer's market, and I was going to make stir-fry. We could have a glass of wine while I get it ready."

That sounded so romantic. Of course, I would have found it romantic if she'd asked me to help unpack and program her VCR. I had no idea whether she was interested in women—let alone me. I couldn't afford to be swept away in a tide of wishful thinking. "I'd like to," I said, "but I've got to get back to my aunt."

As I plodded home my mind moved much faster than my legs. I thought about the fight that was likely to ensue when Zee awoke from her nap, and I thought about why Neale had invited me to dinner. She'd already gotten plenty of information, so maybe she was looking for a friend—or something more.

It had been over a year since Anne left me, and I'd only been on one date since then—the debacle that ended with Vince's drag-queen entourage. Maybe I wasn't ready for romance. Anne and I had been together five years, and after she left, I'd spent many a sleepless night wondering what I did wrong. I didn't want to go through that again. Besides, I was doing great. I had plenty of time for my job, my friends, myself. Of course, I might not have my job for much longer.

I dodged a tricycle that had been left on the sidewalk.

Even if Neale were a lesbian, she wasn't seeking a lifetime companion, just someone to share her stir-fry. Maybe I was subconsciously trying to find an instant partner, someone to replace Anne. Or maybe I was trying to ease my grief about Glad with a crush on Neale.

Or maybe I was overanalyzing things. It's been known to happen.

When I got back to Zee's, she was sitting on the sofa, gazing at a cooking show. Without removing her eyes from the screen she picked up the remote and turned off the TV.

I braced myself.

She turned to me, her brown eyes intent. "I'm sorry about last night." Some of her hair had come out of her braid, and her yellow T-shirt was wrinkled.

I sat next to her. "We've both been under a lot of strain."

"That's no excuse for interrogating my friends."

"But what if one of them—"

"No buts," Zee said.

I stood up.

Zee gently touched my hand and lowered me back to the sofa. "I'm begging you," she said, "No more questions. My friends are grieving, and you're making it worse."

We sat silently. A car drove by, and children laughed across the street.

"Zee," I said, "I love you more than anyone in the world, but I can't do what you're asking. I'm worried about your safety."

She started to protest, but I forged ahead, telling her about the Post-it note suspects and how they all seemed to be lying about their whereabouts the night Glad died. I described Winker's ominous phone call, Stu Two's concern about his father, and Chuck's words to his mother—*If she finds out what we were doing the night of Glad's death, there'll be hell to pay.*

Zee shook her head sadly. "Mara, you don't know the context of those words."

"Neither do you." I told her about the mysterious 9:30 appointments on Charlene's and Stuart's calendars.

Zee frowned. "Mara, you can't just snoop through people's desks. If Charlene met with Stuart—and that's a big if—those two can't stand each other—then that's her business. It had nothing to do with Glad's death. Charlene is one of our oldest friends. She's worked at the station since we opened it. You know that."

"She's been deleting anti–Wal-Mart spots."

"That's enough." Zee barreled toward the kitchen. I followed her, and she whirled around. "I mean it," she said. "Not one word more."

"Promise me you'll be careful around these people."

"I'll do no such thing. Two of them are dear friends. And two of them are children." She pulled a couple of Tupperware containers out of the fridge and shoved the door shut.

I wanted to remind her that the two "children" were gay bashers. I even considered telling her about the note in my car.

She tugged a lid off one of the containers and peered into it. The faint smell of barbecue sauce made my stomach lurch. "I know you mean well," Zee said. "There's nothing I'd like more than to bring Glad's killers to justice, but face the facts, Mara. They're long gone by now." The silverware drawer squeaked as she yanked it open. "I love that you're here, but if you keep poking around ..."

She didn't finish her sentence. There was no need. Now that Glad's funeral was over, Zee wouldn't hesitate to send me back to Iowa City. She'd like to have me with her, sharing her grief and helping with the campaign against Wal-Mart, but not at the expense of her friends.

After Zee picked at some goulash and went back to bed, I went back to stewing. I had no idea how to keep Zee safe. And let's face it, I had no idea how to spend the rest of the evening. Just this morning we'd buried Glad. How could that be?

I went to her office and found her card collection on the floor where I'd left it: a half-full box surrounded by piles of postcards. Sitting cross-legged amongst the piles I went through twenty-some cards addressed to Bill before I found any more of Glad's. She'd sandwiched a snapshot of Judy Garland in between two cards that featured Mount Rushmore. Then there was a commemoration of the Pope's visit to Living History Farms in Des Moines and a scene from Bourbon Street. I'd sent that one during the first long trip Anne and I had taken together.

Quickly, I went to the next card, a photo of the Drake Relays from Parker:

Hey ho, Glad—

Here's one for your collection. I remembered you didn't have any from Drake. College is a lot of work—can't believe how much I'm reading. Miss the station and miss you. Hi to Zee. —Parker

I remembered visiting Zee and Glad during my senior year at Iowa and feeling jealous when Glad baby-sat Parker. She played endless checkers with the eight-year-old and even laughed at his knock-knock jokes. When he was older, she must have shown him her collection, but she'd never shown it to me. Of course, I'd never asked.

Now the least I could do was make sure that part of her collection would be displayed at the Chat 'n' Chew. As I separated her cards from Bill's, I felt a surge of hope. Here was a task I could complete. Better yet, when I returned Bill's cards to Barb and asked what she thought about a commemorative display, I'd give myself a perfect excuse to ask her about the Post-it-note suspects.

I grabbed a card that featured a John Deere tractor. Then I saw it. A yellow envelope with my name. I lifted it out of the box and traced my fingers over Glad's handwriting. No-nonsense, straight up and down. She'd never even written me an entire letter—just an occasional PS to whatever Zee wrote.

Inside the envelope were postcards. Nearly two dozen of them. The top one made my heart race. It was a photo of an Irish castle, and I knew where it had come from—my father.

November 11, 1978

Dear Mara,
I miss you very much.
Let's talk when I get back.

Love,
Dad

He'd sent it during the trip he and Mom took right after I moved out. I'd given it to Glad for her collection—a sort of peace offering for invading her domestic tranquility. She'd been reluctant to take it, and I'd felt rejected yet again. Still, I continued to give her cards, and she'd obviously saved them for me.

Florida, Egypt, Paris, Bath. They were all from my dad. Probably every single card he'd ever sent me. What was Glad thinking? I didn't want them back. Sure, the cards said nice things. Most of them said he missed me, and the early ones said I was always welcome to "come home," as he put it. But mostly they just reminded me that after I'd moved out, he'd continued life as usual without me—long hours with his patients and long trips to Europe so he could peruse Irish castles.

Just what I needed—a long, bumpy ride down memory lane.

I shoved the cards back into the envelope and went to find a box for Bill's collection.

Barb was once again in her terry cloth robe, but she hadn't removed her makeup after Glad's funeral. A frosty lipstick was too bright for her weary face.

"I'm sorry to bother you," I said. "I was going through Glad's things and I found a bunch of Bill's postcards."

The TV murmured in the living room. Barb made no move to take the box of cards I'd brought.

"I thought you'd want them," I said. "Zee says he and Glad were planning a postcard display at the Chat 'n' Chew, but I'm sure you knew that."

She nodded absently.

"I was thinking we could still put together a display in their honor."

She attempted a smile. "How sweet of you. Maybe we can start planning after the Wal-Mart forum."

I shifted the box in my arms; they were starting to tire.

Barb stepped aside. "I'm sorry. I'm not thinking. Please, come in. Have a seat."

I plopped into an easy chair, balancing the box on my lap.

Barb removed a box from her own chair. "I was just sorting through some photos," she said. "I'm going to make each of my grandkids a memory book about their grandfather."

Between scrapbooking and excavating shrubbery, Barb sure kept herself busy.

"They love the books I've already made for them—one for each year of their lives."

I thought of Glad and the postcards she'd set aside for me. You saved things for people you loved, people you cared about. Was it possible I was more to Glad than the kid who intruded on her quiet life with Zee?

"Can I get you something to drink?" Barb headed to the kitchen before I could answer.

Zee was right. Glad had loved me. It hadn't seemed like it, but she had. And I'd never noticed. Maybe she'd never felt my love in return. Blinking back tears, I set Bill's cards on the brown-and-orange shag and tried to focus on the present. Barb's coffee table was still overflowing with desserts. Underneath a miniature loaf of bread was a sheet of pink paper with two rows of tiny, careful script—probably a list of who'd brought what so she could specifically mention rhubarb cobbler or gingersnaps when she sent her thank-you notes. On top of a Saran-Wrapped pie was the same red, white, and blue paperback I'd found in Glad's office and at Neale's: *How Wal-Mart Is Destroying America*.

When Barb returned, I nodded toward the book. "Bet that tops Aldoburg's best-seller list."

Barb cracked a small smile. "Your aunts bought a copy for each of us downtown merchants so we'd be ready for the forum tomorrow night." She handed me a glass and sat on the sofa across from me. "I hope lots of folks will be there to speak out against Wal-Mart."

"I'll be there," I said, "helping Zee."

"Bless your heart."

"Listen," I said. "I don't think Glad's death was a hate crime. I think it had something to do with Wal-Mart."

On the TV, a weather guy babbled gleefully about a storm front.

Barb took a long swallow of ice tea. Her wedding band looked gigantic on her slender hand. "Do you think someone in favor of Wal-Mart killed her?"

I told Barb about the Post-it note and the other things I'd learned. "Do you know why Glad would be having a serious conversation with Stu Two and Collin?"

Barb shook her head. "Parker might, but he's out biking. His father's death has been very hard on him."

"On you too, I'm sure." I sipped my tea and waited for her to gather her thoughts before my next question. "Have you recently sold white spray paint to anyone besides Alex?"

She closed her eyes and tapped her fingernails against her glass. Then she snapped to attention.

"You remembered someone," I prompted.

"Stuart Peterson." She set her glass on the floor. "He was in line behind Alex when Alex bought his."

"Stuart saw Alex buy white spray paint?"

"I remember because Stuart didn't have any paint in his cart until he saw Alex's. Then he sent Stu Two to get some." Barb tightened her robe. "Stu wanted to know what they were going to do with it, but the mayor didn't say."

sixteen

After I left Barb I sat on Zee's front steps to watch dusk overtake the sky. The scent of cut grass gave way to someone grilling a late dinner. Zee's air conditioner hummed, and an elderly couple strolled by with a black terrier that raised its leg and watered what was left of the Honigs' front bushes. Three boys sped past on bicycles, making the most of the remaining light. I'd stay outside until the fireflies appeared, and then I'd get back to the business of bringing a murderer to justice and rescuing small-town America from corporate culture. Or mayhap I should try to salvage what was left of my job. I really needed to talk to Orchid directly rather than leaving her yet another message.

So much for relaxing.

I closed my eyes and tried to forget the mother of all to-do lists. I thought about the cards Glad had saved for me. My dad's cards. Was she afraid I'd grow more and more distant from my parents? Maybe that was one reason she didn't like me living with her and Zee. Maybe saving the cards had been her way of telling me she'd spent time pondering my thoughts and feelings, that she'd known it was hard for me to leave my parents' house.

"Hey!" Talia glided up Zee's driveway on Rollerblades. Her dark ponytail swung back and forth as she skated toward me, carefully skirting the roses that hung over the sidewalk. She wore very short jogging shorts and a tank top—both fuchsia—with nary a knee- or elbow-pad in sight. Nary a bruise either. The last time I Rollerbladed I bruised my butt so bad I couldn't sit for two weeks. I had to wear Vince's pants because my own were suddenly too small.

Talia looked like she'd been born in Rollerblades. She gently stopped and sat next to me. Her lipstick and nail polish matched her outfit. She had a tattoo on her shoulder—some kind of Asian characters.

"You like it?" she asked. "It's my name in Korean. I got it just this spring. My sorority sisters pitched in for my birthday. I was totally excited." Sweat lined the edges of her hair.

"Want something to drink?" I asked.

"No thanks. I'm good." She stared at the cracks in the sidewalk.

Poor thing. Her natural friendliness had brought her to my front steps, but once there she remembered we'd just buried my aunt, and she couldn't think of anything to say. "How's Hortie?" I asked.

"She tries not to show it, but she's totally worried about Alex. Uncle Frank has already hired a criminal lawyer from Omaha." Talia began twisting her ponytail.

"Your uncle is just covering all his bases."

She continued to gaze at the sidewalk.

I wanted to offer her some hope. "Barb just told me that when Alex bought the white spray paint from her, the mayor and Stu Two saw him, and then they bought some themselves."

Talia quit messing with her ponytail and turned to me.

"One of them might have framed Alex," I said. "Probably Stuart."

"Framing someone, that's, like, so cruel."

"Yeah," I said, "there's been a lot of cruelty going around."

We both fell silent. A few fireflies showed their stuff.

"Why frame Alex?" Talia asked.

"Business is slow all over town," I said. "Stuart's not selling much insurance, his oldest son is having financial difficulties, his youngest will be ready for college next year, and to top it all off, he's worried about getting reelected."

She stared at me blankly.

I slapped a mosquito on my arm and continued theorizing. "Stuart thinks Wal-Mart is the answer to all his problems, so he kills Glad and frames Alex. He hopes Zee will be so grief-stricken that she'll back down on her anti–Wal-Mart campaign. If he's really lucky, your grandma will be so worried about Alex that she'll do the same. Maybe even resign her council seat."

Talia twirled her ponytail again. "Sounds like a pretty iffy plan. Besides, Stu Two will probably get an athletic scholarship."

"What about Stuart's other son? Maybe Wal-Mart promised him a management position," I said. "Who knows? Maybe they offered Stuart a large sum of money for his vote."

"Wal-Mart does a lot of crappy stuff, but they're not dumb enough to do something so totally illegal." Talia moved her Rollerblades back and forth on the cement. "I've done some research because Grandma wants me to speak at the forum."

"You all ready?" I asked.

Talia shrugged. "I'll be glad when it's over. Everyone is making such a big deal out of it," she said. "Some people think

Aldoburg will get too big if Wal-Mart comes. Like we might have to install another traffic light."

I chuckled.

"And some people think we'll become a ghost town without Wal-Mart." Talia frowned. "It'll take a lot more than a store to save this place. Most everyone is ancient, and that's a good thing because there's no place to work. There's nothing to do."

Talia was exaggerating, but Aldoburg has lost at least a couple thousand people since I graduated from high school. Half of the hospital has been turned into a nursing home.

"It's kind of sad," Talia said, "but I sure don't want to live here." She met my eyes. "Obviously you don't either." She pushed herself off the step and onto her feet. "I should go," she said. "Don't tell anybody what I said about Aldoburg. It would break Grandma's heart."

"Your secret's safe with me." I didn't want to add to Hortie's troubles, and truth be told, I shared Talia's sentiments about Wal-Mart and Aldoburg. As she skated down the street, I thought of all those Iowa "towns" that consist only of a gas station, a couple of bars, a church, and maybe a grain elevator. Some of them had once been like Aldoburg, but people like me had abandoned them.

I slapped at another mosquito. I'd been elated to leave Aldoburg for a place with more variety and choices: more restaurants and coffee shops, more people who read books for fun, more people and books period. And, last but not least, more lesbians. I'd never once considered moving back to Aldoburg, but I realized it had been comforting to know I could. Someday small-town Iowa would disappear, engulfed by urban sprawl or hog-confinement lots. Had I carried some small part of it with me, or had I been too successful in my desire to leave it behind?

No answers were forthcoming, but several mosquitoes were. I headed inside to phone the dreaded Orchid.

I sat at the kitchen counter, pen in hand. Orchid usually threw me off guard, so I decided to write down everything I wanted to say. So far my legal pad was blank. I was distracted by the mountain of sweets next to me. Forcing my eyes away from a German chocolate cake, I stared at the phone. Then I checked the clock on the stove. 9:56. Maybe it was too late to call.

Oh, what the hell. I punched in Orchid's number. Her phone rang once. Twice. I'd play up the Wal-Mart bit. Orchid would relate to a quest against Wal-Mart. The phone kept ringing. Finally, the machine.

"Hello. You've reached 356-8821. Orchid and Anne can't come to the phone right now."

What? Orchid and Anne? There was no mention of any Anne the last time I called. Had *my* Anne moved in with Orchid? Could my life get any worse?

The machine beeped. I sat with my mouth open, silent. I barely had the presence of mind to hang up. I opened a container of brownies and popped half of one in my mouth. I told myself Anne is a common name. It might not be my Anne. Besides, my Anne wasn't my Anne anymore. She had a right to be with whoever she wanted.

But Orchid? I tore the plastic wrap from the chocolate cake and sampled its coconut topping. Then I called Vince.

He answered on the third ring.

I blurted it out. "Anne has moved in with Orchid."

"Who's this?" a strange male voice asked.

"Who're you? Where's Vince?"

"Who wants to know?" The voice was gravelly and impudent.

"This is Mara. Vince's housemate."

No reaction on the other end of the phone.

"His landlord." I raised my voice.

"No need to get huffy," Gravel Voice said. "Vince is at rehearsal. Then he has a date. Me, I'm just trying to fix the toilet."

"The toilet is broken?" Never assume your life can't get any worse.

"You may need to replace some of the piping."

I couldn't bring myself to ask about the cost.

"You could get estimates, but you can bet I'll be the cheapest on account of I'm just starting out."

Great. Vince had hired a novice plumber who undoubtedly had stellar buns but probably didn't know a plunger from a wrench. I would return to a house filled with sewage.

"You there, ma'am?"

I managed a grunt.

"If you get estimates, you can't use the toilet in the mean time."

"Forget the estimates," I said. "Just fix it." If anything went wrong with the toilet in the next twenty years, I was going to hold Vince responsible.

I hung up and finished my half-eaten brownie. Then I pushed aside my questions about Anne and punched in Orchid's number again. I'd leave her a message, comfort myself with chocolate, and go to bed.

"Hello?" It was Orchid herself.

"Uh, hi, it's Mara." I looked longingly at my legal pad and cursed myself for leaving it blank.

"I'm sorry about your aunt." She didn't sound sorry. She sounded pissed.

"Thanks," I said. "There's sort of a situation—"

"I need you back at the station as soon as possible. We're shorthanded because one of our interns quit."

I was surprised more of them hadn't bailed. I wished I could, but I had toilet bills to pay. "I'm sorry to hear that, but I really can't get away for a few days."

Stony silence on the other end of the line. I imagined Orchid fingering one of her elaborate earrings and glaring into space. Or maybe she was gazing at Anne.

I took a deep breath. "My aunt is real broken up," I said. "She and her partner had been together nearly forty years. The police think her death was a hate crime." It felt gross, distorting the truth to placate Orchid. "My aunts, they were just getting ready to wage a big battle against Wal-Mart. It wants to build in their town. There's a public forum tomorrow night and a vote on Monday. I'd like to see my aunt through that at least." I didn't mention that I was also trying to find a murderer.

"Monday?" Orchid made it sound like I'd asked for the Taj Mahal.

"I'll work extra shifts when I get back." God, I hated groveling.

"I'll expect you here on Tuesday," Orchid said, "and don't worry about the Pride Month reading series. I've got it all taken care of."

As I hung up I forced myself to say thanks even though Orchid was using my absence to maneuver the series away from me. She was good at maneuvering. She'd probably maneuvered herself right into Anne's heart—and Anne into her bed. But I didn't have time for a pity party. What I had was four days to battle Wal-Mart and find a killer.

I studied the live log and clicked on ABC news, but nothing happened. Then I clicked on a Toby Keith tune. Nothing. I tried a PSA. Silence. The phone rang faintly from Charlene's office. Someone was calling to complain about the dead air. I panicked and tried to open my mike. It was stuck. The phone rang again and again.

I jerked awake. The phone rang on the end table by my bed. I tried to reach it, but my arm was wrapped in a sweaty sheet. Squinting through the darkness at the red digits on my alarm clock, I worked my arm free and picked up the phone.

"Hello?" I croaked.

"Mar-Bar?"

I sat up and squinted at the clock again. "Vince, it's 1 in the morning. This had better be important." I grabbed my glasses off the table and put them on.

"George left a note. Something about Orchid and Anne."

"George?"

"The plumber."

I stretched and wondered if George would charge extra for leaving phone messages. "Is the toilet fixed?"

"Not quite. Tomorrow at the latest."

I was too tired to yell at Vince for hiring an incompetent, albeit sensitive, plumber. I just hoped I wasn't paying him by the hour.

"George's note says you sounded upset."

I told Vince about the message on Orchid's machine.

"It can't be your Anne," he said.

I turned on my reading lamp. "What if it is?"

"Then Anne is a fool, that's what. You're a quadrillion times cuter than Orchid. Plus you're a decent human being."

The moon shone through thin white curtains. I started crying. "She said I was emotionally unavailable."

"Oh, Mar-Bar, that's what all lesbians say when they break up."

I tried to laugh, but I couldn't help wondering what Orchid had that I didn't. What had Anne wanted that I couldn't give her? "Vince, do you think I'm a good listener?"

He sighed. "Anne made a big mistake when she left you, and she'll be making an even bigger one if she is indeed with Orchid. But don't worry, girlfriend. I'll discover the identity of the mysterious Anne. You're not the only one who can play Nancy Drew."

"Thanks." I sniffled and looked around the room for a Kleenex.

"Speaking of Ms. Drew, have you unearthed any new evidence?"

I shared my theory about Stuart and the spray paint.

"Watch him closely at the forum," Vince said. "See who he talks to and how he reacts to what's being said. Like Hamlet and Claudius."

I smiled at Vince's enthusiasm, but I didn't share it. Hamlet had only one suspect, and I had at least a handful.

I couldn't sleep after talking with Vince, so I headed to Glad's office to do some more research on Wal-Mart. Zee probably wouldn't need me to speak at the forum, but as Hamlet says, "The readiness is all." Besides, I needed to find something—anything—that could help me believe Zee was engaged in something other than an exercise in futility.

While I waited for the computer to boot up I peered out the

window. The moon shone on Barb taking out more of her hedge—clippers in one hand, a pile of branches at her feet. Once again I quelled the urge to offer her some water or some empty words about the importance of sleep, and I went back to Glad's desk.

There was the pale green Post-it note, taunting me. I peeled it off the front page of the *Aldoburg Times* and stuck it on the bottom of the computer monitor.

WM

SP

CC

Wal-Mart, Winker Mason, Stuart Peterson, Stu Two, and the three Conovers: Collin, Chuck, and Charlene. I was sure one of them held the key to Glad's death. If only I knew what Glad had been thinking when she penned their initials.

The computer beeped and its screen filled with error messages. Could just *one* thing go my way? I rebooted and closed my eyes. Maybe I'd start to feel drowsy and I could go back to bed. Or maybe when I opened my eyes the errors would magically vanish.

Right.

I rebooted a third time and went to the window. Barb had gone inside, but her living room and a couple upstairs rooms were aglow.

Moments later I found myself tapping on her front door. Neighbors borrow things from each other all the time, right? A cup of sugar, a ladder. A little online time in the wee hours of the morning.

Barb pulled me inside, clutching my arm. "What's wrong?"

I instantly regretted my nocturnal impulsivity. "Everything's fine," I said. "I didn't mean to scare you."

Barb released my arm and fingered a pair of gardening gloves she'd shoved into the front pocket of her grass-stained jeans.

"I know it's late," I said. "But I saw you working on your hedge. And your lights were on. Glad's computer isn't working." My voice caught. "I was hoping I could use yours."

She touched my arm again, gently this time. "Oh, Mara, nights are the worst, aren't they?"

I nodded and willed myself not to cry. "I'm sorry," I said, "I shouldn't have—"

"Nonsense." Barb waved her hand through the air. "One computer coming right up." Her voice was falsely perky. "And let's get you a snack too. Have a seat, and I'll be right back."

I sank into a chair, grateful to be mothered. Barb opened the fridge and started chopping something. Her coffee table was still piled with desserts, the neatly scripted list of who-brought-what still in place. On the couch was a nearly empty laundry basket and piles of folded clothes. I moved across the room, studied the mounds of Lycra and spandex, and folded a couple of black leotards that had "legs" no wider than toilet-paper tubes. I don't understand the lure of encasing oneself in shiny fabric—especially in the middle of July.

"That top has the best support." Barb carried a glass of ice water and a plate with apple slices and cheese. "Holds you right up, but you hardly know it's there."

I tried to muster some enthusiasm, but her small talk about shelf bras was too surreal. My whole life was surreal. I'd just been in her living room hours ago, but it felt like centuries.

"You've got to have the right support," she said. "You can't buy bra tops like that at Wal-Mart."

I seized the opportunity to segue. "Have you bookmarked any good anti–Wal-Mart sites?"

"I'm not much of a bookmarker." She handed me the glass of water and gestured to the stairs. "The computer is up in Frannie's old room."

As we made our way up the stairs, Barb said, "The door will be on your right. Parker is right across the hall, but don't worry about waking him."

"You sure?" I whispered.

"He sleeps like a rock."

The doorknob was loose in my hand, and the door squeaked as I opened it. I hoped Barb was right about Parker.

"The light switch is on your left," Barb said.

When I flipped it on I saw that Frannie's room was now mission central for Barb's many projects—and yet another shrine to her grandchildren. The walls on both sides of the window were plastered with their pictures—all in white frames that matched their toothy grins. Underneath Barb's sewing machine was a set of magenta barbells and a bunch of empty picture frames in need of some TLC. In the middle of the floor was a miniature dress pattern pinned to some lacey pink fabric.

"That's for Frannie's youngest." Barb set my snack next to the computer and headed to the door. "I'm finally turning in," she said. "Stay as long as you like. Just lock the door behind you when you go."

I said goodnight, and Barb slipped away. I wondered if she had locked her door before Glad was murdered. Zee hadn't. I rushed to the window and peered out. A streetlight illuminated most of my aunt's yard, and the porch light took care of the rest.

Back at the computer I gnawed an apple slice and got online. The Web site "Against the Wal" had a new story: Wal-Mart had just opened its first store in Beijing. There are twenty-two other stores throughout the rest of China. I scrolled to the end of the piece: Wal-Mart is the world's largest corporation, having recently passed ExxonMobil for the top spot.

Good thing I already had insomnia.

I was familiar with the next story: WAL-MART AGREES TO BAR SEXUAL-ORIENTATION DISCRIMINATION. The headline did not fill with me warm fuzzies. The discount giant had agreed to stop discriminating only because the Pride Foundation of Seattle had bought a lot of its stock. Even then, it took the gay shareholders two years to effect a policy change that included no protection for transgendered people and no domestic-partner benefits. Can we say *shallow victory*?

I sighed and looked away from the screen. The mouse pad bore the Nike swoosh and motto: *Just Do It*. Next to the printer was a diskette box filled with neatly clipped coupons. The rest of the desk was covered with brochures about nursing schools—most of them in the Minneapolis area. If Frannie finally finished her degree, that would bring Barb a lot of joy. During my summers home from college, Barb's standard greeting and farewell was a stern warning—"Don't *you* drop out of college, Mara"—even though I'd never shown the slightest proclivity for prematurely entering the real world.

I clicked on a link and read about a Nebraska town's triumph over Wal-Mart. The deciding vote occurred after a seven-hour city council meeting. I hoped Aldoburg's forum wouldn't last that long. According to Zee, the council had decided to separate the forum from the meeting in which the actual vote occurred so that everyone could have a chance to speak. Nobody ever said democracy was efficient.

Pulling my knees to my chest, I stretched my T-shirt over them and scanned some more of my search results. Bulldozer Blockade, Wal-Mart Trash Page, Wal-Mart: Evil Empire, Wal-Martyrs, and—my favorite—Walmartsucks.com. Maybe I should create some of my own sites. Orchidsucks.com or Orchid's Evil Empire, or Orchid's Control Freak Page. I reveled in my fantasy before clicking on the Wal of Shame. When I could no longer take the litany of women and minorities who'd been harassed or unfairly fired or demoted, I tried another link and found myself reading a former Wal-Mart manager's diary.

His first day of work he was shown a video about the evils of unions. He also had to take a drug test and a personality test before he was hired. He'd included a few questions from the personality test:

A description of my childhood might be:
A. Happy
B. Average
C. Unhappy

I wondered about the preferred answer. Would anyone who had a happy childhood want to work at Wal-Mart? Was it a trick question?

Which of the statements is true of you?
A. I like a neat and tidy home.
B. I don't mind a messy house as long as it's clean.
C. I'm indifferent regarding neatness.

The preferred answer was probably A. I was definitely an A. Vince was a C.

My friends see me as:
A. Tough
B. Average
C. A pushover

Wal-Mart undoubtedly wanted its workers to be pushovers, but would it want them to perceive themselves that way? Maybe with its penchant for conformity, Wal-Mart wanted its workers to see themselves as average.

Me, I was tough. You had to be to track a cold-blooded murderer. But I was also letting an incompetent plumber have his way with my pipes, and I was letting Orchid have her way with my reading series and possibly my ex. Maybe I was a pushover who tried to act tough. I therefore seemed emotionally unavailable to Anne, and that was why she dumped me.

I have felt like breaking something in the past.
A. Agree
B. Undecided
C. Disagree

Who wouldn't feel like breaking something if they had to take such an insulting test? What must it feel like to need work so badly that you'd try to guess the "preferred answer" to multiple-choice questions about yourself, hoping that Wal-Mart would deem you worthy of exploitation?

I sometimes have pretty wild daydreams.
A. Agree
B. Undecided
C. Disagree

Another trick question. On one hand, you'd need wild daydreams to get through the workday at Wal-Mart, but on the other hand, they'd just frustrate you. I should know. My life seemed to consist of nothing but wild daydreams: keeping Zee safe, keeping Wal-Mart out of Aldoburg, finding Glad's killer.

I considered my more modest daydreams: Vince washing his dishes and paying his share of the bills on time, my toilet working, Orchid resigning from the station and moving to another country—preferably one fraught with violence.

Anne coming back to me.

Did I really want that to happen?

What about my other daydream—the one involving a certain blond cop from Chicago?

seventeen

As I trudged past an empty storefront, I longed for a nap. I'd been planning to snooze after my radio shift, but Zee had a list of things for me to do to get ready for the forum that evening. At the top of her list was procuring dowels and masking tape for the signs she'd made with LaVonne and Talia. At the top of my list was a cheeseburger and lots of caffeine.

A blast of air conditioning jolted me as I entered the Chat 'n' Chew. Except for three teenage girls who shrieked and giggled a couple booths down, I was the only customer. I peered through the front window at my car. As usual it was in need of a wash, but nothing else was amiss. Ever since I'd found that nasty note on the front sea,t I'd been bracing myself for something worse—something I couldn't hide from Zee—slashed tires or my sexual orientation carved into the paint. It seemed strange that I hadn't received another warning, but I counted my blessings. Given my defunct toilet I could ill afford car repairs. And I sure didn't want another run-in with Zee.

What I did want was a Coke. I cleared my throat loudly,

hoping someone would hear me above the shrieking girls.

Hortie herself emerged from the kitchen, slid into my booth, and leaned her elbows on the table. She was beaming. "Alex is out on bail," she said, "home safe with his father."

"That's great." I wondered how much money Alex's father had to borrow to pay his son's bail.

"And look at this." Hortie reached into her apron pocket and placed a piece of paper on the table. She smoothed it out in front of me.

It was a credit card statement. Stuart Peterson's. A MasterCard with a balance of $13,846.37.

I glanced around the restaurant. "Where did you get this?" I whispered.

Hortie tucked the paper into her apron pocket and smiled smugly. "His mailbox."

"What?"

"I was taking a walk this morning, and I saw the mailman deliver Stuart's mail. Wasn't nobody to see me, so I helped myself."

The girls kept squealing.

"You can't just take people's mail," I said. "It's illegal."

Hortie frowned. "I thought you'd be grateful. Talia dropped by last night to check in on me. She told me how you think Stuart framed my Alex. She thought it was funny, but I took you serious. I was gathering evidence."

I didn't even want to think about what would happen if Zee knew I'd inspired Hortie to break the law. "What if you'd gotten caught?"

"I didn't." She tapped her cigarettes on the table.

"You could be in jail yourself." I had no idea whether this was true, but I wanted to scare her. "Tampering with the mail is a federal crime. At the very least you could be kicked off city council. Then what would happen with the Wal-Mart vote?"

Hortie puffed on her cigarette, trying not to look worried. "Nobody saw me."

"Did you take the rest of his mail too?"

"Nah. It was just junk."

"What about the envelope the bill came in? Where is it?"

"I tossed it. Didn't think it was important."

"It's not," I assured her. I'd been toying with the idea of sneaking the bill back to Stuart's mailbox but, to be frank, I had better things to do. "Can I have the statement?" I asked, "I'd like to study it in private." No way was I going to risk Hortie getting caught with it.

She put out her cigarette and handed me the bill. "It's good evidence, isn't it?"

I tucked it into my backpack. "Great evidence."

"He owes a pretty penny. And that's just this card. He might have more than one."

I didn't like her train of thought. "Please promise me you won't go near anybody's mailbox but your own. And please, please promise not to tell Zee any of this."

The squealing girls huddled at the cash register, ready to pay. "It's our secret." Hortie winked at me. "But $14,000," she whistled and shook her head.

One more reason for me to watch the mayor's every move at the forum.

Heat rippled off the sidewalk. I was still exhausted despite the Coke I'd guzzled at the Chat 'n' Chew. My braid felt heavy on my damp tank top, and my glasses slid down my nose. I pushed them up and peered into the window of Stuff. There, still, were the humongous red sandals only a drag queen could love. There was also a handwritten sign: CLOSED TO PREPARE FOR THE FORUM. PLEASE COME BACK AGAIN. STUFF APPRECIATES YOUR BUSINESS. I cursed under my breath. Vince's gift would have to wait. Again.

At least I wasn't the only lunatic out in the heat. A couple of women with strollers came out of Dollar Daze. There were also a few cars near Honig's Hardware. I hoped that meant the store was open. Otherwise I had no idea where I'd find dowels and masking tape. Maybe I'd have to drive miles away to the nearest Wal-Mart so I could purchase materials to protest against it.

I was spared that cruel irony by an orange-and-black Open sign. A bell rang as I pulled open the glass door. I paused on the rubber welcome mat and let the air conditioning wash over me. Parker was ringing up some venetian blinds for a stooped old man. Behind him in line was a middle-aged woman with a toddler and a sack of charcoal briquettes.

I began roaming the aisles. Honig's Hardware had been one of my favorite stores when I was a kid, but now it made me claustrophobic. The aisles—with their no-frills concrete floors—were barely wide enough for a single shopping cart, and the ceiling was festooned with bicycles, garden hoses, hunting rifles, wind chimes, sweatshirts, and fans. Honig's used to be strictly a hardware store, but now you could buy practically anything there—that is, if you could find it.

Dowels. Where the heck were they? What did one use them for besides attaching them to anti–Wal-Mart signs? They certainly wouldn't be in the lawn and garden section, although I must admit that the lawn ornaments captured my attention. The trolls reminded me of Orchid.

I strolled past lamps, power tools, plumbing stuff, and paint before finding the masking tape and slipping a couple rolls onto my wrist. Where, oh where, could the dowels be? I was about ready to give up and ask Parker when I spied a sign that said ARTS AND CRAFTS. Glue, balsa wood, miniature clamps, Styrofoam balls. Dowels!

Unfortunately, there were only five that looked long enough for Zee's purposes. I scooped them up along with several shorter ones. Hopefully, the anti–Wal-Mart contingent would boast several tall folks.

Next to the register, Parker sat on a metal folding chair hunched over a book, swaying to some music on his Walkman.

"What are you reading?" I asked.

He shot up, startled. "Just working on my Spanish." He stood up, removed his Walkman, closed his book, and slid them both into the cubbyhole under the cash register. His face was even paler than usual, and dark circles had taken up permanent residence beneath his eyes. "I went to the Yucatan this past spring and tutored some grade school kids in English. If my Spanish improves, the next time I go I can serve as a medical translator." His eyes lit up despite his exhaustion.

"When's next time?"

Parker frowned. "I was planning on next summer, but I'll have to wait and see how the store's doing. See if Mom needs me." He hung his head and tucked his hair behind his ears.

"A lot of things must be up in the air right now," I said.

He nodded. "Dad always said he wanted me to do whatever would make me happy, but I know his big dream was me taking over the store. Mom's too." He pressed his lips together, determined not to cry in front of me. "I'm getting a business degree with my global studies, so I could do it. It's just that—oh, I don't know."

"You don't really want to live here," I said quietly.

"I hope Wal-Mart wins," he blurted. "Then it would just be

over. We've barely been making it. We'd never survive if Wal-Mart came. Then my mom wouldn't have to worry about the store. She could do something else."

Probably work at Wal-Mart, I thought.

"And I wouldn't have to decide between the store and what I really want to do," he said.

"What's that?"

"Travel." His voice brightened. "Translate. Work on my photography." He sighed and slumped back into his chair. "But it would break Mom's heart to lose this store."

I wracked my brain for an appropriate response. Young adults don't often bare their souls to me. "I'm sure your father meant it when he said he wanted you to be happy."

"How can I be happy if I turn my back on the store he worked his whole life to build?" Parker's voice filled with anguish.

I had no answer, so I took the coward's way out and changed the subject. "How's your mom?"

"OK." Parker stared at his feet. "Kind of jumpy."

I thought about Barb digging up her hedge in the darkness. "I returned your dad's postcard collection last night."

Parker managed a half-smile. "It was his prized possession. Besides the store."

I didn't want him to start brooding again. "I was thinking it would be nice to go ahead with the display he and Glad were planning at the Chat 'n' Chew."

"That'd be cool." He gave me a full smile. "But we'd have to decide whether to do it Glad's way or Dad's way. Glad wanted to arrange the cards geographically because she collected them from all over, but Dad wanted to organize them chronologically because he had mostly old ones." Parker shook his head. "Dad was always complaining that Glad had no appreciation for the story his cards told. Can't you just see them fighting?"

I could, and it nearly brought tears to my eyes. I also felt a twinge of jealousy. Parker knew Glad so much better than I did.

The bell rang, and a silver-haired man in overalls entered the store. Parker got back on his feet and rang up my masking tape.

"You sold any white spray paint recently?"

"Mom said you might ask me that," Parker said. "Do you really think somebody who wants Wal-Mart killed Glad?"

"It's possible."

"I don't remember selling any spray paint this summer," he said, "but it keeps forever if you don't open the can."

Great. More suspects. I pushed the thought aside. "What about Stu Two and Collin? Do you have any idea why they'd be having a serious conversation with Glad?"

Parker picked up the dowels. "They're younger than me. We don't have much in common."

"Have you spent any time at all with them this summer?"

He put my purchases in a brown paper bag. "We ran into each other a couple weeks ago. I was feeling restless after closing the station, so I decided to take a long ride even though I usually bike in the mornings. Stu Two and Collin were running, and Collin asked me to pace them." Parker handed me the bag. "Stu Two didn't say a word."

"That's odd."

"Probably just concentrating." Parker grinned. "They're very serious about their training. Collin said they'd been doing the same route all summer, trying to improve their time."

Funny. Neither boy could remember the route when I'd questioned them. "Do you remember the route?" I asked.

"They were almost done when I ran into them, headed back toward town—not too far from the station."

eighteen

Having the Wal-Mart forum in the high school gym was just asking for trouble. The wooden bleachers were filled to capacity, as were the folding chairs on the basketball court. It was already ten minutes past the time the forum was scheduled to start, and folks were still filing in. Some squeezed into the bleachers, ignoring the squished and resentful citizens around them. Some brought lawn chairs and found there was no place to unfold them. One man with a white beard held his green-and-white chair in front of his chest—a shield against the jostling crowd. Others simply sat on the floor around the small stage that had been set up under one of the basketball hoops. So far, no one was sitting on the stage itself. It contained only a podium and microphone.

The gym, like most small-town high school gyms, wasn't air-conditioned, but at least the concrete wall felt cool against my back. I arrived early so I'd have a good vantage point—dead center in the very back row of the bleachers. I not only needed to watch the Post-it-note people, but I also had to make sure Hortie stayed out of trouble.

To my right a woman jiggled a baby on her knee. It kept bawling, and above the dull roar of conversation several infants replied in kind—just like howling dogs.

In front of me a sixtyish woman worked a crossword as her husband read *Farm Journal*. To my left sat a young man with a pierced eyebrow who was inching his hand up his girl-friend's thigh. She had short choppy hair that hovered between purple and burgundy—and she had no problem with public displays of affection.

Several folks were fanning themselves with the neon-green fliers Zee and her comrades had distributed. Talia was using her sign—WAL-MART: LOW PRICES AT A HIGH COST—to fan Hortie in the first row of folding chairs. The center of that row had been reserved for city council members and their families. My father sat smack in the middle. Very symbolic. Mom was to his right. Then LaVonne with her daughter Lucy, and Hortie with an empty chair that must have been Talia's. Several of Hortie's other grandchildren sat behind her. To my father's left was Winker, staring straight ahead with a determined set to his jaw. Next was Stuart, who kept shooting glances between the clock and the people who were still trying to cram into the gym. His wife and kids weren't sitting with him. He leaned over and whispered to a balding man I'd never seen before, possibly a Wal-Mart representative. Next to the balding man sat Father Kelly. He tugged at his collar and adjusted his oversize glasses.

I scanned the bleachers across the gym, keeping my eyes peeled for Charlene. I'd almost given up when a man in a cowboy hat leaned forward to talk with the woman in front of him and I spied Charlene in the second-to-last row, wisely keeping a low pro-file. At this point it was the only way she could help the Wal-Mart cause. She sure couldn't give a speech, because we all knew she favored the store only because she needed to sell her farm.

To Charlene's right sat Chuck and his wife, and on her left were Stu Two and Collin. Both boys wore tank tops in Aldoburg green-and-white. Stu Two blew a large bubble, and Collin stared vacantly into space. The boys had lied about their where-abouts the night Glad was killed—that much was certain. But what about the spray paint? Maybe Stuart had bought it for a home-improvement project and Stu Two had used it for a less innocent one.

I must have stared at the boys a moment too long. Chuck was glowering at me. Struggling to keep my face neutral, I fixed my eyes on him. When he finally looked away, I turned my attention to Zee. She sat at the end of the second row of folding chairs, holding aloft a sign that featured the words *Wal-Mart* with a red slash through them. I wondered if she was thinking about Glad, and I prayed that the evening wouldn't be too hard on her. Next to Zee sat Barb. Her sign— WAL-MART DESTROYS JOBS—rested against her shoulder. She had a lot at stake. Honig's Hardware was Aldoburg's biggest variety store, the store most like Wal-Mart. She leaned back in her chair, and Parker draped an arm around her. In his other hand he too held a sign: WAL-MART SUPPORTS SWEAT-SHOPS. About five rows back was a more succinct sign—VOTE YES—and a banner that proclaimed WAL-MART = ECONOMIC GROWTH. One of the women holding the banner was a regular at Zee and Glad's Sunday brunch potlucks. Lots of friends were butting heads over Wal-Mart.

Stuart stood, and the crowd began to hush. He eased his way to the podium, stepping around folks sitting on the floor. Despite the heat he wore a navy tie and a short-sleeved white dress shirt. He's one of those men who tries to dress a notch better than everyone around him. "Good evening, friends." The PA system whined and crackled, but Stuart kept his smile pasted on. "Before undertaking our important business, I thought it would be a good idea if we started with a prayer, so I asked Father Kelly to say a few words."

Aldoburg has never been big on the separation of church and state.

As Father Kelly made his way to the stage, the people sitting on the floor parted like the Red Sea. The rest of the crowd shifted and coughed. It wanted to debate, not pray.

Father Kelly cleared his throat and nudged his glasses up his nose. "Heavenly Father." His booming voice made the mike shriek. He stepped back and continued as it hummed. "We ask that you send down your spirit of wisdom and tolerance and patience tonight as we struggle to decide what is best for our community."

The woman with the crossword puzzle hissed, "They shoulda got a Protestant too."

Her husband calmly turned a page of his magazine.

I searched the crowd again. Neale hadn't come.

As Father Kelly enumerated the many ways God had blessed Aldoburg, I made excuses for her: She was sick, pursuing a new lead, consigned to a speed trap by the dastardly Chuck. Otherwise she'd be here.

The crowd grew more restless until it finally got the Amen it was waiting for, and Stuart returned to the podium. "I want to thank you all for coming out on such a warm night to share your ideas on the important matter before us," he said. "Your presence here suggests a deep concern and love for Aldoburg." He paused, perhaps for applause, but none was forthcoming, so he cut to the chase. "First let me familiarize you with the ground rules for tonight. Those of you with signs, I ask you to keep them lowered so we can all concentrate on the speakers and so I can identify folks who want to speak."

Zee reluctantly lowered her sign a couple inches. Barb put hers on the floor and tilted her head back against Parker's arm.

"Second of all," Stuart continued, "we want to make sure everybody has their say, so we're limiting speakers to five minutes."

The crowd grumbled, and I said a prayer of my own that not everyone wanted to speak.

Stuart called for quiet. "Nobody gets a second turn at the microphone until everybody who wants to has spoken once."

There were more grumbles from the crowd and more prayers for brevity from me.

"Please be respectful of your neighbors," Stuart continued, "and do not speak unless you're at the microphone." He loosened his tie and ran his hand through his hair. The underarm of his shirt was soaked through. "To start off, we'll have a representative from Wal-Mart explain the proposed project."

Zee furiously whispered to Barb.

"We already know what Wal-Mart wants," called a man from the back of the folding chair section.

Stuart ignored him. "Reginald Daniels is a community affairs director for Wal-Mart. He has been with the company since 1980."

Eyebrow Boy quit sucking on his girlfriend's neck and said, "Just a couple years before Wal-Mart came to Iowa."

His purple-headed girlfriend nodded somberly.

Perhaps the dynamic duo saw the forum as more than a make out venue. "Excuse me," I said, "but you seem to know a lot about Wal-Mart."

Eyebrow Boy put his arm around Purple Hair. "We've been studying it in Current Events, and I'm supposed to give a speech about it in class. If I speak tonight, I get extra credit. It's a big crowd, though, so I don't know."

"You can do it." Apparently Purple Hair was a stand-by-your-man kind of girl.

I turned my attention back to the podium. Reginald Daniels wore a yellow dress shirt—with the sleeves rolled up—and one of those Western ties that looks like a shoestring. His cowboy boots were brand new. Ditto the charcoal dress pants. Their creases were visible from the back of the bleachers. A few strands of his flaxen hair were combed over his bald spot. He was a tall, thin man with just a touch of a beer belly.

"Good evening, ladies and gentlemen. I surely appreciate the opportunity to talk with ya'll about what Wal-Mart can do for Aldoburg." His accent was pure Bill Clinton. He probably worked out of Wal-Mart's headquarters in Bentonville, Arkansas. "As ya'll well know, Wal-Mart wants to become a part of your fine community. Aldoburg is an excellent venue for us. You're near the interstate and smack-dab in the middle of several smaller, more modest towns."

If he were any slicker, he'd slide off the stage.

"But what's in it for ya'll?"

The woman with the crossword jabbed her husband in the ribs. "Can you believe Ron and Charlene are selling their farm to this bozo?"

"It's a shame," the man said.

"A crying shame," she insisted. Several people whirled around and gave her dirty looks.

"The proposed Wal-Mart will benefit you both as a consumer and as a citizen," Reginald said. "In his autobiography, Sam Walton wrote, 'The secret of successful retailing is to give your customers what they want, and really, if you think about it from your point of view as a customer, you want everything: a wide assortment of quality merchandise; the lowest possible prices; guaranteed satisfaction with what you buy; friendly, knowledgeable service; convenient hours; free parking; a pleasant shopping experience.'"

"You can't have everything!" shouted the man from the folding chairs.

Stuart craned his neck and glared in the heckler's general direction. Zee smirked. Reginald used the interruption as an opportunity to drink some bottled water. Sam's Choice, no doubt.

"This Wal-Mart will have almost everything," he said, "except a full grocery." He grinned. "There will be thirty-one departments, including a Vision Center, a pharmacy, one-hour photo processing, and a Tire and Lube Express. The average Wal-Mart carries 70,000 different items. That translates into a lot of choices for you, the consumer."

I didn't follow everything he said about Wal-Mart's hospitality and Always Low Prices because the baby next to me started wailing again. It needed a fresh diaper. I tried to breathe through my mouth.

"The bottom line," Reginald said, "is that this Wal-Mart will create jobs. Lots of jobs. The store will hire approximately 250 associates. As part of the Wal-Mart family, these associates will receive competitive wages, on-the-job training, paid vacations, and a discount on Wal-Mart's already rock-bottom prices." He made a dramatic pause. "They will have a retirement plan, medical and dental coverage, life insurance, and disability coverage. They may also participate in profit-sharing and stock-purchase programs."

Large parts of the crowd buzzed with excitement. A few people applauded. Zee scribbled on her legal pad.

"Wal-Mart will increase Aldoburg's tax base through its large payrolls and through the sales tax it generates." Reginald paused again. "Up front, it will contribute $3 million to improve your community's roads and traffic controls."

Eyebrow Boy stopped fondling Purple Hair. He sniffed the air and grimaced, his eyes landing on the baby with the full diaper. Its mother was completely entranced with Reginald.

"Every year, your Wal-Mart will provide a $1,000 scholarship to a graduating high school senior."

Your Wal-Mart. Reginald was trying to make us feel a sense of ownership. Wal-Mart would not own us; we would own it.

"Wal-Mart is the number-one sponsor of the Children's Miracle Network," Reginald said. "Annually, Wal-Mart sets aside $100 million for charitable donations."

"He's had way more than five minutes." The rebel male from the back row of folding chairs struck again and was joined by several other voices. "No special treatment!" "Let someone else talk!" "We've heard enough!"

Reginald mopped his brow and looked to Stuart. The mayor glanced around the gym. More people started shouting for a new speaker. I joined in. The mother with the stinky baby shot me a dirty look, and I fired one back.

Stuart scurried up to the stage. "Thank you, Reggie."

"Reggie" was not about to surrender the microphone so easily. "Any questions?" he asked. Several hands went up, but protests filled the gym. It sounded like a bad call had just been made against the home team.

Reginald went to his seat, and Stuart asked for the next speaker. Zee and her contingent waved their hands in the air, but Stuart ignored them. "You'll all get your turn," he said, picking a young woman who sat near a pro–Wal-Mart banner.

Very pregnant, she lumbered to the stage, dragging a toddler behind her. She clutched a stack of note cards in her free hand. As she read from them, her limp brown hair covered her face. "Between work and kids, most of us lead very busy lives," she said. "We need the convenience Wal-Mart's one-stop shopping offers. By the time I get off work, the stores downtown are closed, and they're never open on Sundays."

LaVonne cupped her hands around her mouth. "They're

open on Saturdays and Thursday evenings." As a council member she wasn't allowed to give a speech, but she still wanted to make herself heard. Even her red-white-and-blue shirt sent a message: Wal-Mart wasn't the only patriotic merchant.

Onstage the toddler jumped around, pulling his mother's arm taut. She yanked him toward the podium and studied her cards. "Many times the stores in Aldoburg don't have what I need. If Aldoburg had a Wal-Mart, then I wouldn't have to drive clear to Council Bluffs or Carroll to get a better selection. I sure don't like spending the gas money, and I'd rather spend my shopping dollars here." She took a deep breath and reigned in her child one more time. "If we had a Wal-Mart, maybe people would drive to Aldoburg to shop. We could be a regional shopping hub."

The women holding the pro–Wal-Mart banner cheered.

Zee and LaVonne shook their heads in disgust, and Barb shuffled through her own note cards.

Stuart helped the pregnant woman from the stage and studied the sea of raised hands. Once again he ignored Zee's gang and chose Lester Simms.

The funeral director had most likely spent the day on the golf course—his face was sunburned, and his shorts were plaid. "We can't afford to say no to successful businesses that want to locate here," Lester said.

"Give the other side a chance!" The man in back reached his loudest pitch yet. He started chanting, "Equal time! Equal time!" Half the gym joined in, including me.

Lester looked to Stuart for help. He was used to dealing with the bereaved. Angry crowds were not his thing.

A cameraman and reporter from a Des Moines news station entered the gym. The reporter pulled a notebook out of her oversize purse, and the cameraman started filming the chanting crowd. People waved their signs.

The mayor rushed to the microphone. "When Lester here is done, the next speaker will be someone against Wal-Mart."

The interruption had flustered Lester, but he managed a few platitudes about progress before stepping back from the podium.

Zee marched to the stage before Stuart could even begin to choose among the upraised hands. Her hair was in a tight braid, and she'd strategically dressed in Aldoburg school colors. She wore white shorts and a green T-shirt with white lettering. The front of her shirt touted Aldoburg basketball, and the back advertised KGEE. She pulled the microphone down and peered at her audience.

"What Mr. Daniels has promised sounds good," Zee said, "but there are many things he isn't telling us."

Mr. Daniels squirmed. Zee had everyone's attention, including the cameraman's and the reporter's.

"Since Mr. Daniels opened his speech with Sam Walton, that's where I'll start too. A federal court had to order Mr. Walton to pay his employees minimum wage. Apparently it was not *Sam's choice* to follow the law—much less pay his employees a living wage."

Zee's pun brought loud chuckles from the anti–Wal-Mart folks.

"The average Wal-Mart salary is $7.50 per hour. That's $1.20 lower than the average hourly wage in other general merchandise stores." Zee squared her shoulders. "Workers in stores like Wal-Mart average thirty hours a week. At $7.50 per hour, a Wal-Mart employee would make $11,700 a year. That's nearly $2,000 below the poverty line for a single mother with two children."

Reginald leaned over and whispered to Stuart, and Stuart nodded.

"Because of Wal-Mart's low-wage policy," Zee said, "even

employees working forty hours a week are often eligible for welfare. Do we taxpayers really want to make up for Wal-Mart's low wages?"

Zee waited as if the question were more than rhetorical. The reporter and cameraman were recording her every word. I was sure she knew it, and I was proud she had the poise not to glance at the camera. The energy that grief had drained from her returned as she made her arguments. "For every two jobs Wal-Mart creates, it destroys three. I know jobs are scarce, and I feel for those of you who are out of work, but don't take the short view. After Wal-Mart has been here a couple years, jobs will be even harder to come by. Most of them will be at Wal-Mart, and they'll offer less job security, fewer benefits, and lower pay."

Glad used to say the only people who can afford to work at Wal-Mart are teenagers who want spending money and senior citizens who have too much time on their hands.

"As for the benefits Mr. Daniels promised," Zee said, "let's look at health insurance. The average employer asks its employees to pay for twenty-eight percent of their health insurance plan. Wal-Mart employees pay nearly fifty percent."

The mother with the stinky baby mumbled to the woman next to her. "You can lie with numbers."

"Why don't you change your baby's diaper?" I snapped. I was angry because I knew most people in the gym had already made up their minds. We were sitting there sweating for nothing. My father—the one individual who hadn't already made a decision—wasn't going to be swayed by Zee's arguments. He would gauge the crowd and vote with the majority.

The woman grabbed her diaper bag, scowled at me, and made her way down the bleachers. I felt sorry for the folks in her wake.

"Only thirty-eight percent of Wal-Mart employees can

afford the company's health insurance," Zee said. "A Wal-Mart spokesperson admitted that Wal-Mart employees who don't participate in the company's plan use state or federal medical assistance programs. As taxpayers, do we want to foot the medical bills for the sixty-two percent of Wal-Mart employees who won't be able to afford the company's health insurance? Should we have to subsidize the largest corporation in the world?"

In answer to Zee's questions, a woman holding one edge of the pro–Wal-Mart banner yelled, "She's had her five minutes."

Zee feigned innocence and checked her watch. "Oh, my. Look at the time." She shot Reginald an arch look. "Any questions?"

Louann started the applause, and as it died down Hortie rose and put her hands on her hips. "The next two speakers should be against Wal-Mart."

Stuart glanced at Reginald—then at the cameraman—and forced himself to smile at Hortie. "I apologize for inadvertently letting three folks in a row speak for Wal-Mart, but in order to foster debate, it would be best to alternate between the two sides."

"The next two speakers should be against," Hortie said. "Then we can alternate."

The cameraman filmed the standoff, and the reporter flipped a page in her notebook. The crowd hushed, waiting to see what would happen.

My dad stood. With his Mark Twain hair, he strikes a distinguished figure even in a polo shirt and shorts. "Might I suggest a compromise?" he said. "Why don't we alternate for now, and then, since the Wal-Mart folks got the first three slots, the evening's last three speeches can be against Wal-Mart."

The compromise was favorable to Hortie's side—provided that folks stuck around to the bitter end.

She and my dad both took their seats.

Stuart smiled as if to suggest he was pleased with the decision and in complete control. "Who," he asked, "would like to respond to the issues Zee raised?"

Several hands stretched into the air, but Stuart appeared to be looking for someone in particular.

That someone turned out to be Emmet Mason, Winker's oldest son, named after his late mother, Emily. He looked just like his father, except he still had his hair—a light brown ponytail that reached halfway down his back. It had a natural wave most women with straight hair would sell their firstborn for. Instead of raising the microphone to his height, he leaned over it and shoved his large hands into his jean pockets. "What I want to know is, if Wal-Mart's such a crappy employer, how come so many people want to work for them?"

From his seat, Winker gave his son an encouraging nod. My guess was Winker had written the bulk of Emmet's speech. Emmet was a couple years older than me. He'd been a star football player in high school but wasn't the brightest bulb in the chandelier.

"If Wal-Mart pays so little, how come they're able to hire 250 to 300 people for each new store they open?" He cleared his throat, and the microphone whined. "One million people work at Wal-Mart. They're the second biggest employer in America. Only the federal government hires more people. *Fortune* magazine says Wal-Mart is one of the best companies to work for, and by the way, seventy percent of its employees are full-time."

Zee wrote something and passed it to Barb.

Charlene and Chuck smiled appreciatively at Emmet's words, but that came as no surprise.

"'I've been out of work the past four months," Emmet said. "Me and my wife got three kids to feed. I can't afford to take any long view. I got to worry about the here and now." Emmet pulled his hands out of his pockets and rested them on the podium. Then back they went into the pockets. "I got a cousin who works at Wal-Mart in Missouri. He makes ten bucks an hour, and he's not a manager. He works in the warehouse, and he's only been there two years. He gets fifty or sixty hours a week sometimes. His wife started a year ago, and she makes eight bucks an hour. Wal-Mart puts food on their table, pays for their house, their car, everything. They even send their kids to Catholic schools. They got no complaints."

Wal-Mart fans burst into cheers, and Zee nudged Barb toward the podium before Stuart had a chance to pick another speaker.

Barb's dark bangs and small, high ponytail contrasted sharply with her pale skin. She wore a lavender top and a knee-length denim skirt. Her hands shook as she placed her note cards on the podium. She looked toward Zee and Parker for reassurance. Attempting a smile, she read from the paper Zee had handed her. "It would be great if lots of folks in Aldoburg could get jobs like Emmet's cousin," she said, "but that's not going to happen."

I could barely hear her. Zee raised a hand to her ear, and the man from the back of the folding chairs called, "Louder!"

"Why don't she speak up?" whispered the man with the magazine.

"Shush," his wife said. "Her husband just died."

"Zee just lost Glad," the man said, "and she made herself heard loud and clear."

"She's used to talking. Barb's not," the woman retorted. "I don't see you up there giving a speech."

The man returned to his magazine.

Barb glanced up and leaned closer to the mike. "Wal-Mart

defines full-time as twenty-eight hours per week. And the reason Wal-Mart hires so many people is because seventy percent of its employees quit within the first year."

Barb's information was right on the mark, but she sped through it, her voice quavering.

The reporter struggled to keep up, and the cameraman stopped filming. They shrugged at each other and left.

I stifled my exasperation and told myself the woman with the crossword was right: Barb's husband had just died. It was to her credit that she'd even shown up.

"Wal-Mart gets eighty-four percent of its business from existing stores," Barb said. "For each Wal-Mart that is opened, one-hundred family-owned businesses die." She tapped her note cards on the podium, making her words even more difficult to decipher. "We could lose almost every family-owned business in Aldoburg and several in surrounding towns."

Zee smiled and nodded throughout Barb's speech. Parker sat rigid in his seat, his lips pressed tightly together, eyes fixed on his mother.

"Wal-Mart managers have a cheer," Barb said. "It goes, 'Stack it deep, sell it cheap. Stack it high and watch it fly. Hear those downtown merchants cry.'" She swallowed and tapped her note cards again. "They have what's called predatory pricing. First they lower prices—often below wholesale when they can get away with it. And Wal-Mart is able to get much lower wholesale prices than a store like Honig's because it buys in such quantity."

Without taking his eyes off Barb, Reginald leaned over and whispered to Stuart.

"Family-owned businesses can't afford to sell below wholesale," Barb said. "So before long Wal-Mart kills all the competition. Then it has a monopoly, which means it can charge whatever it wants."

The crowd shifted and whispered, tired of straining its ears.

Barb tapped her note cards more quickly. "So if we let Wal-Mart come to our town, eventually we'd have only one place to shop and we'd have to pay high prices. You might think you'll have more choices with Wal-Mart, but you won't. You won't have any choices at all." She tapped her note cards one last time and stepped away from the podium.

Stuart shot out of his chair. "Mr. Daniels is wondering if someone who was planning to speak on behalf of Wal-Mart would forfeit their turn to him."

A round-shouldered woman in the second row said, "He can have mine."

"That's bullshit!" called the man from the folding chairs.

Hortie stood again. "What about the rule that nobody speaks twice till everybody's gone once?"

The round-shouldered woman also rose. "It's my turn, and I should be able to do whatever I want with it. I want Mr. Daniels to speak for me."

The two women glowered at each other. The crowd mumbled as Stuart signaled Reginald toward the podium. Hortie sat down in a huff. Her nemesis smiled smugly.

A strand of hair that was supposed to disguise Reginald's bald spot dangled in front of his face. "When any business closes," he said, "there are always several reasons—a depressed economy, online shopping, shifting consumer tastes. Of course, Wal-Mart will be competing with local merchants, but they can benefit from this competition. It can encourage them to offer special services or merchandise, or it can inspire them to update their marketing strategies."

LaVonne all but bared her teeth, and Parker moved forward in his seat. Barb rested her hand on his back. This was her son's future and her dead husband's legacy that "Reggie" was talking about.

"If Aldoburg doesn't want Wal-Mart, a nearby town will no doubt welcome us with open arms. Then it will be *their* Wal-Mart competing with your downtown."

nineteen

Stuart finally got the applause he wanted at 9:30, when he announced a half-hour break. I wanted to keep an eye on Reginald to see if he was cozy with any of the Post-it-note suspects besides Stuart, but Mr. Wal-Mart slipped right out of the gym. Chuck's eyes were fixed on me, and neither he nor Charlene made a move to follow Reginald. Charlene, in fact, lifted a small cooler to her lap and began distributing sandwiches and pop to Chuck and his wife. Stu Two and Collin had vanished. Stuart remained onstage, fiddling with the microphone. Winker headed toward Zee.

I wanted to check in with my aunt, but I needed a bathroom break so badly I'd have sold my soul to Satan, Wal-Mart, or any other evil entity for instant access to a toilet—even a Porta-Pottie. But alas, there was a line even for exiting the bleachers, and I was in the middle of it.

Fortunately, Zee was surrounded by friends. Hortie and LaVonne stood next to her with their hands on their hips, shooting dirty looks at Stuart. Barb was leaning forward in her chair, her face buried in her hands. Zee began rubbing Barb's neck. That was my aunt—easing a friend's stress when her own was off the charts.

Next to me a forty-something man talked with a buddy. "Trucking is the closest thing to farming," he said. "You got a lot of freedom, and you're out in nature. Sometimes it's pouring sheets of rain."

He sounded wistful, and I wondered how old he was when his family lost their farm. When had large corporations started swallowing Iowa's farms and stores and towns? I squeezed past a chatty woman dawdling near the bottom of the bleachers and made my way toward Zee.

She'd left Barb amongst the folding chairs and was letting Winker have it. "Wal-Mart starts out buying lots of ads," she said. "Color inserts even. But later it rarely advertises in the local paper—not even in Sam Walton's hometown, where his son owned the paper."

Zee was obviously fine without me, so I pushed through the crowd toward the restrooms. By the time I emerged—patience sorely tested, bladder blessedly empty—there were no Post-it-note suspects in sight. At least I could get some fresh air before round two of the great Wal-Mart debate.

The high school parking lot was only a bit cooler than the gym and nearly as crowded. On the sidewalk outside the building, the Aldoburg pom-pom squad was selling pop, cookies, and chips to raise money for new uniforms. From the looks of the crowd around their stand, Aldoburg's youth, unlike its adult merchants, had no need to update their marketing strategies.

Loathe to stand in line again, I opted for a stroll. Several Aldoburgians were firing up their engines and calling it a night. Jealous as hell, I stumbled toward the far end of the lot and leaned against the hood of a car. I studied the sky, but it was too cloudy for any stars to peek through.

My catechism teachers had taught me that people in heaven can see and hear everything we do and say and think. I was never sure whether they were trying to comfort or frighten me. I didn't want Glad to know how cynical I was about the survival of small-town Iowa. Of course, Glad was no dummy. She'd probably seen the writing on the wall. Yet she'd chosen to fight anyway. I gazed at the gym. I wished Glad were here to help Zee battle the superstore.

I turned toward the practice football field at the far edge of the parking lot. Sprawled in the center, barely visible in the moonlight, were Stu Two and Collin. I blame what I did next on the heat, the crowds, the car exhaust, my own sleeplessness and not-so-quiet desperation. I headed straight toward the duo. "Good evening, gentlemen," I called.

Stu Two blew a bubble. Neither boy got up.

"I'm glad I ran into you," I said. "I'm puzzled, and I'm hoping you can help me."

Collin leaned back on his hands. Stu Two scowled and straightened his back.

"You both seem very confused about the night Glad died," I said.

Stu Two's scowl deepened.

"You said you were jogging, but you couldn't remember where. Then Chuck and Charlene told me you were at her house."

"We forgot." Stu Two snapped his gum.

"We all make honest mistakes." I forced a smile. "But then I overheard you telling someone you've been jogging the same route all summer." I left Parker out of it. "So why weren't either of you able to describe your route to me?"

"Are you accusing us of lying?" Stu Two leapt to his feet, and Collin followed suit.

"How can I even be sure you were together that night?" I said. "Maybe one of you is covering for the other."

"You're supposed to leave us alone," Stu Two snarled. "This is harassment."

"Why the mystery about your jogging route if you've got nothing to hide?"

"It's none of your damned business." Stu Two drew closer to me.

I held my ground and gulped, hoping we were visible from the high school.

Collin grabbed his friend's arm. "Come on, Stu. Let's go. We don't have to talk to her."

"Your father also seems pretty confused about where he was that night."

Collin opened his mouth as if he were going to protest, but then he shut it and nudged Stu Two toward the high school.

Their anger confirmed my suspicion that they were hiding something, but I had nothing else to show for my efforts except the strong possibility that the two boys would relay our conversation to their fathers. Best case scenario: Chuck and the mayor would be even more guarded around me. Worst case: Chuck would tell Zee I was jeopardizing his investigation, and she'd ask me to leave. Or maybe that wasn't the worst case. Not if Chuck was the note writer and the murderer.

I rushed back to the gym, wanting to see Zee safe and sound. When I paused at my car to make sure it was unscathed, I noticed someone sitting cross-legged on a car hood about five cars down.

Parker.

I was about to continue dashing to the gym when I noticed him wiping his eyes. Zee was either still arguing with Winker or strategizing with Barb. I strolled over to Parker's perch and called his name.

He nodded and sniffed. Then he pushed a faux-blond lock behind his ears and reached for the Coke sitting next to him on the hood of the car. I wanted to tell him I knew how he was feeling, but I wasn't sure that was true, so I said, "Your mom gave a nice speech."

He gave me a small smile, relieved I'd ignored his puffy eyes. "She was kind of nervous. I told her Dad would under-stand if she didn't feel up to it, but she insisted." He shrugged. "Of course, she said the same thing to me, and I'm still going to speak."

"I'm sure that will mean a lot to her—if Stuart ever calls on you." I wanted to lighten things up.

Parker smiled again and took a long drink of his Coke.

"I'd be up all night if I drank that," I said.

"Not me. I'm like my folks," Parker said. "No matter how much coffee they drink at supper, they still fall asleep in the middle of the 10 o'clock news." He trembled. "Now Mom has trouble sleeping."

"You must miss him a lot." So much for lightening things up.

Parker set his Coke on the car. "This afternoon—what I said about Wal-Mart—I didn't mean it. I don't want it to come here. I don't want our store to close." He stopped his rush of words and looked at me expectantly.

"OK," I said, brilliant as ever in my attempts to be emotion-ally available. Maybe Anne had been right.

I forced my attention back to where it belonged: on Parker.

"Those were terrible things I said." His voice cracked.

"They weren't terrible." I leaned against the car next to him. "It's the choice you're facing that's terrible."

He bit his lip and nodded.

"It would be terrible for anyone," I said.

The cicadas' song mingled with the drone of the crowd near

the high school. "What would you do?" he asked. "Stay and run the store—or go to Mexico?"

I longed for the good old days when I was the baby-sitter and he was the little boy with a bowl cut and the hardest question he ever asked me was whether he could stay up and watch scary movies. "It doesn't matter what I'd do," I told him. "You need to do what's right for you."

"Right." Parker's voice was tinged with hurt and anger. He stood up and started walking away.

I felt ashamed for closing down the conversation with psychobabble. "Wait."

He turned, a slender figure in the dimly lit parking lot.

I took a deep breath. I'd never given a young person serious advice before. "I'd go to Mexico."

He stood motionless.

"Your parents have had their chance to pursue their dreams. Now it's your turn."

Something flickered across his face—a shadow or a smile?—and he dashed back to the gym. As he disappeared into the building, Stuart emerged and strode past the concession stand toward the parking lot. Following him in a none-too-subtle manner was Hortie. I ducked behind a car and considered the situation. She obviously had not heeded my advice. What if she kept following him? What if—in her quest for more "evidence"—she followed Stuart to his house, waited until she thought he was asleep, then checked his garage for white spray paint? If she were caught, she'd get thrown in jail and dismissed from city council. And Zee would blame me.

Was I making a mountain out of a molehill?

Better safe than sorry.

I weighed both clichés and ducked behind a pickup, keeping my eyes on Hortie.

She darted from car to car, glancing behind her while Stuart moved purposefully toward the practice football field. If they continued their trajectory, Hortie would have no place to hide. Surely she'd stop at the edge of the parking lot, where I could talk some sense into her.

Her sense was more lacking than I'd thought, however. She followed him right across the middle of the field. All Stuart had to do was turn around and he'd see the glow-in-the-dark stripes on her tennis shoes.

I hid behind a station wagon in the final row of cars. Should I follow them? In my white tank top and tan hiking shorts I was nearly as easy to spot as Hortie. Besides, the mayor couldn't be going far. It was almost time for the forum to start back up.

He reached the other end of the field, and I could barely see him. As I watched Hortie's glowing shoes chase after him, I pondered the stand of pine trees that lay beyond the field. If Stuart were going out there to get a payoff from Wal-Mart, Hortie could be in danger.

I ran across the field as fast as my Birkenstocks would take me. At the far edge I crouched behind a tree, struggling to control my breath, listening for footsteps. Where were Stuart and Hortie? The breeze rustled the pine branches next to me, and I heard a steady stream. For the record, let me note that there are no bucolic creeks in the vicinity.

twenty

The forum resumed peaceably enough unless you count Purple Hair slapping Eyebrow Boy's hand when it advanced too far up her leg. The couple with the crossword and magazine didn't return, nor did the woman with the stinky baby. All told, the crowd was about two-thirds its original size. I stretched my legs straight in front of me. The Post-it-note suspects were all in their original places, as were my parents, my aunt, and her cronies. Stu Two and Collin riffled through Charlene's cooler. For the moment, they were more interested in filling their bellies than telling Chuck about my sleuthing.

There was still no sign of Neale.

I felt a prickle of irritation as the bank president, Norm Somebody, headed toward the podium. Once again, Stuart was giving extra time to the pro–Wal-Mart side.

Norm's sideburns curved forward at his jawline, and his high-pitched voice vied with the microphone's occasional squeak. "Wal-Mart claims it can increase our tax base, but that's not true."

I was stunned. A banker speaking against big business?

"Sure, the store will have an account with our bank," Norm said, "but we won't get to use the cash. Wal-Mart just uses local banks to transfer its daily earnings to corporate headquarters in Arkansas." Norm scanned the crowd to make sure he had their attention, and he did, as far as the late hour and the heat would allow. "In contrast," he went on, "a dollar spent in a local business like Honig's Hardware will get spent one or more times before it leaves the area."

Parker nudged his mother and smiled. He jiggled his right leg nervously, but there were no other signs of his emotional turmoil.

"A dollar spent at a local store will buy a cup of coffee at the Chat 'n' Chew, or it'll help open a savings account at my bank. So you see," Norm said, "spending at Wal-Mart will not only hurt the downtown stores you're not supporting, but it will eventually hurt all of Aldoburg. If a dollar is spent at Wal-Mart instead of Mumford's Pharmacy, it's not just Mumford's that loses that dollar but also the local trucker who delivers there or the bowling alley where the store's employees go for fun."

Despite his grating voice, Norm was a confident speaker. "Let's talk about Wal-Mart's so-called charitable activities. A hundred million dollars in annual charitable donations sounds like a lot, and so does the $1,000 local annual scholarship—I'd be happy to have that for my own son— but when a family, like the Waltons, is worth billions, these figures are a drop in the bucket. Most other American corporations give more than two and a half times as much as Wal-Mart. Sam Walton himself, whose words have been quoted a lot tonight, wrote, 'Wal-Mart really is not, and should not be, in the charity business.'"

Norm scratched one of his sideburns. "To sum up, Wal-Mart has two main things to offer: an eroding tax base and growing unemployment." He raised a finger. "Oh, and don't forget that

Wal-Mart will also bring a lot of traffic to the south edge of town, which will lower property values there and cover rolling fields with asphalt. The land next to this gigantic slab of concrete will be bathed in polluted runoff: engine and asphalt oil, sand, and salt."

I gazed across the gym at Charlene. Chuck put his arm around her and stared daggers at Norm. Charlene's head was lowered, so I couldn't read her expression, but I imagined it was a mixture of wrath and regret. She had a perfect right to sell her farm—how could anyone dare suggest otherwise? Yet she didn't want to sell. She simply saw no other way to help her ailing husband.

The next speaker was a woman with iron-gray hair cut short and shapeless. Flabby arms emerged from a sleeveless checkered blouse. Beneath navy polyester shorts her legs were crisscrossed with varicose veins and her ankles were swollen. She'd brought Zee a pie a few days ago. "As most of you know, Marv and I own a farm a few miles south of where Wal-Mart wants to build, and let me tell you, we're not going to mind the traffic one bit. The past six years, I've been driving to Des Moines every weekday. I got to so we can have health insurance." She rested her elbows on the podium and leaned forward. "I'm mighty sick of that two-hour commute—and you know I'm not the only one around here that makes it. Let me tell you, I'd be very happy to get on at Wal-Mart. It would save me a lot of time and gas money."

I wondered if she had any children, and I thought about how tired she must be. She probably had farm chores to do before she even began her commute to Des Moines.

"Maybe a bank president can afford to worry about a little traffic, but, Norm, I say it's pretty selfish to deny 250 people good jobs so you can enjoy a view of some corn fields."

I had no idea where Norm was seated, but odds were he wasn't enjoying himself right now.

"Those 250 people will put their money in your bank, Norm. They'll have to since it's the only one. I don't understand all that gibberish about an eroding tax base." She eased herself away from the podium and stood tall. "Most of us are not bank presidents. We need to make our money go as far as it can. We look for the lowest prices because they're all we can afford. Nobody has a right to criticize us for that."

Part of the crowd burst into applause. When Stuart asked for the next speaker, volunteers were less eager than they had been.

Hortie poked Talia, and she piped up, "I'll go."

She wore camel-colored Capri pants, a bright orange spaghetti-strap top, and thick-soled white sandals that clomped as she ascended the stairs to the stage. Her hair was in two French braids, making her look younger than her twenty-some years. She smiled at her grandma. "A study published by the Institute for Women's Policy Research ranked Wal-Mart last among retailers in terms of equity and fairness for women." Talia's voice rang out clearly.

I'd expected her to be timid, but if nothing else, her cheerleading days had taught her to project.

"The National Organization for Women has named Wal-Mart a 'Merchant of Shame,'" she said.

The crowd murmured at Talia's mention of NOW. To Aldoburg's many pro-lifers the organization is synonymous with the devil.

The farm-wife who'd just spoken stood up and shouted. "She shouldn't get to speak! She's only here in the summer!"

Talia ignored her. "Women make up seventy-two percent of Wal-Mart's sales staff, but only thirty-three percent of its managers."

Purple Hair sat up straight and extricated herself from Eyebrow Boy's grasp. You never know where you'll find a feminist.

"The few women managers are not even paid fairly," Talia continued. "One woman, Gretchen Adams, worked for Wal-Mart for ten years in five different states. As a comanager she helped open twenty-seven Supercenters. But she saw men with little or no relevant experience earn starting salaries of $3,500 more than her own."

"That sucks," Purple Hair whispered.

"Wal-Mart refuses to sell emergency contraceptives, and one store even refused to sell T-shirts that read SOMEDAY A WOMAN WILL BE PRESIDENT. They said it went against 'family values.'"

Somebody coughed loudly, a baby started whimpering, and makeshift fans worked furiously.

Talia raised her voice. "Wal-Mart often violates its workers' privacy. Prospective employees have to submit a urine sample for drug-testing, and if hourly workers want to date each other, they have to get permission from the district manager."

"Creepy," Purple Hair said.

"Totally," agreed Eyebrow Boy.

"Wal-Mart is also racist," Talia said. "After learning store managers were regularly making insulting remarks about Mexicans, the Mexican-American Political Association urged a boycott of Wal-Mart all over the Southwest." Talia paused and studied the crowd. "The store has been successfully sued by several Hispanics and African-Americans." She raised her voice yet another notch. "In 1998, a jury found that Wal-Mart fired a white female employee because she was dating a black man."

The crowd continued fanning itself. Except for the right-eous indignation of the make-out duo, Talia's revelations didn't spawn much reaction. She scowled and clomped back off the stage. One more reason to leave Aldoburg behind.

Stuart slowly stood, sweating through his dress shirt. "Before I select the next speaker, Reginald wanted me to note that Wal-Mart is the largest private employer of African-Americans and Hispanics."

The crowd was too hot and too tired to protest this bit of unfairness on the mayor's part. Eyebrow Boy directed his attention back to Purple Hair's thighs.

Father Kelly stood. His large glasses slid to the very edge of his nose. "If I might," he said, "I'd like to raise a point on both sides of the issue."

Stuart was not inclined to argue with a priest, so Father Kelly once again took the podium. "It's not my job to choose sides." He pushed his glasses up his nose. "But I'd like you all to prayerfully consider a couple issues. First of all, do we really want a store that's open all the time—especially on Sundays? If parents work evenings, when are they going to spend time with their children? If students work evenings, when are they going to study? And if people work Saturday evening and Sunday morning, when are they going to worship?"

"Lots of us already work evenings," yelled the farm-wife.

Father stopped. His glasses slid back down his nose. He wasn't used to being interrupted. "I'd also like to say that a community is more than its stores." Father raised his voice. "A community is its people. Parks, libraries, churches, county fairs, high school band concerts, and athletic events—those things don't change."

"What if there's nobody left to go to them?" challenged the man from the back of the folding chairs.

Father Kelly made the mistake of pausing to think about the question.

"How are you going to like it," the man called, "when nobody has any money to put in the collection plate?"

Eyebrow Boy stopped pawing Purple Hair. "They're heckling a priest," he whispered. "I better give my speech before things get really ugly."

I suspected he was already too late. Stuart stood and asked for quiet, but the farm-wife had already accused the folding-chair man of paranoia, and he replied that she had her head in the sand. Father Kelly slunk to his seat.

"Would anyone else like to speak?" Stuart's weary tone suggested he hoped they didn't.

Purple Hair raised her hand and pointed to Eyebrow Boy. He gave her a weak grin and made his way to the podium. He wore lots of jewelry: a couple of rings, a large gold chain around his neck, and a black leather strap with green and purple beads around one of his ankles. Of course, there was also the ring in his eyebrow. His baggy shorts looked as if they could slide off his bony frame at any moment. He glanced at his note cards and smiled at the audience.

Purple Hair smiled back.

"Lots of stuff has already been said, so I'm going to start with censorship. Wal-Mart refuses to sell music with warning labels, and John Mellencamp had to airbrush Jesus and the devil from the cover of his new album in order to meet Wal-Mart's approval."

One of the classes Eyebrow Boy must have skipped was the one about knowing your audience. If Aldoburg was unconcerned about sexism and racism, it was even less concerned about the artistic freedom of rock stars.

"Wal-Mart also removes magazines from its shelves when it finds them offensive." Eyebrow Boy squeezed one of his hands into a fist. Whether to soothe his nerves or emphasize a point, I couldn't tell. "You might go to Wal-Mart and not even be able to buy *Rolling Stone* or *Cosmopolitan*."

Cosmo, I assumed, was Purple Hair's contribution to the speech.

"Wal-Mart will also ruin the appearance of our town. At

best," he said, "we'll be a cookie-cutter town. We'll look like every other town with a box-store at its edge."

Zee jabbed Barb in the arm and grinned. Reginald whispered to Stuart, and Winker scowled.

"Despite what Father Kelly said, when we lose family stores we'll lose part of our uniqueness. Do we really want Aldoburg to look like every other town?"

"Hell, no," called the man from the folding chairs.

"Shut up," shouted the farm-wife.

Father Kelly rested his head in his hands as if he were praying—or nursing a headache.

Eyebrow Boy briefly stepped back from the podium, surprised and pleased he'd generated a reaction. "Wal-Mart could also decide to abandon the store when it wants to build a bigger one nearby. It does this all the time. There are already 380 empty or 'dead' stores, and Wal-Mart plans on closing over a hundred more. If this happened to us, we'd be left with no stores at all. No shopping choices. Just a big empty box and acres of asphalt." By way of conclusion he nodded grimly, but when he walked away from the podium, he could barely contain his glee. He'd not only earned his extra credit—he'd reveled in the attention.

Stuart made a huge show of looking at his watch. "Anyone else?"

Purple Hair gave Eyebrow Boy a big hug, and a busty woman in a lilac-print dress charged the stage. Her short, dark curls were beginning to gray at the temples. "I'll be quick," she said. "Lots of you are criticizing Wal-Mart for being good at what they do. Businesses are supposed to compete with each other. It's the American way. And I, for one, appreciate the fact that Wal-Mart keeps smut out of its stores. I like a business that promotes good morals." She marched back to her seat, sure she'd persuaded the entire crowd to her point of view.

"Speaking of morals," Parker said. "I have something to say." He stepped toward the stage with no trace of nerves or uncertainty. He carried a yellow legal pad and wore cutoff jeans and a purple T-shirt that said PAZ CON JUSTICIA: PEACE WITH JUSTICE. He smoothed his hair behind his ear and gave his mom a tiny smile.

She beamed at him.

"If we allow Wal-Mart to come to Aldoburg, we'll not only hurt ourselves, but we'll hurt people all over the world. Wal-Mart imports over eighty percent of the clothes it sells. That's way more than other retailers. As a result, thousands of Americans have lost their jobs to overseas sweatshops." Parker paused. "Just like lots of you lost your jobs at IBP."

"That's a great intro." Eyebrow Boy was suddenly more interested in rhetorical strategies than in his girlfriend's thighs, and he was right. Parker had captured the tired crowd's attention with his IBP reference.

"I'm sure you've all heard about sweatshops," Parker said. "In Honduras, twelve-year-old girls sew $20 Kathie Lee pants for 31 cents an hour. They work seventy-five hours a week. They get only two bathroom breaks a day, and they're not allowed to talk with each other while they work."

Stu Two whispered to Collin and glanced at me. I had a sinking feeling they weren't discussing sweatshops.

Parker turned a page on his legal pad. "Wal-Mart ran 'Buy American' and 'Buy Mexican' campaigns at the same time while reinvesting overseas—mostly in China, the country with the world's largest forced-labor population." Parker bit his lip and tucked his hair behind his ear again. "Wal-Mart is now the world's largest importer of Chinese-made goods. Even though China's minimum wage doesn't begin to cover anyone's living expenses, Chinese workers who produce toys for Wal-Mart are paid 18 cents *less* than the minimum wage. They earn only 13 cents an hour."

Winker pulled a pen from his pocket protector and grabbed a notebook from beneath his chair. He began writing as Stuart took a long drink of water. Charlene handed Chuck another sandwich. Unless you count Chuck's scowls and Stu Two's temper tantrum, none of the Post-it-note suspects had revealed any murderous impulses. Even though I was slowly but surely sweating away half my body weight, I was none the wiser about Glad's killer.

"China not only uses slave labor," Parker continued, "but during the last fifty years it has also killed over one million Tibetans, and it has destroyed all but thirteen of Tibet's nearly 6,000 monasteries. When you buy from Wal-Mart, China's number one importer, you support the destruction of Tibet, and you drive down wages and living conditions worldwide."

Winker's son Emmet stood so quickly he knocked over his chair. "I don't need some college boy telling me I'm ruining the world."

Barb shot to her feet. "Don't you interrupt my son." She spoke each word deliberately through clenched teeth.

Parker stood silently at the podium.

Emmet glanced between mother and son. "You can't blame the whole world's problems on a single store," he said. "I got a girl and two boys and a wife who need to eat. I can't afford to turn my back on a job because of folks halfway around the world."

"You've already spoken!" Barb's voice rang out loudly.

Zee stood up next to her, but no one else moved. Emmet Mason was easily the biggest man in the room, and at the moment he was also the angriest.

"I got news for you folks who think shopping at Wal-Mart is

going to ruin Aldoburg," Emmet said. "Most of us already shop there because the stores downtown are too damned expensive."

Parker rallied. "We keep prices as low as we can," he said. "We lose money on some things."

"That's right," Barb said. "And Bill worked himself to the bone to keep down the overhead." She burst into tears, and Zee wrapped an arm around her.

Parker and Emmet both gazed at the two women, stricken.

"I didn't mean your store," Emmet said. "Honig's is a good place."

Barb blew her nose, and Parker rushed to her side.

"The thing is," Emmet continued, "I got high blood pressure, and my wife and daughter have diabetes."

Parker and Zee eased Barb back into her chair.

"We got medicine to buy every month, so we drive to the Wal-Mart in Carroll. Saves us $20. I got to wonder why prices are so high in Aldoburg. Maybe there's not enough competition."

LaVonne whirled around and faced Emmet. "Are you accusing me of price-gouging?"

Emmet shrugged. "If the shoe fits."

LaVonne's mouth hung open.

Stuart stood and attempted a smile. "Perhaps we should just call it a—"

"The city council is supposed to represent the people." The farm-wife pointed a finger at LaVonne. "But everybody knows you're going to vote against Wal-Mart to protect your own self-ish interests."

Hortie stood next to LaVonne. "Don't you accuse my friend of being selfish. We've also got to vote our conscience—consider what's best for the town."

"You don't think we know what's best for ourselves?" The

farm-wife narrowed her eyes and put her hands on her hips.

Emmet shook his head in disgust. "That's just a fancy way of saying they'll vote how they want. Both of them." He plopped back into his seat.

When he was in high school, Emmet bussed tables at the Chat 'n' Chew, and Hortie went to all his football games. I couldn't believe they were fighting.

My dad stood. "Since the council is representative, I'd like to ask those of you who are here tonight to vote on the issue. I know several people have already left, but it would still be helpful to me."

Stuart seized the opportunity to regain control. "Shall we have paper ballots or a show of hands?"

"Paper takes too long," called the folding-chair man. "I ain't ashamed of my vote."

"Me neither," said the farm-wife.

Hands it was, and, unfortunately for my father, they were evenly split.

The farm-wife stood again. "This wasn't a true vote," she said. "Lots of folks that are for Wal-Mart didn't even come tonight. They're quiet people, afraid of being criticized by those that are against the store." She glared at Zee. "Your radio ads kept lots of them away. You've made it sound like folks who want Wal-Mart don't know their head from their ass—like we don't care about our town. It ain't right, intimidating people like that."

A few days ago this woman had brought Zee comfort by way of a homemade pie, and tonight she was yelling at her in front of half the town. I wondered if the two women would ever speak to each other again. One thing was for sure: Regardless of the council's decision, Wal-Mart had already torn Aldoburg apart.

twenty-one

Despite the air conditioning and ceiling fans at Mitzi's, my glass of Miller Lite was sweating. But better my beer than me. I tried to buck up and listen to LaVonne sputter about predatory pricing. Zee nodded sympathetically, Hortie puffed on a cigarette, and I took a long drink. They would undoubtedly rehash the evening until the bar closed.

"Barb sure was riled up," Hortie said.

LaVonne cracked open a peanut. "She always was tough as nails when it came to her kids."

Zee stared vacantly at her beer. I hoped she was OK.

"Remember what she did when Coach Jorgenson wouldn't let her Frannie play during the district basketball tournament?" LaVonne asked.

I remembered that myself. Barb had circulated a petition, trying to get him fired. She'd almost succeeded too.

Hortie smiled and flicked her cigarette into a plastic ashtray. "She was one proud mother when Frannie won the tournament with that last-second steal. Screaming her head off and jumping up and down."

"Wish she'd had that kind of oomph tonight," LaVonne said. "I could barely hear her speech." She dissected another peanut and began detailing what she would have said if she'd had a turn at the mike.

I tuned out. I love LaVonne, and I love words, but I'd had way too many for one day. They were everywhere, even carved into the wooden booth where we sat.

NEBRASKA SUCKS

FOR A GOOD TIME CALL 243-5566

SARAH
+
JAMES
4-EVER

Poor Sarah and James. So naïve.

I wondered if Vince had learned anything about Orchid and Anne.

The Coors clock that glowed above the bar registered a little after midnight. It was Friday—or technically speaking, early Saturday morning—so there was little chance Vince would be home. If he were, he'd be too, shall we say, *engaged* to answer the phone. Maybe the plumber would answer. I imagined him puzzling over my toilet in the middle of the night, charging overtime.

There wasn't much at Mitzi's to keep my mind off my financial doom. Three other booths were filled with people, and a couple of men in their late twenties were shooting pool. An older man hunched over a drink at the bar. The bartender, a morose girl who didn't look of legal drinking age, gaped at a boxing match on TV. Another woman leaned over the jukebox, reading its titles. She wore extremely tight jeans, but the sight did nothing for me. All I wanted was sleep.

Since that wasn't one of my current options, I tried following my mother's favorite piece of advice. "Look at the bright side," she'd say, as if the Bright Side were an actual place, a scenic beach resort where one could feel instantly restored. I tried looking at my own bright side:

1. The forum was over.
2. Zee was safe and sound where I could keep an eye on her.
3. Ditto for Hortie. As long as she was with me, she couldn't stalk Stuart.

I tried to think of a fourth positive point. Honest, I did, but I was in a glass-half-empty kind of mood. My actual glass was more than half empty. I thought about ordering another, but I had to be back at KGEE in about five hours. If I stayed here with Zee until closing time, I'd get three hours of sleep max.

"Mara, how do you think the forum went?" Zee asked.

I wanted to say it seemed like a no-win situation.

Smoke from Hortie's cigarette curled around Zee's tired face.

"You did Glad proud," I said.

"How do you think your father will vote?" LaVonne asked. "Did you talk to him about it?" The neon light in the window blinked on her patriotic shirt.

"He's a hard man to persuade." I didn't mention I hadn't actually tried to persuade him.

"It's too bad the vote turned out so even-steven." Hortie lit another cigarette.

"That Emmet Mason makes me so mad," LaVonne said, but

before she could start up again, Emmet himself sauntered into the bar with his father.

I felt like we were in a low-budget Western. The two men stared at us. We stared back. Everyone else picked up on the tension and fell silent. A pool ball rolled across the pool table, clicked against another ball, then quieted with a soft thud. On TV, the boxers kept duking it out.

Winker gave us a cool nod and followed his son to the bar. I thought about all the beers Winker had shared with Zee and Glad, and I blinked back tears.

Zee was doing the same.

"Maybe we should just go home," I whispered.

"Not until I finish my drink."

So far, she'd barely touched it. She just didn't want Winker to think he could chase her out of the bar.

I weighed my options. I could enable Zee's stubborn pride amidst the tension and smoke, or I could walk home and go to bed.

When I left, my aunt and her two friends were glaring at Winker's and Emmet's backs. I hoped Mitzi's would remain a peaceable establishment.

As I crossed the muggy parking lot, Neale's badge flashed underneath a streetlight. My stomach fluttered.

"I was hoping I'd find you here. I've got some information." She lowered her voice. "About the bat."

"Was it the...?" I couldn't bring myself to say *murder weapon*.

Neale glanced over her shoulder. "I'd rather not talk right here," she said. "Someone might see us."

The evening was turning out to be a veritable movie medley. I'd gone from a showdown at the saloon to a spy thriller.

"We could go to my place," Neale said.

I looked around the lot, but I didn't see a police car.

She followed my gaze. "I just got off work. I drove my own." She nodded toward a black Mustang.

I count myself lucky if my car moves me from Point A to Point B without breaking down. Neale was obviously of a different school. She opened the passenger door for me, and I sank into a real leather seat. As she pulled her own door shut and slid under the wheel, her uniform stretched against the slight curve of her hips.

She caught me looking, and I had to try three times before I could fasten my seat belt.

"I would have waited and talked to you at the radio station in the morning," she said, "but I was afraid Charlene might be there." She slipped the key in the ignition, cranked the air conditioning, and we were off.

All the windows on her block were dark, but she signaled for me to be quiet as we entered her house. Her caution seemed a bit over the top, but I wanted her information. And let's be frank—I wanted her too. A girl will put up with a lot to satisfy her lust.

I snuggled into her sofa as she disappeared into the kitchen. In the soft lamplight I could see there were still plenty of boxes to be unpacked. Her fireplace mantle was graced with ferns—plants I've never been able to keep alive.

She returned—minus her gun and her hat—and set two beers atop the newspaper on the coffee table. Then she sat on the other end of the sofa and kicked off her shoes. She leaned forward, putting her elbows on her knees.

A clock ticked loudly, but I couldn't see where it was.

"The blood on the baseball bat matched your aunt's."

I took a long drink. No way did I want to think about Glad's blood. "What about fingerprints?"

"Alex Riley's weren't on it."

I smiled and set my drink back on the table.

"But Chuck thinks Alex wore gloves."

"I didn't know he found gloves," I said.

"He didn't."

Unbelievable. I shot up and strode toward the picture window. Chuck was planning to use his lack of evidence to make a stronger case against Hortie's grandson. Given the heat index, wearing gloves would suggest a lot of premeditation. I peered out the window and watched a car inch its way down the street. "Why would he return the bat?" I asked. "Why not bury it somewhere in the country?" I whirled around to face Neale, and she flicked her eyes away from me.

"Chuck thinks Alex wanted to cast suspicion on one of the baseball players," she said.

I folded my arms over my chest.

"One of them is dating a young woman Alex was interested in." Neale tried to look me in the eye but didn't quite make it. Exhaustion made her face seem softer, more open than usual. Or maybe it was her stray wisps of hair. I returned to the sofa.

Neale grabbed her beer, but she didn't drink it.

"Were there *any* prints?" I asked.

"Lots." Neale said. "Probably the entire baseball team's." She started pulling the label off her beer, still avoiding my gaze. "I was hoping the bat would tell us more."

"You can't order up your clues on a silver platter, can you?" I stopped, surprised by my own irritation.

Neale quit fussing with her beer label and met my eyes. The silence between us was laden with desire. I longed to touch her or to say something beautiful and extravagant that would give her the courage to touch me.

Instead, I told her what I'd learned since we last talked, ending with Stu Two's outburst in the parking lot.

"I've learned something else too," she said. "Chuck is tired of small-town police work. He's been gunning for a job with the Phoenix force."

Chuck, the devoted son. Charlene was always bragging about how he helped on the farm and how he sometimes gave her flowers just for the heck of it. "I guess he's hoping his parents can sell their farm so they can all move west together," I said.

"Looks like it." Neale crossed her legs underneath her.

I didn't ask where she got her information. She hadn't asked how I learned about Stuart's credit card debt, and I wanted to keep it that way.

Rubbing her eyes and yawning, Neale pulled her hair from its knot. It fell past her shoulders, and she shook it free.

I closed my eyes and forced myself to focus. Chuck wanted to impress Phoenix. Maybe he murdered Glad so he'd have a big case to solve.

"We have so much information but no idea what is significant." Neale gazed at the notebook on her end table. "We don't even know how many killers we're looking for."

Maybe I'd been too intent on finding a single killer. I'd considered the possibility that Stuart killed Glad, intending to frame Alex. And I'd all but decided that once Glad was killed, Chuck seized the opportunity to arrest Alex. But I hadn't put these scenarios together. "What if Stuart and Chuck worked as a team?" I asked. "They both believe Wal-Mart will solve their problems. They think if they kill Glad, Zee will stop her anti–Wal-Mart campaign. They decide Stuart will kill Glad and Chuck will make sure he doesn't get caught."

Neale started taking notes.

"Then Stuart sees Alex buy the spray paint," I said. "He realizes Glad's death can have an added benefit. They can frame Alex and hope Hortie will be so worried about her grandson that she'll resign her council seat. Lester will take her place. He's a Wal-Mart fan, so my dad's vote will no longer matter."

Neale glanced up, and I forged ahead, my theories making me giddy. "Wal-Mart arrives in Aldoburg. Stuart is reelected mayor. Chuck basks in the publicity of solving a murder and earns a spot on the Phoenix police force. Stuart and Chuck live happily ever after."

Neale swept her hair behind her shoulders and frowned. "Why the fake hate crime? Why cast suspicion on their sons?"

"They had to divert attention from the Wal-Mart issue," I said. "It was the best way to frame Alex. Chuck knew he'd be in charge of the investigation. Their sons would be in no real danger. It would be natural for their prints to be on the bat." I took a long swallow of beer, waiting for Neale to voice her awe and appreciation for my mind-boggling deductive powers.

She put her notebook aside. "The plan didn't work," she said quietly.

"They underestimated Zee and Hortie."

"No," Neale said. "They grew up here. They've known those two women their whole lives."

"They were desperate." Who was I kidding? I was the one who was desperate. If Wal-Mart wasn't behind Glad's murder, I had no idea what was. "Grasping at straws is thankless work," I said.

Her eyes swept over me and lingered on my lips. Or did I imagine it? "I should go," I said, "I have to open the station in a few hours."

"When are you going back to Iowa City?"

"Bright and early Tuesday if I want to keep my job."

She smiled and moved next to me on the sofa. My palms started sweating.

"What else is waiting for you there?"

"My housemate Vince and a broken toilet." Was Neale trying to find out if I was available? "There's also the possibility that my ex has moved in with my evil boss. My ex," I said. "Anne."

I wondered what Neale would do with the obviously feminine name, and I sipped my beer.

Neale sipped hers.

Why had I even considered the possibility that she might be attracted to me? Could I be a bigger glutton for self-punishment?

"I wish we'd met under different circumstances," Neale said.

I gazed into her eyes. They were the deep green of early July cornfields.

I cataloged all the reasons why I should leave. Neale had just moved to a strange new town. She was lonely and closeted. I was obsessing about a woman who left me a year ago. My aunt had just been murdered, and the killer—or killers—hadn't been caught.

Yet when Neale extended her hand and our fingers touched, I couldn't help it. My soul leapt up. Soon the rest of me wanted in on the action. My free hand, for instance.

I caressed Neale's face and traced her jaw with my finger. She lowered her head and took two of my fingers, gently, in her teeth. Her breath was warm and slow on my hand as she squeezed her lips around my fingers and eased them out of her mouth. Then she moved her cheek against my hand, and I heard her swallow. I leaned in and brushed my lips against hers. Sweet hesitation, then no going back.

twenty-two

If I ever have my fifteen minutes of fame, it will be for breaking the world's record in coffee consumption. I set my mug next
to a turntable and checked the clock above the live log. 10:12.
The Brownfield News was nearly finished. Bean prices were up;
corn was down. I was somewhere in the middle, basking in the
afterglow of my time with Neale. But that didn't erase the fact
that I hadn't slept in more than forty-eight hours. I stood up,
placed my hands on my hips, and cracked my back. My spine felt
better, but not my psyche. I'd had a delightful night, but what did
it mean? Was it a one-night stand or the start of something new?
Which did I want? All I really knew about Neale was that she was
a beautiful and persistent cop from Chicago.

And that she didn't buy my theories about Stuart and
Chuck.

Maybe my dislike of the two men had obscured my thinking. In all honesty, I didn't know them very well. I'd fully
expected the indignant father routine after my most recent
Q&A with their sons, but—knock wood—neither Chuck nor

Stuart had called to complain. Still, both men had strong motives.

I needed a fresh perspective, so I called Vince, hoping against hope that the plumber wouldn't answer. He didn't, but neither did Vince. I hung up on the machine and—God forgive me—clicked on Air Supply. Enveloped in their crooning, I closed my eyes and pulled my legs to my chest.

A sharp knock. Then another.

I whirled around and peered through the vines that surrounded the back window.

Neale pointed to the back door, wanting in. Air Supply had about a minute left, so I headed to the back. Last night she was afraid of being seen at the station with me, yet today passion overwhelmed her better judgment. She found me utterly irresistible.

My thoughts halted when I opened the door. Neale's face was etched with worry. Her cop uniform was wrinkled and spotted with raindrops. She locked the door behind her. "I can only stay a minute," she said.

Air Supply was winding down, so we headed back to the studio. I announced the time and clicked on Billy Joel. As he began singing "Piano Man," Neale paced in front of the bulletin board. "I have some bad news," she said. "The mayor is dead. Murdered."

Someone had murdered Stuart? How could that be? I thought *he* was the murderer.

"It was a hit and run."

He'd just led the forum. How could he be dead? "Maybe it was an accident," I said.

Neale moved toward the orange vinyl chair and collapsed into it. "He was walking home from the forum. Someone hit him right in front of his driveway."

Stuart lived on a dead end. No one would accidentally speed there. "Maybe one of his neighbors didn't see him in the dark."

Neale's eyes met mine. "He was hit hard." She bit her lip. "And then backed over. That's what it looks like, anyway."

I tried not to go there, but I couldn't help imagining Stuart's flattened body.

"His son found him this morning," Neale said.

"Stu Two?"

"His dog woke him up early. Around 6."

A young man's life changed forever as he stepped out his front door half asleep, his dog barking. I faded out Billy Joel and clicked on a PSA. "When did it happen?"

"We won't know for sure until DCI is done, but probably some time around 1. A Wal-Mart representative says Stuart was in the gym, reviewing the zoning ordinance until about 12:30."

"Reginald Daniels?"

Neale nodded. "He offered Stuart a ride home, but Stuart wanted to walk."

I clicked on an ad, and a jingle for toilet bowl cleaner filled the room. "Do you want me to announce it on the news?" I asked.

"There are still relatives to contact." She sighed. "Chuck's afraid the town's going to panic when word gets out."

I started a feed company ad and scrolled through the music list, searching for a long CD so we could talk uninterrupted. And so I could gather my thoughts. If the same person had killed Glad and Stuart, the motive couldn't have been Wal-Mart. I'd been wasting my time. I needed to find a new motive—and fast.

"Who would want to kill Stuart?" I said, not expecting an answer.

"One thing is for sure. Alex Riley didn't do it. He has an air-tight alibi."

I selected a Dan Fogelberg CD. "That's great. "Hortie will be so relieved."

Neale gazed at the floor and fussed with a wisp of hair.

"Don't tell me Chuck still thinks Alex killed Glad?"

Neale's silence said it all.

"How likely is it that sleepy little Aldoburg spawns two murderers in the course of a week?"

"Don't shoot the messenger." Neale glanced at me and then at her watch.

Why had she come? Was she worried about my safety, or did she simply need to see me? I wanted to say something about our night together, but it didn't seem appropriate given the situation. "So who does Chuck think killed Stuart?" I asked.

Neale crossed and recrossed her legs at the ankle, refusing to meet my eyes. She cleared her throat. "I'm afraid," she said, "that he suspects your aunt and a couple of her friends."

"What?"

Neale jumped back in before I could work myself into a frenzy. "Winker claims your aunt and her friends left Mitzi's shortly after you did. That would give them plenty of time to kill Stuart. None of them has an alibi. They all say they went home and went to sleep by themselves."

"Where else would they go?"

Neale ignored my outburst. "Your aunt and her friends were angry at Stuart because of the forum."

"Of course they were," I said, "but so was half the town. That doesn't mean they killed him. Stuart's death isn't going to change the council's vote on Wal-Mart. Lester Simms will simply take his place, and he's just as big a Wal-Mart fan."

Dan Fogelberg declared himself a living legacy to the leader of the band. His plaintive voice jangled my nerves.

"Chuck doesn't actually suspect LaVonne Mumford." Neale

fingered another unwieldy curl. "He thinks Hortie may have killed Stuart, hoping it would get her grandson off the hook for Glad's murder."

I started to protest, but Neale raised her hand. "She was following Stuart around."

My stomach tightened. I should have insisted that Hortie stop trailing the mayor. It was my fault she was a murder suspect.

"And Chuck thinks you convinced Zee that Stuart killed Glad." Neale spoke slowly. "He thinks Zee wanted revenge."

I'd tried to find Glad's killer so Zee would be safe, and I'd wound up getting her accused of murder. Her and her best friend.

"I'm afraid," Neale said, "that Chuck also suspects you because of all the questions you were asking the mayor." Neale looked past me toward the live log. "Stuart knew you'd visited his office. And he told Chuck you'd harassed his son even after he asked you not to."

So Stu Two did run to Daddy after our encounter in the practice field. I turned down the volume on Fogelberg and glanced underneath the soundboard at my backpack. It still contained Stuart's credit card statement. "Lucky me," I said, "I have an alibi."

Neale smiled uneasily. "Listen, about last night, I was wondering if you could keep our time together quiet unless you really need to bring it up."

I couldn't believe it. She'd come to see me for purely selfish reasons. She didn't care about my safety or my feelings. She only cared about her precious career. "How will I know when I need to bring it up?" I asked. "When I'm being handcuffed or when I'm thrown in a cell?"

"Chuck won't have any hard evidence against you." Neale's voice was annoyingly calm. "He'll check your car, and it'll be clean."

That wasn't the point, and she knew it.

"I won't let you go to jail," she said.

"But you'll let Chuck treat me like a murder suspect—which, by the way, will really upset my aunt, who is already grieving. And you'll let him waste his time—and mine—while someone gets away with murder?"

"We could keep working together to find the killer," she said.

"You have got to be kidding." Our night together had obviously meant nothing to her.

"Please," she said, "don't be like this."

"Like what? Angry that someone I just made love with is willing to cast me as a murder suspect rather than admit she shared a bed with me?" I swiveled my chair and pretended to inspect an old tape deck. "I have work to do." I kept my back to her until she left.

Fogelberg sang about meeting his high school sweetheart in the parking lot of a grocery store. When he finished, I opened the mike and told my listeners it was still raining. Then I clicked on Fleetwood Mac's "You Make Loving Fun." I couldn't bear to listen to the lyrics or think about Neale, so I switched to problem-solving mode.

Maybe Chuck was partially right. Maybe there were two murderers, but neither of them was Alex. The first murderer—maybe Stuart himself—was a Wal-Mart supporter. The second murderer's motive was anybody's guess. Who knows? Maybe Lester Simms had a lifelong ambition to be a council member. Or maybe business was slower than he'd like at the funeral home, and he'd decided to help things along. I was never at a loss for wild theories. My mother used to tell me I had quite an imagination. She didn't mean it as a compliment.

Zee burst into the studio. "Mara," she gasped. "Have you heard about Stuart?" Her clothes were flecked with rain. She took off her glasses and furiously cleaned them with the bottom of her T-shirt. "Chuck thinks one of us did it." She stopped wiping her glasses. "I told him you were asleep when I got home from Mitzi's, but your bedroom door was open, so I know you weren't there."

Zee had lied on my behalf. She slipped her glasses back on, waiting for me to say something. I felt no need to protect Neale, but I was embarrassed about having a one-night stand the day after Glad's funeral. I hoped Zee wouldn't notice I was still in the same tank top and shorts I'd worn to the forum. "I took a long way home," I said. "I felt restless."

As Fleetwood Mac faded out, I announced the time and clicked on an ad for Lasik surgery. "And don't worry about your alibi—or Hortie's," I said. "Chuck can't do anything without hard evidence." I didn't like echoing Neale's words, but I needed to comfort Zee. "Besides, Chuck is full of shit."

I was rewarded with a small smile. Zee sat down and folded her hands in her lap.

"Why don't you go home?" I said. "You've had a rough morning, and you were up late last night. I'll take your shift."

"Mara," she said, "I really appreciate all the work you've done at the station. I couldn't have kept it open without you." She leaned forward, resting her elbows on her knees and studying me. "But Jack's mother has taken a turn for the better, and he'll be back on Monday. I can manage the station by myself until then. I want you to go back to Iowa City before you get yourself in more trouble." She straightened her back and flipped her braid over her shoulder. "Before you get *me* in more trouble."

That stung. I clicked on an ad for Honig's Hardware. "Don't you want to know who killed Glad?" I asked.

"It's not going to bring her back." Zee locked eyes with me.

"She wouldn't want you to wind up in jail. Or worse. And she wouldn't like you upsetting her friends with your questions."

"She cared about the truth." I clicked on the ABC news, and the announcer began his litany: bombs, hurricanes, mounting death tolls. "What about you?" I asked. "Glad wouldn't have wanted me to leave you all alone with a murderer running loose."

"I'm not alone." Zee stood. "I have plenty of friends."

Most of these friends had strong motives for murdering Glad, but I refrained from saying so. "I can't leave when things are so unresolved." I pushed aside the fact that I'd have to leave on Tuesday if I wanted to remain employed. "Please," I said. "Can't you understand?"

Zee left the studio, muttering something about stubbornness.

A chipper meteorologist predicted more rain, and the phone started blinking. I wasn't in the mood to answer it. I'd had enough bad news for one day. But the masochist in me picked up the receiver anyway.

"Miss Gilgannon?" asked a quavering voice.

"Who is this?" I hate being called Miss Gilgannon. It makes me feel old.

"Collin Conover." His voice was thick with tears. Obviously, he knew about Stuart's death. "I'm sorry to interrupt you at work, but I need to talk to you."

"OK," I said.

"In person," he said. "Somewhere private?"

I briefly wondered if he was trying to lure me to a remote place in order to kill me, but I told myself to get a grip. Nonetheless, I suggested somewhere public. "How about the Chat 'n' Chew?" I offered. "If we meet there after my shift, the lunch crowd will be gone."

As I waited for his answer, I clicked on an ad for Stuff. It reminded me of the sandals I wanted to buy for Vince.

"What time?" Collin asked.

I'd expected him to disagree. Where was the quietly confident young man who had assured his friend they didn't need to talk with me? Why was he so eager for a *tête-à-tête*? "1:30," I said. "Does this have something to do with Stuart's death?"

He hung up, leaving me with yet another unanswered question.

twenty-three

When I arrived at the Chat 'n' Chew, Collin was in a corner booth, stirring his Coke with a straw and watching for me. His menu lay unopened. The one other diner, an elderly man at the counter, posed little threat to our privacy. Wild horses couldn't drag him away from his mashed potatoes.

I peered at Collin over the top of my menu. Even in the midst of pain and gangly adolescence, he was a lovely young man, blessed with honey-blond hair and deep brown eyes. But they were completely swollen and red.

"I'm sorry about Stuart," I said. "You must have known him pretty well."

He nodded. His Adam's apple bobbed up and down.

"I'll treat you to lunch." It was the only comfort I could offer.

"No, thanks." He gazed despondently into his Coke.

I felt like an ogre, wanting to eat in the midst of Collin's sorrow, but my stomach wouldn't let me concentrate if I didn't. I settled on a bacon cheeseburger platter and cleared my throat obnoxiously, hoping whoever was in the kitchen would hear.

Talia emerged, waitress cap perched atop her ponytail. Her makeup, as usual, was flawless. She seemed surprised to see me with Collin but said nothing other than hi as she gave me a water and took my order.

Collin and I sat in silence until she brought my Coke. I took a sip and waited for him to begin. He looked everywhere but at me.

"What did you want to talk about?" I asked gently.

He took a drink, either stalling for time or working up his courage. "This will be confidential, right? You won't tell anybody?"

"Unless it has something to do with Glad's death."

That wasn't the answer he wanted. His Adam's apple bobbed some more.

"Please tell me," I said. "I'm not a gossip."

"You've got to stop asking Stu about Glad's death," Collin said. "He had nothing to do with it. He's really broken up over his dad, and he doesn't need any more trouble." His lip trembled.

I wanted to reach out. Pat his hand. Offer him a Kleenex. Anything. But he had information I needed—I was sure of it. "I'd like to believe you," I said, "but I have no reason to. You and Stu—and your fathers—have lied about the night Glad died."

Collin folded his arms over his chest and glowered at me.

"You know the station well because your grandmother has worked there your whole life," I said. "People saw you and Stu having an intense conversation with Glad before she died. And you beat up a young man simply because he was gay. It all adds up."

Collin lowered his eyes. "Things aren't what they seem."

"Why don't you tell me how they are." I waited for him to meet my gaze and gave him an encouraging smile.

He turned to the framed photos on the wall, rows and rows of grinning girls and boys with champion cattle. The man at the counter stacked a pile of change next to his empty plate and left. Collin looked over his shoulder. Talia was nowhere in sight. "Glad was helping us with something personal."

Dishes clattered and the grill hissed as I waited for him to continue.

"This is what happened." He bit his lip and blushed deeply. "Stu and I are more than friends." He glanced at me to make sure I got it.

It caught me off guard. I've always prided myself on my gaydar. This time it was clearly out of whack.

"Last spring I talked Stu into going to a gay dance in Des Moines. Tim O'Rourke was there."

The boy they'd beaten up.

"Stu went ballistic. He thought O'Rourke would tell everybody—our parents would find out."

I could see where this was going, but I didn't interrupt.

"He said if we beat up O'Rourke, nobody would believe him if he told about the dance." Collin swallowed and took a deep breath. "I didn't want to do it, but Stu begged me. He said we wouldn't hurt him very bad." Collin took a deep breath and clenched his fist.

I waited for him to regain his composure. Talia laughed with someone in the kitchen.

"O'Rourke told Glad about the whole thing. She was fuming."

I wondered what had prompted him to seek Glad's help.

"But in a way," Collin said, "it was a relief—having an adult who knew about us. Stu really needed somebody to confide in. He was terrified of people finding out. He was afraid it would wreck his chances of getting a football scholarship. And he was so worried about his dad."

I recalled the snippet of conversation Talia had overheard: *I'm afraid of what my dad will do.* Stu Two had been afraid for himself—not Glad.

"Glad talked to O'Rourke on our behalf and—somehow—she got him to keep our secret. She said she'd never tell anybody—not even Zee—as long as we never bothered anybody again. She wanted to talk to our parents. Not tell them anything. Just feel them out." Collin paused for air. "Stu wasn't so sure about the parent part. He doesn't think of himself as gay. Says it's just me. That except for me, he likes girls."

"That must be hard." I tried to concentrate on Collin, but I was puzzled. Glad had been close to all sorts of young people—Collin, Stu Two, Parker, O'Rourke. She'd had heart-to-hearts with all of them, but not with me.

Talia brought my food, and a woman entered with a baby in a carryall and two small boys. She sat the carryall in a window booth and yelled at the boys to join her, but they seemed more interested in running around the restaurant.

I salted my fries and studied Collin. He gripped his Coke with both hands. "How did it go with your parents?" I asked.

Collin shrugged and pushed his Coke aside. Then he grabbed it again and took a long drink.

I waited for the words to come.

"Glad said we shouldn't come out to them until we were on our own. Stu got even more freaked after that."

Collin kept the focus on Stu, his own hurt and anxiety bottled tight inside. I wanted to tell him I knew what it was like to grow up gay in a small town, to hide a new and blossoming part of yourself. But I said nothing. I also knew that sometimes you just have to ignore your pain and bluff your way through.

"Don't you see?" Collin gazed at me expectantly.

"Me and Stu had no reason to hurt Glad," Collin insisted. "She was trying to help us. She was our friend."

I took a bite of my burger. I finally understood why he and Stu Two had taken Glad's death so hard, but I still wondered about Stu Two. If he'd had doubts about whether Glad would keep their secret, he had a motive for murder. "So why all the mystery about your jogging route?"

Collin blushed again and studied the table. "It's got nothing to do with Glad's death."

I thought about Stu Two's unfriendliness when Parker encountered them on his bicycle. Maybe jogging was the only time Stu Two and Collin had alone together. "Look," I said, "I don't want to believe you or Stu hurt Glad, but I have to wonder why you both pretended you couldn't remember your jogging route the night she died."

He kept his eyes on the table.

"You've got to admit, it looks suspicious—especially since your regular route goes right past the station."

"We weren't running," he said abruptly.

"Then why did you say you were?" I hoped I wasn't pushing him too much. I took another bite of my burger. "If you really want me to stop asking Stu questions," I said, "you need to tell me why you lied."

One of the little boys jumped off the seat of his booth, shrieking for his mommy to watch. She gave him a tired smile.

Collin met my eyes. "You can't tell anybody—especially Zee."

I agreed. What could be a bigger secret than his relationship with Stu Two?

"Promise?" Collin asked.

I nodded. I had to know what happened that night.

He glanced over his shoulder again. "I was at Stu's, and he asked his mom for the car. She said his dad needed it for a meeting at my grandma's."

I nibbled a fry and thought about Stuart's and Charlene's calendars, both with a 9:30 notation the night Glad died. "Was it a late meeting?" I asked. "After 9?"

Collin nodded slowly, puzzled. "Stu went postal. He was sure my grandma had found out about us and was going to tell his dad. I told him no way—Grandma would never do that—but he wouldn't listen. Finally, I agreed to bike out there with him just so he'd chill." Collin sipped his pop. "And I was a little curious. I mean, Grandma never had anything good to say about Stu's dad, so I couldn't figure out why they'd be getting together."

"There was a light on in the living room, so Stu wanted to hide our bikes and watch through the window. I thought it was a dumb idea, but we'd already biked out there, so why not?"

"What did you see?"

"Nothing at first. Just Stu's dad having coffee with Grandma. Real low-key. Then *my* dad came. I was afraid he'd see us, but he didn't. He was real preoccupied, and I started worrying that maybe Stu was right." Collin suddenly stopped talking and began twirling his straw around in his Coke again. His Adam's apple was doing its thing.

He leaned toward me and lowered his voice. "Then Winker came. He was with the Wal-Mart guy. You know, the man from the forum."

Finally, I understood Chuck's comment: "If she finds out what we were doing the night Glad died, there'll be hell to pay." *She* was Zee, and she would have been rabid if she'd discovered a Wal-Mart representative was secretly meeting with two council members and the family that wanted to sell its land to the store. And she would have made sure everybody knew.

"The meeting wasn't illegal or anything," Collin said. "Just informational."

I wondered if Collin really believed that. He seemed smart, but we believe what we need to. "Who told you that?" I asked.

"My dad." Collin smiled. "When we saw Winker with the

Wal-Mart guy, we knew they didn't know about us, and Stu was so relieved. He forgot to be quiet, and my dad came outside and found us."

Talia delivered steaming plates to the window booth. One of the boys began throwing his fries on the floor, one by one.

"Dad said their meeting was totally aboveboard, but that it might look bad if people found out about it."

It probably was aboveboard. Barely legal but certainly not ethical. I imagined the meeting: Reginald saying Winker's and Stuart's oldest sons *may* earn managerial positions at Wal-Mart. Not a bribe but damn close. I imagined the group formulating strategies for promoting Wal-Mart. Not a proper activity if you're Stuart and Winker, council members duly sworn to represent the wishes of the people.

"Miss Gilgannon?"

I returned my attention to Collin.

"Now you see why me and Stu lied, right? We promised not to tell about that meeting." He stuck his chin out defiantly. "And you can forget about your idea that my father is a murderer."

Then it struck me. All the Post-it-note suspects were at Charlene's at 9:30—half an hour before Glad was murdered.

"Me and Stu were still outside," Collin said, "and Dad was explaining why we should keep quiet about the meeting when his phone went off. It was about Glad." He looked apologetic for mentioning her death, but then perked up. "So you see," he said triumphantly, "me and Stu couldn't have killed her and neither could our dads."

My head was reeling. I popped a cold fry in my mouth and slowly chewed.

"You're not going to tell anybody about the meeting, are you?" Collin's triumph vanished.

I usually keep my promises, no questions asked. But this one gave me pause. If I revealed Winker's collusion with Wal-Mart, he'd surely be removed from the council. Maybe his replacement would be someone who would vote against Wal-Mart.

"You promised," Collin said.

He'd taken a big risk trusting me, and he'd done a brave and remarkable thing: broken a promise to his father in order to protect his boyfriend. I didn't want to break my promise to him, but if I didn't, wouldn't *I* be in collusion with Wal-Mart? I couldn't keep a secret that might help Zee win her battle. "I won't ask Stu any more questions," I said, "and I won't tell anyone about your relationship."

"But what about the meeting?"

The boy at the window booth finished flinging his own fries and began eyeing his brother's.

"If you tell," Collin said. "I'll deny it, and it'll be your word against mine." He tossed a couple dollars on the table and left.

The floor under the window booth was covered with fries. The woman gazed at them in defeat. I knew the feeling. If Collin was telling the truth, I was fresh out of suspects.

twenty-four

My to-do list was not for the faint of heart: catch Glad's murderer and buy shoes for Vince. Apparently, I wasn't destined to accomplish either. In the window of Stuff, the mannequin's toeless bare feet mocked me. She still gloried in her bright green tube top, but gone were the clunky red sandals I'd planned to buy for Vince. If the road to hell is paved with good intentions, I was creating an eight-lane interstate to eternal damnation.

I stood in the drizzle and gaped at the headless mannequin. No doubt she had more brains than I did. I'd been so sure the murderer was one of the Post-it-note suspects, but Collin had jettisoned that theory.

If he had told the truth.

It started to rain harder as I headed toward the *Times* office. In the window of Dollar Daze, a woman was arranging spiral notebooks into a rainbow. This back-to-school display might be her last if Wal-Mart won, and each time a store like Dollar Daze had its final going-out-of-business sale, Zee's heart would break.

OK, so I had more than two items on my to-do list: help Zee

defeat Wal-Mart and deal with her grief, keep Zee safe, keep my job, protect my reading series from my evil boss, discover whether my ex was cohabitating with my evil boss, pay for my new toilet, avoid Chuck, avoid jail, avoid Neale, avoid my anger at Neale.

As I crossed the street, my rain-spattered glasses blurred the brick *Times* office. I had a niggling feeling someone was following me, but when I turned around, nobody was there.

I dreaded my confrontation with Winker. If he denied Collin's story, I wouldn't know who to believe, and I'd still have to suspect Winker and Charlene of murder. On the other hand, if Winker confirmed Collin's story, I'd have to face the fact that a man I'd known and loved my whole life had acted like a sneak. I'd have to decide whether to tell anyone about it. And I'd have no suspects for Glad's murder.

When I opened the glass door, a bell jingled and the air conditioning assaulted me. Shivering in my damp clothes and listening to the rain beat against the windows, I waited for someone to come to the front office. Framed front pages of the *Times* lined the walls. A few of the older ones were yellowing, even under glass. They featured mostly state and local news: the close of the Rock Island Railroad, a tornado that uprooted several houses on Oak Street, the state champion football team from 1973. My favorite item was a photo of Winker shaking hands with Jimmy Carter before he was elected president. As head of the Aldoburg Democrats, Winker had almost sent someone else to meet with Carter because he didn't think the guy stood a chance. Winker told that story almost every time he had a few too many beers with my aunts. He also used to tell me I should come work for him at the paper instead of wasting my time in radio. Then he and my aunts would fight about which was the better medium.

I headed past the secretary's desk to Winker's office. The beige walls of the hallway were smudged, and a couple cracks snaked their way toward the ceiling. The door to Winker's office was open, and the light was on. Winker himself was punching numbers on an adding machine. It looked too small for his large, cigarette-stained hands. He sat at a metal desk that was just like himself: solid, large, no frills. His wooly eyebrows drew together as he frowned. Behind him was a floor-to-ceiling window, but it was closed, and the room reeked of cigarette smoke. The walls were covered with Winker's treasures: his diploma from the University of Iowa, a shelf with bowling trophies, another copy of the photo with Jimmy Carter, a photo of Emmet in his high school football uniform, and a picture of Winker with one of his grandsons on his lap. The largest photo was a family portrait taken when Emmet was in junior high. Winker still had hair, and his wife was still alive.

He was so absorbed with his adding machine that he didn't notice me. He was always proud of how hard he worked. It must have torn him apart when his son's job went kaput.

"Hey," I called.

He stopped punching numbers, his hand poised above the machine. "Mara, what are you doing here?"

I deserved the brusque greeting. After all, I'd accused him of murder. "We need to talk."

Winker grabbed a pack of Camels out of his shirt pocket.

I took it as an invitation to sit in the overstuffed chair across from his desk. I didn't let myself slide all the way back into the chair's comfort, though. I needed to stay alert.

"Nothing's wrong with Zee, is there?" he asked gruffly.

"She's fine," I said. "Shaken up over Stuart's death." I put my hand to my mouth.

"Don't worry. I know," he said. "I do run a newspaper." He tried to sound casual, but his hands shook as he lit his cigarette. "You didn't come here to talk about Stuart."

237

Fluorescent lights hummed, and a clock on the wall behind me ticked loudly. "Collin Conover told me about the meeting the night Glad died."

Winker puffed on his Camel. "You going to tell Zee?"

"I don't know."

The floor on one side of Winker's desk was covered with stacks of scratch paper. Once, when I was a kid, I sat next to him in church, and he made me a small hat out of the bulletin. He seemed magical to me then. All-powerful with his booming voice. Now I had the power to get him kicked off city council—to disgrace him in front of the community he loved. "I'd like to hear your side of the story," I said.

Winker smiled sadly. "There's no sides." Rain pounded against the window. "You don't have any kids," he said, "so you don't know what it's like. The minute they're born, you can't stop thinking about them. You'd do anything to make sure they're OK. To make them happy."

"So you're hoping Wal-Mart will give Emmet a good job?"

"As good as they got." Winker perched his cigarette on an ashtray that was already heaped with butts. "I saw a chance to help my son and keep my paper afloat, and I took it. Wal-Mart is going to hurt Aldoburg one way or another. You heard the man. If they don't come here, they'll go to the next town over."

I eased back in my chair and let its softness envelop me. "Do you believe all those things you wrote in your editorials?"

"Course not," he said. "I wrote them for Emmet. His wife and kids." He leaned forward and put his elbows on his desk. "But understand—nobody took a bribe. The Wal-Mart rep simply said there was a strong possibility my son would be hired as a manager if I voted for Wal-Mart and praised the store in my paper."

"What about the others?"

"You going to spread this around?"

I wondered whether the information could tilt the scales against Wal-Mart. "What's going to happen with the council now that Stuart—now that he's gone?" I asked.

"I'm the new mayor." Winker smiled wryly. "Lester Simms will take my place."

"What if you were off the council?"

Winker slowly put out his cigarette. "Your dad would be mayor, and Aggie Schumacher would take his place."

Aggie Schumacher. The proud proprietor of Stuff. She had an anti–Wal-Mart poster hanging next to the headless mannequin. If Aggie were on the council, my dad's vote would no longer matter. Aggie, LaVonne, and Hortie would all vote against Wal-Mart. Lester would be the only one for it.

"It's not going to matter," Winker said. "Wal-Mart will get us one way or the other."

"Not if neighboring towns fight Wal-Mart."

Winker lit another cigarette. "Most towns near here are even worse off than Aldoburg."

"At least Wal-Mart wouldn't be *here*." I slid forward in my chair.

Winker narrowed his eyes. "Telling about the meeting isn't going to do anybody any good."

"You mean it's not going to do *you* any good."

"What about Zee?" he said. "How do you think she'll feel if you tell her? What about Charlene?"

"Why was she at the meeting?"

Winker ignored my question. "What about my son?" His voice was steely. "He'll be humiliated. And for what? Nothing."

Revealing Wal-Mart's underhanded tactics didn't seem like nothing to me. It wouldn't have seemed like nothing to Glad. But I wondered. Would it have been worth the unhappiness of a dear friend, someone who—except for the Wal-Mart issue— had always been there for them? And not just for them. Winker had cosigned his son's mortgage. He delivered Meals on Wheels to shut-ins. Every Christmas he donned a lopsided Santa hat and distributed gifts at the elementary school.

Winker tapped his cigarette over his ashtray, and rain pummeled the window.

Zee always liked to think the best of people—especially her friends—and she would need Winker's friendship now more than ever. I couldn't tell her about the meeting. Not to save all the mom-and-pop stores in the world.

But Winker didn't know that.

"My lips are sealed," I said, "if you answer my questions and promise to vote against Wal-Mart."

Winker scowled. "I already gave my word I'd vote for it."

"You also gave your word you'd represent the wishes of the people."

"They're divided."

I stood and turned toward the door.

"Wait," he called. "Give me a day to think about it."

I turned back. "If you answer my questions now."

He snuffed out his cigarette. His jowls and eyes sagged more than usual. Two deaths in one week. "What the hell," he said. "You always were a smart girl. You probably already figured most of it out."

"Collin said the meeting was about strategizing. What was the strategy?"

Winker refused to meet my eyes. "Stuart and I were to vote for Wal-Mart," he said, "and I was to run pro–Wal-Mart ads and write pro-Wal-Mart editorials."

"What about Charlene?"

Winker tapped his cigarette pack.

"You said you'd answer my questions." I hated bullying a man I loved so much, but I needed answers.

Winker continued to stare at his desk. "She was supposed to convince your aunts to stop their anti–Wal-Mart programming."

"She didn't succeed," I said, "so she settled for deleting anti–Wal-Mart PSAs from the live log."

Winker nodded and finally looked up. "We were all going to work on persuading your father to vote for the store. Chuck especially."

I raised my eyebrows.

"A while back one of your father's patients got arrested for shoplifting at Dollar Daze. Your dad talked to Chuck—explained how the guy had mental problems—and Chuck convinced the store not to press charges." Winker pulled out another Camel. "So Chuck figured your dad owed him one."

"What about the note in my car?" I asked. "Was that Chuck's idea too?"

Winker paused in the middle of lighting his cigarette and frowned. "We never talked about any note."

Surely he wasn't playing dumb after all he'd told me. Maybe Chuck had taken matters into his own hands and decided to scare me. I wanted to believe I'd solved at least one piece of the puzzle. "So," I said, "were you all at Charlene's when Chuck received the call about Glad?"

"What kind of note?" he asked.

"Just a note," I told him. "Times Roman twelve point on white office paper."

Winker refused to smile. "Let me guess," he said. "You got some kind of threatening note, and you just kept nosing around?"

I didn't know what to say.

"Jesus," he said, "you're just like Glad." He lit his cigarette. "She'd find herself a cause and the rest of the world be damned. Never knew when to call it quits."

My chest and throat tightened, full of unshed tears. The rain had stopped, but several drops rolled down the window. Winding paths of water going nowhere.

"Mara." Winker's voice was firm. "We evil Wal-Mart folks were all at Charlene's when Chuck received the call about Glad. Some crazy stranger killed her. You're not going to find him."

"What about Stuart?" I said. "Did the same crazy stranger just happen to kill him?"

"You let Chuck worry about that," Winker said. "Take care of yourself and Zee."

"Had Stuart received any threats?"

Winker took a drag of his cigarette. "Mara, just let it go."

"You said you'd answer my questions."

Winker sighed and closed his eyes. "The mayor and I weren't friends. He didn't tell me his deep, dark secrets. We worked on Wal-Mart together—that's it."

"Was he behaving strangely?"

"He was the same as always." Winker hunched over his desk, his voice weary. "Pestering me to buy some newfangled kind of insurance. Said he'd sell me some if it was the last thing he did." Winker's voice caught.

I studied his desk in order to give him some emotional privacy. A half-full Coke bottle towered over a stack of mail. There were a couple postcards on top.

Postcards. Caffeine. Insurance.

Suddenly, I knew who killed Glad and Stuart. But I'd have to wait until dark to prove it, and I'd have to ask Neale for help.

twenty-five

Nothing is eerier than a silent radio station. Especially if you're waiting for a murderer. I checked my recording equipment for the umpteenth time. The three tape decks that towered on the left counter were all hooked up to my microphone. When the front-door light signaled the killer's arrival, I would open my mike and start the tapes. Then I would cleverly extract a confession. The killer would be none the wiser because I had draped a tarp over the tape decks and made sure they ran quietly. No one would interrupt the confession. I'd told Zee I was going to visit a high school buddy. Then I biked to the station and brought the bike inside with me. The station's front lights were off, so there would be no reason for Chuck or anybody else to stop by.

Of course, I'd told the killer I'd be there. Late at night and alone.

But that last part wasn't true. Neale crouched between the towering tape decks and the wall of records. The killer wouldn't be able to see her from the studio door, and from the back window there would be nothing visible but the tarp she was hiding under.

I was glad my plan required her to hide. I didn't feel like talking about *us*, as she put it. I wasn't even sure why she'd agreed to help. Part of me wanted to believe she cared about me and was eager to show me she was sorry. But another part of me knew she cared only about herself and her career. If my plan worked, she'd be a hero—and a huge step closer to becoming a homicide detective.

"What time is it?" Neale's voice was muffled.

"Nearly 11:30."

She rustled around under the tarp. We'd been waiting for way over an hour. What if the murderer didn't take my bait?

Keeping an eye on the front-door light, I stood and tried to crack my back. It wasn't easy with the bulletproof vest Neale had made me wear. "You really think we need the vests?" I asked.

Neale shifted again, and the wind whistled against the back window.

"Glad and Stuart weren't shot," I said.

"Mara." Neale sounded weary.

The front-door light flashed.

"It's time," I said. I opened my mike, flipped on all the tape decks, and put the tarp back over them. I gazed at the computer next to the live log, pretending to study a list of ads. The studio door opened.

There was Barb. Her hair was in a ponytail, and her toothy smile made her look deceptively young and innocent. The sheen of sweat on her face told me she'd biked or jogged to the station. She didn't want anybody spotting her car, and she didn't want anybody spotting her. Despite the heat, she was encased in a black leotard. I'd folded such a garment in her living room, never thinking she might have worn it when she killed Glad.

She was also wearing a black jacket that was baggy enough to hide a gun.

Neale had told me to expect anything, but I hadn't wanted to believe her. Sure, I knew Barb had often gone hunting with her husband, but Barb and bullets just didn't seem to go together. She was a grandma. I tried not to think about the fact she was in better shape than me—and that she'd already killed Glad and Stuart.

I swallowed and forced a hello.

"Hope I didn't startle you," she said. "Parker left a book out here. I couldn't sleep, so I grabbed his key and biked out here to get it for him." As she spoke she edged around the counter. "He left it near the soundboard." She stood right next to me.

I'd imagined the counter between us as I accused her of murder, but what the hell. Now the mike would pick her up more clearly. I stood and squared my shoulders. I hoped she couldn't see the vest underneath my oversize T-shirt. "You didn't need Parker's key the night you killed Glad," I said. "You just waited outside until she decided to have a smoke."

Barb pursed her lips. "Grief can make people do crazy things, so I'll pretend you didn't say that."

"Was it grief that made you kill Glad?"

Barb slipped her hands into her jacket pockets.

I tried to think of a way to let Neale know that Barb was standing right next to me—maybe ready to draw a gun—but my mind was a blank. Besides, Neale and I had agreed that unless I was in immediate danger, she wouldn't surface until Barb had confessed.

So I had to make her. "Glad knew the truth about Bill," I said, picking up a notebook. "I read it in her journal." The "journal" was really a blank spiral-bound I'd bought at Dollar Daze, but Barb didn't know that.

She raked her eyes over it.

"Glad thought Bill was suicidal," I said. "He was depressed because your store was barely breaking even. Wal-Mart would force you out of business."

Barb shook her head as if I were crazy.

"Glad knew he was sleeping a lot because he was depressed," I said, "so she was puzzled when she saw him buy sleeping pills at Mumford's Pharmacy. Then a few days later, he did something even more unusual. He brought Glad his post-card collection, and even though they'd been arguing about how to display their cards at the Chat 'n' Chew, he asked her to take charge of the project."

Barb's arms tensed.

I needed to make her angry enough to say something incriminating but not angry enough to kill me. A fine line if ever there was one.

"The card collection was the last straw," I said. "Glad went to your store to warn you that Bill was planning to kill himself. Who knows? Maybe he did it as you two were talking."

Barb flinched. I'd hit the mark.

"He'd purchased a hefty life insurance policy from Stuart," I said, "but the company wouldn't pay if they knew Bill had killed himself. They asked Stuart to look into his death—maybe because Bill had recently purchased the policy—or upgraded its death benefit." I waited for Barb to say something, but she stared at me, her blue eyes fierce whirlpools.

"You were in a tough spot," I sputtered. "You needed the money to keep the store going. Bill intended it as Parker's legacy, and you wanted to honor your husband's wishes. You also want-ed to keep Parker in Aldoburg. If the store closed, he'd leave, and you'd be alone."

I was sweating under my vest. "Your daughter and her kids

also needed money. You were trying to do what was best for your family," I said. "You wanted them to have the insurance money, and you didn't want them to know Bill killed himself. You were afraid Glad would talk—your kids would lose all the money Bill wanted them to have." My throat tightened. "So you killed her."

"What?" Barb cried. "And destroy the woman who was trying to keep our downtown alive?"

Thank God, she'd finally spoken. I waited for more, but Barb simply curled her lips around her teeth.

"You knew if you murdered Glad, you'd give Wal-Mart's proponents an edge, so you tried to make her death look like a hate crime. Then Stu Two and Collin would be the top suspects. Their fathers would be preoccupied, worried about their sons. They'd have less time for the Wal-Mart debate. Chuck would be distracted as he investigated Glad's death, and Stuart would be too busy to look into Bill's."

I waited for her to protest again, but she remained silent, a horrible smile pasted on her face, her hands planted in her pockets.

"You knew in the long run no harm would come to the boys. There'd be no hard evidence against them."

The wind beat against the window.

"Then I came along, suspicious of Chuck and Stuart themselves. I played right into your hands."

"Don't be ridiculous," she said. "I was in my room the night Glad was killed. You can ask Parker."

"You climbed down that beautiful old oak outside your window, and he was none the wiser."

Barb forced a laugh. "He would have heard me open the garage and start the car."

"You didn't need to open it," I said. "Your car wouldn't fit. You told me so yourself the day I rescued your tools from the rain."

Barb's smile faded.

"You also told me Parker sleeps like a rock, but even if he was awake—and not wearing his Walkman—why would he notice an engine starting? He would have had no reason to think it was you."

She inched closer to me. I wanted to step away, but I was cornered.

"After you murdered Glad, you climbed right back up the tree," I said. "You're in better shape than most twenty-five-year-olds. Scrambling up and down must have been a snap."

Barb whipped out a gun and pointed it at me with both hands.

I could see down its barrel.

"You're wrong," she said. "I didn't plan to kill Glad." Her hands trembled.

Maybe I shouldn't have pushed her so hard.

"I just came out here to talk," she said. "I didn't intend to hurt her. I just wanted to ask whether she'd told anybody else her suspicions about Bill." Barb bit her lip, and the gun shook harder. "I explained how important it was that my children and the insurance company not find out about Bill, but she said that would be fraud." Barb's voice was flat and calm, an odd contrast with the quivering gun.

I tried to squelch my panic. I needed to think. Keep her talking. "Glad refused to go along with your plan?" I asked.

"She needed to think about it." Barb tried to steady her hands. "Some nonsense about secrets—they could fester, and maybe it would be better in the long run if Parker and Frannie knew the truth about their father. How could it possibly be better?" Barb narrowed her eyes. "I couldn't afford to let Glad think about it. I couldn't wait for her to decide my family's fate."

A confession. I hoped the mike had captured it. "If you

weren't planning to kill her," I asked, "why did you hide your trip to the station from Parker? Why bother with the tree?"

"I didn't want him asking any questions about why I needed to see her." Barb smiled sadly. "He's a smart kid. He might have figured things out."

"You just happened to have a baseball bat with you?" I didn't bother masking my sarcasm.

Barb stepped aside. "Walk," she said. "We're going outside."

"What about the spray paint?"

"Move it," Barb barked.

I stood still, waiting for Neale to save the day. She leapt from her hiding place and leveled her gun at Barb.

Barb grabbed my shoulder and yanked me toward her. She wrapped one of her arms around my neck and pressed her gun against my head.

So much for my bulletproof vest.

"Drop it," Barb said, "or I'll shoot her."

Neale didn't budge. She clasped her gun with both hands, her arms perfectly parallel to the floor, her knees bent, ready to spring.

"I said drop it." Barb's breath was on my neck. I could smell her fear. Or mine.

I gazed at Neale—her wrinkled uniform, her disheveled hair. The wind rattled against the window. She slowly lowered her arms.

"Put it on the floor," Barb said, "gently."

Neale looked at me and obliged.

"Kick it over here," Barb said. "No funny stuff."

Neale nudged the gun with her foot. It barely moved.

"Closer," Barb snapped.

Great. Barb was going to kill us, but first we'd have a little game of soccer with a SIG Sauer.

Neale kicked the gun harder. It slid across the scuffed floor and stopped a few inches short of my feet.

"Get back," Barb said, "against the wall."

Neale hesitated, and Barb pushed the gun so hard against my temple that I had to tilt my neck to relieve the pressure.

"I'll kill her," Barb said.

Neale stepped back, and Barb stretched a leg toward the gun and kicked it behind us. It thudded against something. "OK, lady-cop," Barb said, "bend over slowly and roll up your pant legs. I want to be sure you don't have another gun."

Neale did as she was told. There, in a black holster on her calf, was plan B.

"Put it on the floor. Kick it over."

Once again, Neale kicked the gun toward Barb, and Barb kicked it behind us. I probably couldn't reach it even if I managed to escape Barb's hold.

"You two are going to be victims of another hate crime," Barb said.

Her matter-of-fact tone sent chills down my spine. I had to catch her off-guard or Neale and I would both die.

"The light that's connected to the front door is on," Neale said. "Someone's entering the building."

twenty-six

It was Zee, mouth scrunched up, ready to chew me out. But then she saw the gun. Her eyes widened in horror, and she slowly raised her hands to her mouth. "We're neighbors," she whispered. "Friends."

Barb stiffened. Now she would kill Zee too if Neale or I didn't think of something fast.

"We baby-sat your children." Zee found her voice.

Neale tried to shush her, but Zee ignored her and stepped toward Barb. "We played your ads and let you pay whenever you could."

"Stay back." Barb's forearm crushed my voice box.

"Glad spent her final months working against Wal-Mart. She tried to protect the downtown—your store—she was trying to save your way of life."

"Not *my* way of life," Barb snarled. "I hated that damned store."

What? Had she completely lost it?

"It made Bill old before his time," she said. "It killed him."

Zee gaped at Barb, and Neale gazed at the gun.

"Stupid place was more important to him than his own family."

"But you've devoted your life to that store," Zee said.

"You got that right. It took everything—time and money. We had to take out a second mortgage, and we still couldn't give Frannie anything for college. What kind of life is that?" Barb was breathing faster and faster as her words spilled out. "We were only a five-hour drive from our grandkids, but how often did we visit? I can't even remember the last time Bill went. And whenever I went by myself, he complained about it for weeks after. Said it was too hard to run the store without me. Only way I'd get to see my grandkids more than once a year is if Wal-Mart drove him out of business."

I thought about the memory books Barb had made for her grandchildren and the postcard she'd sent Bill when she visited them. The card seemed so innocuous—cheerful even—but it masked years of resentment.

"You were *for* Wal-Mart?" Zee was incredulous.

Barb tightened her choke hold. "I didn't want Parker wasting his life trying to keep his father's store afloat."

I had utterly misread Barb—her inaudible speech at the Wal-Mart forum, her tears when Parker tried to defend their store.

"What about Alex?" Zee asked. "How can you let an innocent boy go to prison?" She narrowed her eyes. "Hortie's grandson."

"What about my kids?" Barb's voice rose. "They need that insurance money."

"Insurance?" Zee's brow furrowed, and then it dawned on her. "You killed Stuart too."

The wind hammered against the window screen.

Barb dug her fingernails into my shoulder. "Open the studio door, Zee. It's time to head outside."

Zee shook her head, stunned. "He had a wife and kids."

"You don't have to kill anyone else," Neale said. "Extenuating circumstances made you kill Glad. Any jury will see that."

"And then what?" Barb snapped. "I get put in the loony bin, and me and my kids lose all that money? Oh, no—I've got plans. I'm going to sell our house and get rid of that damned store. Then I'm going to move to Minneapolis so I can be near my grandkids."

So that was why she was digging up those bushes. She was getting her house ready for the market.

"I may even go back to school and become a nurse. I always wanted to be one, but Bill needed me at the store."

I'd seen piles of brochures about nursing programs at her house, but I'd stupidly assumed they were for Frannie.

"Now's my chance," Barb said. "I'm going to make something of my life. I'm going to help people."

With her gun to my head, I couldn't help note the irony: a murderer who wanted to enter a helping profession.

"I'm going to make sure Parker gets to travel and take pictures. My boy could be in *National Geographic* someday."

I thought about Barb's pride in her son's photography and her willingness to battle for her children. Why had I assumed—why had Parker and the whole town assumed—that Barb and her husband shared the same dreams? That they wanted the same thing for their son?

"I'm going to set up saving accounts for my grandkids' college," she said, "and help Frannie buy a car that's not a death trap."

"Those sound like nice plans," Neale said.

They were nice plans. If Barb hadn't panicked, Glad would surely have agreed to keep her secret. Anger seized me. "Why didn't you give Glad some time to think?"

"Shut up." Barb's fingernails dug deeper into my shoulder. "OK, Zee," she said. "You and lady-cop—open the studio door. Mara and I will be right behind you."

"How many more people are you going to kill?" Neale asked.

She no doubt intended it as a rhetorical question, but I imagined Barb counting: one, two, three.

Three. It was three against one. If I was going to die anyway, maybe I could do something to save the others. I could ram my elbow into Barb's stomach, and Neale could grab her gun. I glanced at Neale out of the corner of my eye. She was looking past me and Barb.

"The phone is blinking," Neale said.

Barb slowly turned me toward the phone.

Its red light pulsed off and on.

I tried to speak, but Barb's choke hold was too much for me. She released my throat and quickly wrapped her arm around my chest.

"I told an old friend I'd be here," I lied. "If I don't answer, she'll get worried. She may even call the cops."

The phone kept blinking.

Barb thrust me toward it, keeping the gun to my head. My legs were sandwiched between her and the counter.

"Answer it," she barked, "but mind what you say."

I snatched the phone and moved the receiver to my free ear, the one that didn't have a gun above it.

"Mar-Bar?"

Vince!

I jammed the receiver against my ear so Barb couldn't hear him. "I'm afraid the station is closed," I said.

"I'm in back," Vince whispered. "I've called the police."

"I can't help you tonight. I'm going to check the rain gauge out back and then go home." I prayed Vince would pick up on the words *out back*.

"Hang up," Barb hissed.

"Thanks for calling," I said.

Barb jerked me away from the phone. "Zee," she said, "open the studio door."

Zee's eyes darted from me to Neale.

Neale nodded, so Zee opened it. I tried to catch Neale's eyes, but she and Zee entered the next room, Barb guiding me after them. They stood in front of two computer monitors with dark and empty screens. Barb steered me toward the metal door that led outside. Soon she would force us through it.

Vince was waiting on the other side, but he didn't have a gun. What could he possibly do to stop Barb? Our only hope was to stall until the police arrived. "Barb," I said, "did you plan Stuart's death, or was he just in the wrong place at the wrong time?"

She jabbed my head with her gun. "You don't know when to stop, do you?"

"You're the one who keeps killing people." Maybe I could entangle her in an argument.

"If you hadn't asked so many questions," Barb said, "none of you would be here right now. None of you would have to die."

Tears sprang to my eyes. She was right. If only I'd listened to Zee and left well enough alone.

"Don't blame your sickness on her." Zee put her hands on her hips.

Neale reached for Zee's elbow, trying to calm her, but Zee shook her off, intent on Barb. "Are you going to try to make this look like a hate crime too?" Zee's voice oozed bitterness.

"You're going to get caught," Neale said. "It's just a matter of time. If you kill us, you're only going to make it harder on yourself and your family."

Barb took a deep breath and cocked her gun.

I gasped.

"Open the door, Zee," Barb said.

Zee rushed to it and pushed it open. Then she stopped in the door frame, looked back at me, and gave me a firm nod. She was being strong for me. Sweet Zee, my anchor.

"Outside," Barb said. "You too, lady-cop."

Neale backed toward the door, keeping her gaze fixed on me. This couldn't be the last time I'd ever see her beautiful green eyes. It just couldn't.

"Turn around," Barb said.

As I gazed at Neale's ashy knot and Zee's silver braid, I prayed Vince had a really good trick up his sleeve.

"Take it slow," Barb ordered. "Stay near that little light so I can see you."

Before the door could close behind Neale, Barb wrenched me through it, banging my knees against its metal. I longed to hear police sirens, but all that greeted me was the wind and Barb's shallow breathing.

At the edge of the patio, Zee hid behind Neale. Where was Vince?

Barb trembled and pressed her gun harder against my skull. I tensed my sore knees and summoned my strength, ready to throw us both back against the station wall. If I could knock Barb off balance, even for a moment, Zee and Neale might have a chance. I closed my eyes and imagined them running for the cornfield.

The station door clicked shut.

Barb grunted and dropped her gun.

I leapt away and ran toward Zee and Neale.

"Look," Neale said.

There Barb lay, crumpled on the cement. Out cold. In the dim light, Vince stood above her, brandishing the chunky heel of a bright red sandal.

twenty-seven

The next morning in Zee's dining room, Vince and I confronted yet another green bean casserole and several other cholesterol-laden delights courtesy of Hortie, whose praise and admiration flowed more freely than her coffee and maple syrup. We had saved her grandson from prison; we had—thank God—made the streets of Aldoburg safe for decent folks again.

"How'd you know it was Barb?" Hortie passed some raspberry Danish to me and some chicken to Vince. Then she filled Zee's mug with coffee.

I wondered if my aunt had slept. She picked at her eggs and stared blankly at the pitcher of orange juice.

I sipped my coffee. My throat still hurt from Barb's choke hold.

"Mar-Bar," Vince said, "a sleuth such as yourself needn't be modest." The sun shone on his red silk pj's and lethal bed head. On one side his dark hair jutted out wildly. On the other side it was smashed flat.

I glanced at Zee again and launched into my story. "The

Coke and the postcard on Winker's desk made me realize I'd been wrong about the Post-it note. It was an important clue, but I'd misinterpreted it."

Vince cut in. "I was there when she found it on Glad's desk. It said, *WM, SP, CC*. Without much ado, we determined *WM* must stand for Wal-Mart."

Vince had conveniently forgotten he'd called me crazy when I suggested that Wal-Mart could inspire a murder. He began gnawing on a drumstick, so I assumed it was my turn to talk again. "I was right about Wal-Mart, but wrong about the other two sets of letters. They weren't people's initials. The Coke on Winker's desk reminded me of a conversation I'd had with Parker. He was drinking a Coke—and we were joking about caffeine—and he said his mom and dad always fell asleep during the evening news even if they'd just had a lot of coffee. Then I knew. *SP* stood for sleeping pills."

Hortie rested her elbows on the table. "You got all that from a Coke?"

"And from a conversation with LaVonne. She saw Bill and Glad at her pharmacy a few days before Bill killed himself. He was buying sleeping pills, and Glad was right behind him in line. Glad knew Bill well," I said, "and she knew he was sleeping extra because he was depressed about Wal-Mart."

"She knew he didn't need sleeping pills," Vince said, reaching for another piece of chicken.

I wondered if he was congenitally unable to let someone else finish a story. "Then," I said, "Bill gave Glad his beloved postcards, and she started to put two and two together." I slathered butter on my pancakes. "*CC* stands for card collection. I can't believe I missed that—after all the time I spent looking at Glad's and Bill's cards."

Hortie tucked her napkin into the top of her daisy-print

blouse. "So when Glad wrote those letters on the Post-it, she was trying to figure out what was going on with Bill?"

"Voilà!" Vince said. "She deduced that Bill might kill himself, but when she warned Barb she was already too late."

We all fell silent.

"That poor family." Zee stared at her plate.

"But what about Stuart?" Hortie said. "How'd you know Barb killed him?"

"Right before I figured out the Post-it note, Winker mentioned that Stuart had really been pushing his insurance. I'd heard this before." I nodded toward Hortie. "From you. And Stuart had mentioned life insurance to me at Glad's visitation."

I glanced at Zee, hoping I wasn't upsetting her. My pause seemed to bring her back to the present. She looked up and cleared her throat. "Stuart convinced Glad to increase her coverage just a couple months before..." Zee's voice faltered.

I put my arm around her.

"Mara started wondering whether insurance had anything to do with Stuart's death," Vince said. "Then she realized Bill wouldn't have left his family with a failing store and no resources. He'd bought more life insurance from Stuart, then killed himself so his family would receive his death benefits. Sort of like in *Death of a Salesman*."

Hortie frowned. "I still don't see why Barb killed Stuart."

"His company wanted him to investigate Bill's death," I said. "Barb was afraid Stuart might discover the truth. Then she and her family wouldn't get the money. Insurance companies don't pay for people who kill themselves right after increasing their coverage."

Hortie ladled some gravy onto a biscuit. "I can't believe Barb was actually *for* Wal-Mart."

"She fooled everybody," I said.

"What a great actress." There was a note of admiration in Vince's voice. For him, all the world truly was a stage, and Barb was simply one of the finer players. "She fooled her husband and kids too," he said. "She must have been acting 24–7."

Hortie thrust the ladle back into the gravy. "How can you trust anybody?"

Things were never what they seemed. Stu Two seemed like a gay-bashing jock who cared only about his football scholarship. Wal-Mart—with its red-white-and-blue folksiness—seemed like a champion of small-town America and the little guy. Barb had seemed like a woman devoted to her husband's dream—to the family store—and to Aldoburg itself, but underneath she was seething with rage and a need to carve out her own dream. I thought about the shrubs she'd been digging up. Some of their pale orange roots were wider than my arm. Who knew how deep they went?

"Sometimes you've got to take a leap of faith," Vince said. "Mara trusted me to save the day, and I did."

I'd actually been scared shitless, but I kept my mouth shut and let Vince sing his own praises. Nibbling on a bacon strip, I pondered leaps of faith. I'd taken a huge one when I'd swallowed my pride and asked Neale to help me catch Barb. If I took any more leaps with this lovely, ambitious cop, would I just keep wondering whether she cared more about her career than about me?

The doorbell rang.

I waved Zee back into her seat and hurried to answer it. Neale had promised to come by if she learned anything new.

There she stood on the front porch. Her green sundress matched her eyes and showed off her biceps. Her hair tumbled over her shoulders. You'd never guess she'd spent the night before hiding under a tarp, then catching and interrogating a murderer—except her face was pale and somber. I wanted to talk with her alone, but Hortie was at my heels, ushering us toward the feast.

For a moment I wished I'd stayed at the station the night before so I could have heard Neale and Chuck interrogate Barb. But I'd done the right thing—getting Zee out of there as soon as I could.

"I'll set another plate," Hortie said. "You must be famished."

As Neale settled into a chair next to mine, I realized I was still wearing yesterday's clothes (minus the bulletproof vest, of course). I'd fallen into bed with them on and hadn't stirred until I'd smelled Hortie's sausages simmering. The scent had distracted me from my morning ablutions, so there I was in a wrinkled tie-dye T-shirt, my braid half undone, looking like pond scum. But what did I care? I was still angry at Neale for wanting me to lie about our night together. Sure, I was grateful she'd helped me catch Barb, but that didn't erase her earlier betrayal. All I wanted from Neale Warner was information. No way was I going to pine away over her.

She smiled at me over a mound of mashed potatoes.

I smiled at Hortie. "This is so delicious. You must have worked for hours on all this food."

"Oh, it's nothing." Hortie beamed. "Especially compared to what you girls have been up to." She picked up her fork and turned to me. "How'd you lure Barb to the station?"

I wanted to question Neale, but she was digging into her potatoes, so I figured I might as well answer Hortie. "First, I made sure that Neale—Officer Warner—could help me," I said.

Hortie studied Neale. "How'd she convince you? You two barely know each other."

Neale blushed slightly, but she didn't miss a beat. "Mara told me about all the clues she'd uncovered. We both connected the dots the same way."

Vince grinned mischievously. It would serve Neale right if he attempted a sexual innuendo involving the connection of dots, but I leapt back into my story. "I went over to Barb's on the pretext of borrowing some milk. We chatted, and I told her I'd just found Glad's journal and that I was going to read it at the station that night while I recorded some music for the live log."

Vince chimed in again. "Mara made sure Barb knew she'd be at the station alone for several hours after dark."

"That was so clever," Hortie said. "I bet Barb was scared to death you'd read the journal and figure everything out."

"Glad never kept a journal," Zee said. "I was lucky if I could get her to write a grocery list." She smiled sadly.

Hortie gave her hand a supportive squeeze before quizzing Vince. "What were you doing at the station? I thought you left town after the funeral."

Vince cleared his throat. He's never shy about telling stories that make him look good. "After Stuart's death Zee called and asked me to convince Mara to come home. Wisely knowing my powers of persuasion were no match for Mar-Bar's stubbornness, I returned to fair Aldoburg so I could watch over her myself." He helped himself to the last drumstick. "And, I might add, I risked the role of a lifetime. In order to protect our dear Mara, I skipped a crucial technical rehearsal of the show I'm currently starring in, *La Cage aux Folles*." He frowned. "At least, I hope I'm still starring in it. The director is an unforgiving man who—"

This time I interrupted Vince. "Vince arrived in town yesterday before I left the station and followed me to my meeting with Collin Conover at the Chat 'n' Chew."

Vince gave me a dirty look and plunged back into his tale of heroism and derring-do. "When I saw Mara was settling in for a repast, I decided to use my time wisely and do some shopping. As fate would have it, my only purchase, a pair of lovely red sandals, turned out to be the weapon with which I slew the murderess and saved the day."

"Slew?" I said.

Vince shrugged and patted his lip with a napkin.

"They don't make sandals like that anymore," Hortie said, "sturdy and built to last."

"Sexy too," Vince said.

Neale chuckled.

"How'd you manage to hit her?" Hortie asked.

Vince puffed himself up. "I hid behind the station door until everyone was outside. Then I let it shut, crept behind her, aimed for her head, and unleashed my formidable strength."

"Then what?"

"Neale slapped handcuffs on her faster than you can say *denouement*. When Chuck and another cop finally arrived, it was completely anticlimactic. They couldn't believe I'd saved three lives with a sandal."

"Chuck just stared wide-eyed at the shoe," I said. "He kept saying, 'You hit her with a woman's shoe?'"

"He has issues with his masculinity," Vince said. "It really bothered him that Mara figured out who the killer was." He gave me a sly grin. "How macho can you be when a girl and a flaming queen do your job for you?"

I peeked at Neale to see how she was taking Vince's assault on her boss. She was smiling.

"At first," Zee said, "Chuck refused to believe Barb was the murderer, so Mara played the tape she made."

"Oh, Mara," Hortie cried, "what a plan!"

I hadn't planned on Zee showing up, but no doubt Zee had already told Hortie that part of the story. My aunt had been agonizing over the Wal-Mart forum, so she'd headed out to the station to make some new PSAs denouncing the store.

Hortie scooped some more potatoes onto Neale's plate. "Is it really true that Barb didn't plan to kill Glad?"

"That's what she claims," Neale said.

"But what about the baseball bat?" Finally, a chance to ask my questions. "Did she just happen to have it in her car?"

"It was a softball bat," Neale said. "She's in a slow-pitch league."

"Oh, sure," Hortie said. "Honig's has a team."

"What about the bat you found at the baseball complex?" I asked. "The one that had, you know, evidence on it—wasn't that a baseball bat?"

Neale met my eyes. "You were right about Barb wanting to keep Stuart busy and worried."

"Because of the insurance," Hortie proclaimed, proud of herself.

"Right. So the night after she killed Glad, Barb took her bat to the baseball complex," Neale said. "She wore work gloves and managed to transfer some of the evidence onto one of the baseball bats."

"What'd she do with her bat?" Hortie asked.

Neale placed her fork on her plate and glanced nervously at Zee. "She buried it in her front yard underneath those shrubs she was digging up."

Bile rose in my throat. I may have been watching while Barb buried the bat. I'd felt sorry for her. I'd almost taken her a drink of water.

"What about the spray paint?" Vince asked. "Why did she have that with her?"

"She said she'd been meaning to brighten up some picture frames," Neale said.

I'd seen those frames underneath Barb's sewing machine, and I'd noticed they'd needed work. I'd also noticed the rest of the pictures in the room had white frames. Yet I hadn't made the connection. It hadn't occurred to me that Barb—the owner of a hardware store—had ready access to all kinds of spray paint.

"But why'd she bother with the paint?" Hortie asked.

"An excellent question," Vince said. "The paint makes it seem premeditated—like she planned on framing those two boys all along."

"She says she didn't intend to frame anyone. Not at first." Neale looked at Zee out of the corner of her eye.

Zee leaned forward, her hands wrapped around her coffee mug.

"But after she killed Glad, she panicked. She was terrified she'd get caught. Then she remembered the spray paint in her car, and she used it to write the nastiest thing she could think of." Neale paused for air. "To throw everybody off."

I stiffened. Barb knew nobody would suspect her of writing such a hateful thing because she was supposedly Glad and Zee's friend. I hadn't suspected. I hadn't noticed that the cramped script on the back of the station resembled the tiny letters on Barb's thank-you list and on her postcard to Bill. If I'd figured things out sooner, maybe Stuart would still be alive.

I poured more syrup on my already soaked pancakes.

"Later," Neale said, "when Barb discovered Stuart was looking into Bill's death, she remembered what Stu Two and Collin did to the O'Rourke boy. That's when she planted evidence at the baseball complex and made sure Mara knew what Collin and Stu Two had done."

"What about Alex?" Hortie asked. "Did she mean to get him in trouble?"

"Once Barb started thinking about people she wanted to distract, you came to mind. Barb was hoping you'd be so distraught about your grandson that you'd resign your council seat. Then Wal-Mart would be a sure thing."

My "wild theory" had been right, but I'd never connected it with Barb.

Neale took a drink of coffee. "She'd probably never have thought of such a scheme except she sold Alex some white spray paint the day Bill died. She hoped Alex would still have it in one of his motorcycle saddlebags, so she sent an anonymous note to Chuck, saying she'd seen Alex out by the radio station the night of Glad's murder."

"And Chuck wanted to believe it," Hortie said. "He's always had it in for Alex, and he sure didn't want his Collin considered a suspect." She chopped a piece of sausage into tiny bits. "I thought Barb was my friend. She kept asking me about Alex. She even sent him cookies when he was in jail."

"Guilt cookies," I said.

Vince passed Hortie a plate of muffins. "She did try to save him with that note she left in Mara's car."

Neale poured herself some coffee, unfazed. Barb must have told her about the note. But as far as Zee and Hortie were concerned, I had some explaining to do—thanks to Vince, the ever-flowing fount of information. "After Alex got arrested, Barb left a note in my car," I said, "sort of a threatening one."

Vince opened his mouth, and I kicked him under the table. "I think Barb was hoping I'd take the note to the police and Alex would be cleared."

"No one ever said anything to me about it," Hortie slowly pulled her napkin away from her blouse, her gaze fixed on me.

"Mara never told the police," Neale said.

I couldn't read her tone, but I figured a closeted cop didn't have much room to criticize me for withholding information. "Chuck was one of my suspects," I said.

"But what about me?" Hortie said. "Why didn't you tell me?"

"All's well that ends well," Vince announced. He forced a smile, and we all stared at our plates. The murderer had been caught and Alex was cleared, but it was an overstatement to say things had ended well.

"What about Stuart?" I said. "Was that premeditated?"

Zee stood. "I'll make some more coffee."

I watched her head for the kitchen, telling myself she needed a moment alone.

"Barb was upset after the Wal-Mart forum," Neale said, "so she took a drive in the country. As she was coming back into town, she saw Stuart walking and assumed he was headed home. She drove to his street—"

"Arbor Lane," Hortie volunteered.

"Right," Neale said, "it goes for three or four blocks, then dead ends."

Zee's coffeemaker began to gurgle and hiss.

"Barb shut off her lights, drove to the dead end, and turned her car around so she could see Stuart coming. The houses were all dark. She could wait as long as she liked."

I imagined Stuart as he unknowingly strolled toward his death—reviewing the forum, hoping his wife would still be awake, maybe planning to take Stu Two fishing the next day. And Barb. Calmly sitting in her car, her motor humming, waiting to kill the mayor. A woman who used to leave me milk and cookies when I baby-sat her son.

"When Stuart rounded the corner," Neale said, "Barb was ready. She hit him at a high speed, then backed over him."

Hortie started passing bowls and plates around the table again. Her hands shook.

"He died right away," Neale said kindly.

I passed a mound of cold scrambled eggs to her.

Zee emerged from the kitchen with a pot of coffee and red eyes. Catching Glad's killer had brought her little comfort. She hadn't wanted to believe she knew anyone capable of murder, and now she had to absorb the fact that her next-door neighbor had killed Glad and Stuart. Evil had been homegrown after all.

The wooden floor of Glad's office felt cool on my bare feet. Downstairs, Vince's voice mingled with the clatter of silverware as someone—probably not Vince—tackled all the dirty dishes left in our wake. Outside, sunlight flickered on the Honigs' giant oak. I didn't want to think about Barb climbing down its branches on her way to the station. I didn't want to think about anything.

I knelt on the floor next to Glad's box of postcards and pulled out a handful. Parker had sent a bunch from Drake, and somebody named Lynn had sent several from Iowa State. *Glad, you're the best*, she wrote. *I learned so much from you—and not just about radio.* I vaguely remembered Lynn, a cheerful girl who worked at the station a few years after me.

I studied some more cards and found several others from young people who'd worked part-time at the station since I'd been there. I told myself Glad had loved me—I shouldn't be jealous—but it seemed she'd been much more of a mentor to other young people than she'd ever been to me. She'd grown much fonder of young people after I'd left for college. She seemed so close to Parker—and to Stu Two and Collin.

Embarrassed by my resentment, I eased myself off the floor

and went over to Glad's desk. I moved aside a stack of papers, and there by her pencil holder was the photo of me, pigtailed, laughing, riding on her back.

Then it hit me. Glad had grown much fonder of young people after I'd left. My presence had somehow changed her.

I walked back to the box and pulled out the envelope she'd left for me. Maybe she missed me after I'd left home. Maybe she was just as sorry as I was that we hadn't been closer, so she'd reached out to other young people.

"Mara?" Neale leaned around the door frame. "Zee said you might be up here." Her voice was tentative.

I sat in Glad's office chair and gestured for Neale to have a seat. She sat primly on the edge of Glad's easy chair and tried to meet my eyes.

I looked away. "I don't want to talk about us right now."

"Me neither."

I felt a pang of disappointment.

"I want to sometime," she said quickly, "but that's not why I came up here."

I waited, trying hard to keep my face neutral. Outside, two dogs barked at each other.

"There's something more about the murders that I wanted to tell you when we were alone."

I rubbed my finger around a corner of Glad's envelope.

"Usually when a person dies unattended there's an autopsy," Neale said, "but there wasn't for Bill." She took a deep breath and sat up straighter. "Mara, I'm afraid your father falsified Bill's death certificate. He claimed he was present when Bill died and listed heart failure as the cause of death."

I heard her words, but they didn't make any sense. "My dad would never do anything like that," I said. "He does things by the book."

Neale met my eyes. "Bill left Barb a note explaining there couldn't be an autopsy or they'd lose the insurance money. He told her to ask your dad for help. Barb showed your father the note and pleaded with him."

I tried to imagine the two of them—Barb hysterical, and my dad... What? How had he felt?

"Your dad thought he was doing the right thing," Neale said. "He didn't want Barb's children to know their father committed suicide."

My father had delivered those children, and he'd been dear friends with their parents. He had no fondness for Stuart and, like most doctors, no fondness for the insurance industry. "Did you see the note?" I asked.

Neale nodded. "And I was there when Chuck questioned him."

So it was true. "Will he go to jail?"

"No," Neale said, "but he could lose his license."

My dad had risked his practice and his reputation in order to protect a family he loved. He'd chosen to honor his heart rather than his duty as a physician. I'd drastically underestimated his devotion to his patients. Maybe I'd misunderstood him entirely.

"So how did he seem?" I asked.

"Shaken," Neale said, "but hanging in there."

My poor dad. There was no way he could have known his choice would pave the way for two murders and a town full of grief. I squeezed Glad's envelope in my hands and wondered if the cards inside would help me understand my father and his choices. Tears sprang to my eyes.

Neale got up and wrapped her arms around me. I clung to her for a moment then pulled away. I needed to sort through everything she had just told me. I needed to see my dad.

As Neale left, I gazed at Glad's bookshelves. When you

read a mystery, the case is solved. You close the book and go about your business. In real life, there are always more questions, and you have to live with the truth you uncover.

epilogue

I was hitting every red light in Iowa City, but I didn't mind, because everything else was going my way. Wal-Mart had been voted out of Aldoburg, and for the first time since Glad's death, Zee sounded happy. As Hortie put it, she was "tickled pink." My dad had voted against the store in honor of Glad's memory, and then he resigned his seat. He was also closing his practice. Rather than lose his license, he took matters into his own hands and opted for early retirement. He seemed ecstatic, although my mother was less than thrilled with abandoning her post as Aldoburg's alpha church lady. Still, she managed to console herself with the fact that she'd be golfing in the Florida sunshine, chasing her grandkids around the beach, and buying them season passes to Disney World. My dad offered to buy me a plane ticket so I could come visit. When I agreed, he even offered to buy a ticket for my "friend."

I assumed he meant Anne since I still hadn't told him she'd left me. Alas, my ex-lover is indeed living with Orchid, but the gay grapevine reveals that the hapless duo is already in couples counseling. Either they've already fallen prey to lesbian bed death or they soon will in their pursuit of a "healthy rela-tionship": two emotionally available lesbians who don't eat meat, drink coffee, or do anything "patriarchal," even if it's a lot of fun. Let's face it, none of us stands a chance of being emotionally available—or even civil—without coffee and an occasional orgasm.

I'm no longer worried about Orchid firing me. She's been walking on eggshells because I've become a local celebrity: IOWA CITY WOMAN SOLVES DOUBLE MURDER. Ah, the power of the press. Not only did she relinquish control of my reading series, but she also offered me an hour-long weekly feature slot and told me I could do whatever I want with it. The slot wasn't accompanied by a raise, but my financial situation isn't as dire as I once feared. George the plumber has a crush on Vince, so he fixed my toilet for free.

I noted another red light and slowed my car to a stop. Best news of all: There in my passenger seat was Neale, wearing a skimpy black dress and holding a doggie bag. Some would say the bag contained leftover chicken curry, but to me it contained the remains of a romantic first date. She had arrived in the late afternoon with chocolate, flowers, apologies, explanations, sweet nothings, lingering kisses, and the aforementioned skimpy black dress.

I decided to let bygones be bygones.

Neale and I savored Vince's triumph at the opening night of *La Cage aux Folles*, complete with his Queen Elizabeth wave dur-ing the standing O. Then we enjoyed a late dinner at the Sanctuary, where we exchanged amorous glances and carefully avoided discussing Neale's career plans. Having solved two mur-ders fresh out the academy, she could easily get a job wherever she wanted, and I assumed that wouldn't be Iowa City. I told myself that a long-distance relationship might be just what I needed. Then I told myself to slow down. I sure didn't want to be one of the women in the old lesbian U-Haul joke. I told myself to live in the now.

Neale and I were mere blocks from my house. Vince would be at a cast party, and we'd have the place to ourselves.

The light turned green, but one of Iowa City's many suicidal pedestrians (a.k.a. college students) dashed across the street. I spared his life and tried to decide what CD I'd put on once we got to my place. Torn between Melissa Etheridge and Enya, I turned onto my street.

There were cars parked on both sides. Somebody was having a party.

I pulled into my driveway. As soon as I killed the engine, I heard it. Music. Loud music. Coming from *my* house. My heart sank. I'd promised Neale a romantic evening alone. Vince had promised me he'd be in absentia, but now another one of my dates would be scared away by his entourage of drag queens.

Vince was going to pay.

I threw open the front door, barely aware of Neale behind me. Our ears were assaulted with an old disco tune: *Boom, boom, boom, let's go back to my room.*

If only.

You couldn't walk through my living room without bumping into a pair of falsies. I peered through a sea of big hair, searching for Vince. He was lying on the sofa, having his toes painted by a scrawny man in a Marilyn Monroe wig. Marilyn was perched on the edge of my coffee table, which was overflowing with bottles of nail polish and plus-size pumps. It also looked like a set of boobs—and maybe a girdle too—had detached themselves from their owner.

I forced my eyes away from the carnage and glared at Vince.

He batted his false lashes at me. One of them tilted precariously.

I turned to Neale.

She gazed at the pile of shoes with a bemused expression. Then she grabbed a glittery green pair with stiletto heels and held them aloft. "Hey, Mara," she yelled over the music. "Killer shoes."

acknowledgments

As I wrote *Death by Discount*, I enjoyed the support and encouragement of many friends, colleagues, and students. I'd especially like to thank Angela Brown at Alyson for her enthusiasm and helpful ideas; the members of Creative Girls—Mary Helen Stefaniak, Eileen Bartos, Kris Vervaecke, Tonja Robinswood, Mo Jones, Ann Zerkel, and Jane Olson—for workshopping two drafts of my novel; Helen Keefe for proofreading; Liz Noyes for reading my second draft and always asking about my writing; Sheri Morris for her advice on the scenes between Mara and Neale; Mount Mercy College for granting me a sabbatical so I could have time to write.

And finally, I'd like to thank B.D. Thiel—editor, proofreader, muse, and partner extraordinaire.